Th

Roughest

Draft

The *Roughest* Draft

Emily Wibberley &
Austin Siegemund-Broka

PAN BOOKS

First published 2022 by Berkley, an imprint of Penguin Random House

First published in the UK 2023 by Pan Books
an imprint of Pan Macmillan
The Smithson, 6 Briset Street, London EC1M 5NR
EU representative: Macmillan Publishers Ireland Ltd, 1st Floor,
The Liffey Trust Centre, 117–126 Sheriff Street Upper,
Dublin 1, D01 YC43
Associated companies throughout the world
www.panmacmillan.com

ISBN 978-1-0350-1864-2

1 3 5 7 9 8 6 4 2

A CIP catalogue record for this book is available from the British Library.

Printed and bound by CPI Group (UK) Ltd, Croydon, CR0 4YY

This one could only be for each other

Every secret of a writer's soul, every experience of his life, every quality of his mind, is written large in his works.

—Virginia Woolf

1

Katrina

THE BOOKSTORE IS nothing like I remember. They've remodeled, white paint covering the exposed bricks, light gray wooden shelves where there once were old metal ones. Cute candles and Jane Austen tote bags occupy the front table instead of used books.

I shouldn't be surprised it looks different. I've pretty much given up buying books in public in the past three years, including from Forewords, where I've only been once despite the bookstore being fifteen minutes from our house in Los Angeles's Hancock Park. I don't like being recognized. But I love books. Doing my book buying online has been torture.

Walking in, I eye the bookseller. She's in her early twenties, not much younger than me. Her brown hair's up in a messy bun, her green nose piercing catching the overhead lights. She doesn't look familiar. When she smiles from the checkout counter, I think I'm in the clear.

I smile back, walking past the bestseller shelf. *Only Once* sits imposingly right in the middle, its textured blue cover with clean white typography instantly identifiable. I ignore the book while I move deeper into the store.

This visit is something my therapist's been pushing me to do for months. Exposure therapy, conditioning myself to once more find comfortable the places I used to love. Pausing in the fiction section, I collect myself, remembering I'm doing fine. I'm calm. I'm just me, looking for something to read, with no expectations pressing on my shoulders or stresses jackhammering in my chest.

Covers run past me in rows, each waiting to be picked out. Everything is crisp with the scent of pages. I knew the Los Angeles independent bookstore scene well when Chris proposed we move here from New York for the job he was offered in the book department of one of Hollywood's biggest talent agencies. Each shop is varied and eccentric, indignant icons of literacy in a city people say never reads.

Which is why I've hated avoiding them. The past three years have been a catalogue of changes, facing realities of the life I no longer knew if I wanted and the one I decided I didn't. I've had to remember the quiet joys of my ordinary existence, and in doing so, I've had to forget. Forget how my dreams hit me with devastating impact, forget how horrible I felt coming close to what I'd once wanted. Forget Florida.

Everything's different now. But I pretend it's not.

The bookstore is part of the pretending. When I lived in New York on my own, before Chris, I would walk to Greenpoint's independent bookstores in the summer, sweating into the shoulder strap of my bag, and imagine the stories in the spines, wondering if they'd lend me inspiration, fuel for the creative fire I could never douse. Reading wasn't just enjoyment. It was studying.

I don't study now. But I never lost the enjoyment. I guess it's too integral a piece of me. Reading and loving books are the fingerprints of who I am—no matter how much I change, they'll stay the same, betraying me to myself for the rest of my life. And bringing me into this bookstore, wanting to find something new to read until Chris gets home in the evening.

"Can I help you find anything?"

I hear the bookseller's voice behind me. Instinctive nerves tighten my posture. I turn, hesitant. While she watches me welcomingly, I wait for the moment I've been dreading since I decided earlier today I needed something new to read *tonight.* Why should I wait for delivery?

The moment doesn't come. The bookseller's expression doesn't change.

"Oh," I say uncertainly, "I'm not sure. Just browsing."

The girl grins. "Do you like literary fiction?" she asks eagerly. "Or is there a subgenre you prefer?"

I relax. The relief hits me in a rush. This is great. No, wonderful. She has no idea who I am. It's not like people overreact in general to seeing celebrities in Los Angeles, where you might run into Chrissy Teigen outside Whole Foods or Seth Rogen in line for ice cream. Not that I'm a celebrity. It's really *just* bookstores where the possibilities of prying questions or overeager fans worry me. If this bookseller doesn't know who I am, I've just found my new favorite place. I start imagining my evening in eager detail—curling up with my new purchase on the couch, toes on our white fur rug, gently controlling James Joyce so his paws don't knock green tea everywhere and stroking him until he purrs.

"Yeah, literary fiction generally. Contemporary fiction more specifically," I say, excitement in my voice now. I'm going to enjoy telling Chris tonight that I went to Forewords and no one knew who I was. It'll probably piss him off, but I don't care. I'll be reading while he's working out his frustration on his Peloton bike.

"I have just the thing," the girl says. She's clearly delighted to have a customer who wants her recommendation.

When she rushes off, my nerves wind up once more. The horrible thought hits me—what if she returns, excited to pitch me the book she's chosen, and she's holding *Only Once*? I don't know what I'd say. The couple seconds I have right now aren't enough for me to come up with even the first draft of how I could extricate myself from the conversation.

Instead, it's worse.

"Try this." The clerk thrusts the hardcover she's chosen toward me. "It came out last week. I read it in, like, two days."

Under the one-word title, *Refraction*, imposed over moody black-and-white photography, I read the name. Nathan Van Huysen. I look to where she got the book from, and I don't know how I didn't notice when I walked in. The cardboard display near the front of the store holds rows of copies, waiting patiently for customers, which tells me two things: high publisher expenditure, and it's not selling.

His name hits me the way it does every time I see it. In *New York Times* reviews, in the profiles I try to keep out of my browser history—never with much success. The first is wishing those fifteen letters meant nothing to me, weren't intertwined with my life in ways I'll never untangle.

Underneath the wishing, I find harder, flintier feelings. Resentment, even hatred. No regret, except regretting ever going to the upstate New York writers' workshop where I met Nathan Van Huysen.

I was fresh out of college. When I graduated from the University of Virginia and into the job I'd found fetching coffee and making copies in a publishing house, I felt like my life hadn't really started. I'd enjoyed college, enjoyed the rush I got learning whatever I found genuinely interesting, no matter the subject—fungal plant structures, behavioral economics, the funeral practices of the Greco-Roman world. I just knew I wouldn't be who I wanted to be until I wrote and published. Then I went upstate and found Nathan, and he found me.

I remember walking out of the welcome dinner, hugging my coat to my collar in the cold, and finding him waiting for me. We'd met earlier in the day, and his eyes lit up when he caught me leaving the restaurant. We introduced ourselves in more depth. He mentioned he was engaged—I hadn't asked. I was single—I didn't volunteer the information. It wasn't like that between us. While we walked out to Susquehanna River Bridge in the night wind, we ended up exchanging favorite verses of poetry, reading them from online on our phones. We were friends.

For the whole lot of good it did us.

When I take the copy of *Refraction*, the clerk's voice drops conspiratorially. "It's not as good as *Only Once*. But I love Nathan Van Huysen's prose."

I don't reply, not wanting to say out loud his prose was the first thing I noticed about him. Even at twenty-two, he wrote with influences fused perfectly into his own style, like every English course he'd ever taken—and Nathan had taken quite a few—was flowing out of his fingertips. It made me feel the things writers love to feel. Inspired, and jealous.

In my silence, the clerk's expression changes. "Wait," she continues, "you have read *Only Once*, haven't you?"

"Um," I say, struggling with how to reply. *Why is conversation way easier on the page?*

"If you haven't"—she starts toward the bestseller shelf to fetch the paperback. I know what'll happen when she catches sight of the back cover. Under the embarrassingly long list of starred reviews, she'll see the author photos. Nathan's blue eyes beneath the immaculate black waves of his hair, the dimple he only trots out for promotional photos and press tours. Then, next to him, she'll find his coauthor, Katrina Freeling. Young woman, sharp shoulders, round features, full eyebrows she honestly loves. Professionally done makeup, dark brown hair pressed and polished, nothing like it looks when she steps out of the shower or she's reading on the patio on sweaty summer days.

The differences won't matter. The bookseller will recognize the woman right in front of her.

My capacity for speech finally returns. "No, I've read it," I manage.

"Of course," the girl gushes. "Everyone's read it. Well, *Refraction* is one of Nathan Van Huysen's solo books. Like I said, it's good, but I wish he and Katrina Freeling would go back to writing together. I've heard they haven't spoken in years, though. Freeling doesn't even write anymore."

I don't understand how this girl is interested enough in the writing duo to know the rumors without identifying one of them in her bookstore. It might be because I haven't done many signings or festivals in the past three years. Following the very minimal promotional schedule for Nathan's and my debut novel, *Connecting Flights*, and then the exhausting release tour for our second, *Only Once*—during which I made my only previous visit here, to Forewords—I more or less withdrew from writerly and promotional events. It was difficult because Chris's and my social life in New York centered on the writing community, and it's part of why I like living in LA, where our neighbors are screenwriters and studio executives. In LA, when people learn you're a novelist, they treat you like a tenured Ivy League professor or a potted plant. Either is preferable to the combination of jealousy and judgment I endured spending time with former friends and competitors in New York.

If you'd told me four years ago I would leave New York for the California coast, I would've frowned, or likelier, laughed. New York was the epicenter for dreams like mine, and Nathan's. But I didn't know then the publication of *Only Once* would fracture me and leave me reassembling the pieces of myself into someone new. Someone for whom living in Los Angeles made sense.

While grateful the Forewords bookseller hasn't identified me—I would've had one of those politely excited conversations, signed some copies of *Only Once*, then left without buying a book—I don't know how to navigate hearing my own professional life story secondhand. "Oh well," I fumble. "That's too bad." No more browsing for me. I decide I just want out of this conversation.

"I know." The girl's grin catches a little mischievousness. "I wonder what happened between them. I mean, why would such a successful partnership just split up right when they were really popular?"

The collar of my coat feels itchy, my pulse beginning to pound. This is my least favorite topic, like, ever. *Why did you split up?* I've heard the rumors. I've heard them from graceless interviewers, from comments I've happened to notice under online reviews. I've heard them from Chris.

If they're to be believed, we grew jealous of each other, or Nathan thought he was better than me, or I was difficult to work with. Or we had an affair. There'd been speculation before our split. Two young writers, working together on retreats to Florida, Italy, the Hamptons. Photos of us with our arms around each other from the *Connecting Flights* launch event—the only launch we ever did together. The fact *Only Once* centered on marital infidelity didn't help. Nor did the very non-fictional demise of Nathan's own very non-fictional marriage.

This is why I don't like being recognized. I like the excited introductions. I love interacting with readers. What I don't like is the endless repetition of this one question. Why did Katrina Freeling and Nathan Van Huysen quit writing together?

"Who knows?" I say hastily. "Thanks for your recommendation. I'll . . . take it." I reach for the copy of *Refraction*, which the girl hands over, glowing.

FIVE MINUTES LATER, I walk out of the bookstore holding the one book I didn't want.

2

Nathan

I'M ON MY third iced tea. I would order coffee, except it's gauche to order iced coffee from the bartender. Fuck, though, I'm exhausted. I feel sleeplessness singeing my corneas, the small revolt they're staging for the post-midnight hours I spent in front of my new manuscript. It's this thriller I'm working on, where the wife of a federal agent stumbles onto the possibly criminal secret he's hiding.

I look like hell, the product of being on a plane yesterday, then writing into the night, then getting shitty sleep in my non–Four Seasons hotel. It leaves me undeniably out of place in O'Neill's, the trendy bar where I haven't set foot in years. When I lived in New York, I'd come here to meet other writers. With gold-rimmed mirrors, marble tabletops, and cocktails named after playwrights, O'Neill's was the place to be seen. Which I liked. But it's been two years since I left the city I could feel turning on me, needing a fresh start following my divorce.

"Sorry to make you wait." My agent sits down across from me. Jen

Bradley is middle-aged, fearsome in negotiations, and fantastic with working out plot holes. She's the second agent I've had in my career. After *Only Once*, I had my pick of literary agents. I chose Jen for her straight-shooting sensibility and her intelligence, which she's shown in selling my solo manuscript.

"It's fine," I say, washing the words down with iced tea. "How are you?"

"Busy," Jen replies. "How was your tour?"

I have to smile. Straight to the point. I just wrapped a weeklong book tour for my new novel, *Refraction*. It was a whirlwind of bookstores in Midwestern cities, nondescript hotels, dinners of room-service Caesar salads every freaking night. Hour-long flights between airports named for one president or another, which were the best parts of my day for the refuge I could take in writing on the plane, running wild on this new thriller. "Fewer stops than the last one," I admit. "Pretty good turnout, though."

Jen eyes me.

"Okay, mediocre turnout," I amend. "They did crap marketing, and you know it."

I was prepared for *Refraction* to get less promotional support than *Only Once*. When we sold the book, it was clear my publisher was settling. What they wanted was another Katrina and Nathan book. It was Jen who convinced them this was the next best thing. One-half of the duo whose book sold fifteen million copies and counting wasn't someone to turn down.

Her mouth flattens. She's displeased. "First week numbers aren't what they'd hoped." She lets the sentence hang in the chatter of the room.

I nod. While I suspected sales numbers were low, I don't like having my suspicions confirmed. In the pause, I drift from the conversation. I have this problem—at least my ex-wife, Melissa, would say "problem"—

where when I'm not immediately engaged in what's in front of me, my mind returns to whatever I'm writing. Which right now is the critical scene where Sarah confronts her husband. It's a referendum on their marriage with huge, high-intensity implications, and I'm hungry to put it on the page.

"Will the numbers hurt their offer?" I ask, remembering I haven't yet sold the book I'm working on now. I submitted the proposal months ago, and we've heard nothing since. Jen's explained the publisher didn't want to offer until they had sales information on *Refraction*. Truthfully, I don't even care what they pay me. It's not like I need the money. I've never needed the money—a trust fund and an Ivy League education took care of that long before *Only Once* was an idea in the back of my head. Even with the divorce, in which I willingly gave Melissa half of *Only Once*'s royalties, I still don't *need* money.

What I need is to write. I'm not me if I can't write.

Jen frowns. Her fingers worry her delicate gold watch. She says nothing.

It scares me. "Don't sugarcoat it now."

While she hesitates, my mind rehashes the scene I'm working on. It feels less like a reverie now, more like a coping mechanism. Sarah's in their kitchen, the domesticity of the setting purposeful. She doesn't need to speak. He knows. He says, *They're going to pass on the proposal.*

Wait.

I refocus on Jen. The words I just heard weren't in my head. They were from her.

They're going to pass on the proposal.

The weight of it settles on me. They're rejecting me. I wasn't rejected from Dartmouth, wasn't rejected when Katrina and I queried our agent, wasn't rejected when we sold *Connecting Flights* or *Only Once* on proposal. I haven't been rejected from anything.

No, that's not true.

It hurts. No matter how much success you've had, insecurity is never far from reach when you're being judged on pieces of your soul. If you won't kill your darlings, I guess someone else will. There's no indignation where I expected there to be, only whispers of doubt newly insistent in my head.

I force my next words past them. Wallowing won't help. "Okay. It's a setback, but I'll write something else. What're they looking for?" This is how I'll fight those whispers. I'll write. I have enough ideas in my head to fill my hard drive. It's not difficult to imagine, if given the time, loving one of them the way I do this one.

"Nathan." Jen says my name forcefully. It's her reality-check voice.

"What? I have the 1950s novel I was developing—"

"They don't want another book from you."

I've never felt O'Neill's was small. The extravagance is part of the point. The grandeur of the floor plan, the glittering shelves of liquor, the expensive suits and handbags of the patrons.

With Jen's words, the place feels small. The walls press inward, warping nauseatingly. I fight the sensation. "So we'll submit wide," I say. "Send the manuscript everywhere. I'm a *New York Times* bestselling author. I have a movie in development. I've had other publishers salivating over me for years." I'm half convincing her with my confidence, half convincing myself.

"We could," Jen replies levelly. "You won't get a good offer, though, which could eventually kill your career. Your sales are dropping, and your reviews are lackluster."

I clench my hand reflexively on my drink. I know she's right. What's more, I know why. Anything I write is compared to *Only Once*. Which is unfair. It's ridiculous to compare me to one of the most successful books of the past five years. I wrote it, but not alone. Of course it's better. Katrina's a genius. It's why I walked up to her on the first day of the New York Resident Writers' Program, dazed from the power and clarity of the excerpt she'd read, and practically prostrated myself telling her I wanted to collaborate. I remember how surprise didn't enter her round eyes. How she'd said yes like it was easy.

The first night out there in Cooperstown, New York, we left the introductory dinner with our workshop classmates together. We introduced ourselves for real, got to know each other. She was fresh out of undergrad, unlike me. I kind of figured she couldn't be single, though the question only crossed my mind objectively—I'd proposed to Melissa three months prior and was enjoying the post-engagement rush of pride and promise. While we walked, Katrina read me her favorite poetry from off her phone. I found myself loving her choices, understanding what resonated for her in each of them.

It wasn't romantic, Katrina and me. It was romantic when Melissa would come home from one of her work events in her semiformal dress and I couldn't decide whether I was more eager to hear how her day went or run the zipper down the black-diamond ski slope of her backside. (I ended up doing one then the other, though the order changed often.) It was romantic when we'd count down from three and simultaneously say the same movie we wanted to watch on Friday nights.

But with Katrina—was it romantic when you instinctively knew someone's very existence fascinated you, made you grateful? Finding it romantic would be missing the point, like valuing the sun because it was bright. I'm glad for the light, but really, I'm grateful for the fact it sustains life on Earth.

Not that Katrina sustains my life on Earth. I— No. Inelegant metaphor.

It's over with Katrina. That's what's important. And, presently, damning. Being compared to her and what we did together for the rest of my career is a death sentence.

"What're you saying, I'm finished?" Hearing the words out loud nearly paralyzes me. It sends me back to those years in high school, before I'd shown anyone my writing. I wasn't athletic, wasn't particularly good-looking or funny. I had trouble talking to my peers. Even the wealthy family I came from didn't exactly distinguish me in the marble halls of my prep school. I was no one.

Until I sent a short story to the *New Yorker.* I couldn't talk to my peers, but I could write for them. I could write my way onto their breakfast tables, next to their parents' grapefruit. Into their older brothers' bedrooms, in piles they'd catch up on over winter breaks home from college. Nathan Van Huysen—the Nathan I was meant to be—was born on those pages, his life written in fine black print. Elegant and undeniable. "I'm not going to quit, Jen," I say. "I'll write the best fucking book they've ever read."

"You're not finished," Jen says. "I have a plan."

"Fine. I'll do it. What's your plan?"

"You're not going to like it," she warns.

"I can handle whatever—"

I cut myself off, realizing what she has in mind with the penetrating clarity people probably have right before they're hit by an oncoming car.

"No." I drop the word onto the table between us.

"Hear me out." For once, Jen sounds gentle, persuasive. "You still have a contract for one more book with her."

Her. Jen's probably wise not to use her name. The visceral reaction I'd have would not help her case. "I'm not the one holding things up," I say. "If Parthenon wants Katrina, then they need to call Katrina."

"Parthenon's passed on your book because they're trying to force you to fulfill your contract with her." In my silence, Jen continues. "If we can deliver something to them, I'll have the leverage to sell more of your solo titles."

"Fine." I falter on the syllable. "Like I said, *I'm* perfectly able to deliver another Freeling–Van Huysen book. It's Kat who will never agree." I wince, hearing myself use her shortened name. I shouldn't have said

Kat. We're not friends. I don't need to have spoken to her in the past four years to know she won't do it. She made it painfully clear on the night we finished *Only Once*. Finished everything, really.

"I've already discussed it with her agent. He thinks he can get her on board."

Discussed it with her agent? I'm irritated Jen's gone behind my back, opening this conversation with who knows who. She might've even gone to Parthenon. This ends here. "Bullshit," I say.

"Are you calling me a liar?" Jen isn't offended. She raises her eyebrows dryly.

"No," I reply. "It's Chris you shouldn't believe." I know Katrina's agent. He used to be *our* agent. Chris Calloway would promise whatever to whomever if it would put him ahead.

"He *is* her fiancé," Jen reminds me. "Presumably, he has some insight into what she will and won't do."

I crack a couple knuckles under the table. Why Katrina got together with Chris is outside my comprehension. "She's retired," I say firmly. Katrina Freeling is retired. If the man she's marrying hasn't gotten the memo, I guess she'll need to write it in words with fewer syllables next time.

Jen watches me. "Respectfully, you haven't spoken to her in years," she says. "How would you know?" The ice in my drink shifts suddenly, tumbling down like it's punctuating her point.

"I know her." I hate how well I know her. It's not the fundamental things I wish I could unlearn—her resoluteness, her intelligence. They're the things everyone knows. I wish I didn't know she's restless on planes, even a little fearful. I wish I didn't know she hates the word *always*. I wish I didn't know what time she showers, what she wears to bed.

Jen's inquisitiveness turns delicate. "I don't want to invade your privacy," she starts. "You know I don't give a shit about the gossip. But this is a *good* move for your career. I need to know if there's a reason I shouldn't pursue it." I open my mouth. "Not this retirement nonsense. A real reason," she preempts me.

She's not asking whether Katrina's hard to work with, whether our styles no longer mesh, whether we just don't like each other. I know what she's asking.

I finish my drink, the memories of our final night writing *Only Once* rolling over me, smothering like the Florida heat outside the house where we wrote the manuscript. Pages with her handwriting and mine scrawled on top of each other, the strokes and curves of the letters crossing like in a dance. Waiting in front of her door. A fire dying in the fireplace, the ashes of charred paper in the air. Returning to writing with Katrina would be a nightmare.

No. Not writing is the nightmare. What's left of my career if I refuse? I'm only thirty-one years old. I've been writing since I was seventeen. It's the only thing I've ever wanted to do. The only thing I *can* do.

"Is there really no other choice?" I ask, my voice low. Jen shakes her head. I stand, placing cash on the table. *Is there a reason I can't work with Katrina?* I have reason enough to fill books I'll never write. "If Chris can convince her—and that's a big fucking if—then I don't have a problem with it."

Jen hefts her purse onto her shoulder, standing up. "Great. We'll make it happen. Start developing ideas. This'll be huge."

"It'll be something." I head for the front of the bar, not waiting for Jen's reply. Pushing open the burnished gold handle on the black door, I walk out, terrified by and taking comfort in what I know fundamentally to be true. Kat—Katrina—will never want to work with me.

3

Katrina

When I walk in my front door, I stop in surprise, smelling coffee. In the kitchen, I hear the Nespresso machine spitting out cappuccino, and I have the mental image of some under-caffeinated burglar who's stolen into our place and decided to whip up some joe while going to work on our valuables. Then I—the place's well-meaning and coffee-hating co-occupant—would surprise *him*. It would be the perfect inciting incident.

It's not my cappuccino burglar, of course. It's Chris, who I realize in seconds has come home in the middle of the day. I walk into the living room, where he's spread out his laptop and contract pages into an impromptu workspace.

He comes out of the kitchen carrying his coffee and sits on the couch, hardly glancing up. "Where were you?" he asks.

I hold up the bookstore bag. "I went to Forewords. When did you come home?" Chris doesn't work from home often. Every chance he gets, he's in the office or riding the endless carousel of networking with editors and authors.

"Had lunch with a client nearby, then needed to take a call. It was just closer to come here." Chris's voice is deep, declarative. It's like everything about him—conventionally desirable. Golden hair, green eyes, sharp jaw, former-Duke-quarterback shoulders. It's funny, having a handsome face in front of you for years, you start to lose the whole for the composite parts. It's like how if you focus on each individual word in a gorgeous passage of writing, they cease to have lyricism or meaning.

I sit on the ottoman, pulling off my flats. I don't exactly get lonely while Chris is in the office—I enjoy the freedom to organize my own days—but I do miss my fiancé. The chance to talk to him isn't one I'll pass up. "Was it for the Vincent Blake book?"

He grimaces. "He turned me down. Signed with someone else."

"I'm sorry," I say, meaning it. I respect Chris's drive, despite how his work life occupies his *entire* life. I shrug my jacket off, moving to sit next to Chris on the couch. When I entwine my arm with his, he looks down and unlinks our elbows. While he doesn't move away from me, I'm pretty sure he's leaning imperceptibly in the opposite direction. It dims my enthusiasm.

"He'll regret it," Chris intones.

James Joyce darts out of the hallway, finding my feet immediately. Well, *someone's* glad to see me. I stroke his head, his ears flicking while I do. "Yes, I'm sure he will," I say.

Chris scoffs. It's pointed, purposeful. Not just from professional dejection.

I furrow my brow. "What's that for?"

"You make it sound like you respect me."

His words hit me like a slap. Chris and I fight every now and then. Unremarkable fights—whether I'm "meddling" when I urge him to network less, if I'm pushing him too hard to set the date for our wedding, whose family we're visiting for the holidays. It's never about whether I *respect* him. I'm reeling slightly from this jab out of nowhere.

"Of course I respect you," I say. "Why would you think otherwise?" We've been engaged for two years. He was Nathan's and my agent for the three years before that. I respect him professionally and personally, though it's not why I fell in love with him.

When I was a kid, I would go hiking in the hills outside our house. South Dakota is humid in the summers and hilly twelve months out of the year. My mom would serve us vanilla ice cream when we got home, hot and exhausted. It was from the rectangular Dreyer's container, the cheapest from the grocery store, I guess, and with four kids in the house, vanilla was a safe choice everyone would enjoy. I remember the way the perfect, cold sweet would melt in my mouth while sweat stuck my hair to my forehead. In those moments, vanilla ice cream was the greatest ice cream flavor—the greatest food in the whole world. When people asked me what my favorite ice cream flavor was, I would say vanilla without considering the question.

Chris was vanilla ice cream.

The hiking days were the pre-publication fervor of *Only Once*. Nathan and I were no longer speaking. We'd finished rounds of developmental and copyedits and were in the crush of publicity and meetings for other opportunities, which we did over the phone whenever possible. Every day, instead of writing or reading or just enjoying my downtime, I was watching what was only a Word document on my computer grow into this monster of epic promotional proportions.

I wasn't well. I woke up with cold in my fingers and my feet and went to bed exhausted from worrying and inexpressibly grateful for the reprieve of sleep. I googled "post-success depression" from my phone under the covers. I sought out my therapist in New York, who I still call, though less often now. Interviews were grueling—I, who once wrote hundreds of words per hour, struggled to push single sentences past the cage of insecurity and uncertainty in which I lived.

I'm under no illusion that what stressed me out was watching the success of *Only Once*. It wasn't humility. It was fear. I hadn't felt this way with *Connecting Flights*, with its modest deal, its respectful but ordinary reviews. But with *Only Once*, I was close to having what I wanted, and if I had what I wanted, I could lose it. The possibility felt like radioactive material, and I was certain it would chew up my insides or make me lose my hair or whatever holding onto plutonium would do. I hated it.

The fear was what caught me in the women's restroom of one of LA's film and TV agencies, where I was pitching *Only Once* for development. It was an important meeting, hence my flying out, and on the same day as one of Nathan's divorce mediations, hence his not. The restroom was entirely white stone, like a spaceship or something. The lights were iridescent. When I stopped in front of the sink, feeling the sweat sliding down my sleeves, the idea of charmingly reproducing our pitch points overwhelmed me. I worked to even my breathing, and I . . . couldn't. Then I was crying, hiccupping, gripping the sink like the seat of a crashing plane.

I called Chris. Not out of some instinct for his comfort or whatever. We weren't dating, wouldn't be for several months. I just wanted to cancel the meeting. Pretend I had the flu, or wasn't stomaching the sushi from the reception dinner with Hollywood agents the night before. I didn't care. I guess he heard the waver in my voice or the sob waiting in my throat because he spoke calmly instead of wondering why I wanted to cancel. He said, *Today isn't your entire life. Today is one day of your job. Do your job the best you can, then do the next thing. Okay?*

In short, it worked. I did what he said. I did the meeting. I called my Uber. In my hotel I wrote four interview question responses I hadn't finished. I had a sandwich. I read Celeste Ng's new book and focused on her use of prepositional phrases. When I got in bed, I felt calmer, more cohesive. The next day, I did the same thing.

Chris made me feel like I could be okay. I wanted very much to return to being okay and with him, I could. In the years that followed of his encouragement, patience, and support, I was, or close.

I wondered if Nathan would've done the same. I'll never know.

I love vanilla ice cream. I do.

Right now, however, my fiancé is watching me with impassive, resentful eyes. "Why would I think you respect me, Katrina?" It is pointedly rhetorical. "You won't let me sell books for you," he continues.

The realization dawns on me where this conversation's headed. "Chris, I don't have books *for* you to sell. If I did, believe me, you'd be my pick. You're always my pick," I say delicately, struggling to keep my voice in a reasonable register. He only rolls his eyes. It's what pushes me over the edge. I stand up, yanking my jacket from the couch cushions. "My decision to stop writing has nothing to do with you. You know that." Irritation wraps around my words. His audacity, that he would make this about himself, is unnerving.

"You have ideas, though," he says as I walk over to the hall closet and shove my jacket inside. The hangers rattle, and I still them with my free hand.

"Nothing I want to write," I say, holding in my indignation. It's not untrue, though I know I'm hiding the nuances of the problem. I've had concepts for new novels, characters I've daydreamed of. I just don't know if I want them published.

While I'm more confident I could face the fear I felt when *Only Once* was coming out, I'm not certain I want to. Not certain it's worth it. I enjoy my life. I enjoy perusing wedding venue possibilities and presenting the occasional writing workshop for an MFA program or high school class. I enjoy the freedom I have to read, even to outline in my head or draft pages nobody'll ever read. I don't know if I want to catapult myself once more into the heights of publishing, only to wrack myself with the fear of falling.

I face Chris on the other end of the room, finding him watching me. He's discarded his laptop next to him. "Why are we even talking about this?" I'm getting the uneasy feeling this conversation was planned, scheduled into his day with his other meetings and obligations. *Lunch with editor. Call with Vincent. Guilt-trip fiancée.*

Chris is a chaser, which I do respect in my partner, the way he will fix his gaze on the horizon until the sunlight sears his eyes. He comes from high-pressure parents who live outside New York City in a house with a stone driveway. Every minute of his childhood was spent in competition with his older and younger brothers, and I remember Chris telling me he and his siblings were the only kids whose parents would bring them to back-to-school nights so the Calloway children could hear their teachers' feedback in person. Psychotic.

The problem is, Chris wants me to chase with him. Chase bestseller lists, chase publishing prizes and other prestigious recognition. Chase a solo career. For me, the stability I found in our relationship was the destination. For him, it was only one stop on the journey somewhere shinier and sleeker and *more*.

While I've known deep down it irks him I gave up writing, he's never pressed me on it. Until now, anyway. As my partner, if not my agent, I assumed he understood. I head for the kitchen, needing aspirin.

"I've had a call with Liz," he says.

It halts me. Liz is the editor at Parthenon Books who bought *Connecting Flights* and *Only Once*. When she and I last spoke, I told her I was taking time off from writing. I round on Chris, not liking his fixed stare. He's serious. "Oh yeah?" I ask hesitantly.

"I raised the possibility—"

"Why?" I cut him off. "There is no possibility."

"You're technically under contract with Parthenon," he replies, like I hoped he wouldn't. When Parthenon bought *Only Once,* it was a two-book deal, meaning they also bought another yet-to-be-written book from me and Nathan and paid us an advance. We discussed ideas, worked up a synopsis, but we never wrote the book. Parthenon never pushed because the advance was next to nothing compared to the huge earnings of *Only Once.*

They'll never cancel the contract, I know they won't. *Only Once* continues to pull in good sales, though not quite like they once were. While the film in development with Miramount probably won't ever happen—they often don't, Chris cautioned me—it would return Nathan and me to prominence. Parthenon doesn't want to pass up the possibility.

Nevertheless, our deal has left Nathan and me and our publisher in a complicated, motionless dance. They won't force us to write. It's not unheard-of for successful authors to take several years between books, and there's no writing police they could have bang down our doors demanding pages. Nathan and I won't cancel the contract, for different reasons. Nathan is a workaholic and would never pass up the opportunity to write something. I haven't had the heart to tell my literary agent–fiancé it's never going to happen. As long as the contract isn't canceled, it's left our publisher with the rights to the next Freeling–Van Huysen book. If there ever is a next Freeling–Van Huysen book.

"Fine," I say, feeling less generous now. "Let's pay back the advance."

"Why won't you just consider it?" Chris is using his phone voice, velvety and persuasive. He never uses it with me.

"Because I don't want to."

"What about me?" He's no longer nonchalant. His eyes are hard and defensive. "I'm your fiancé. Do my feelings mean nothing?" Hearing raised voices, James Joyce, who was curled up on the foot of the couch, races from the room.

"*Your* feelings? On *my* writing career?" I fire back.

"We could use the money," Chris says.

I laugh. He flew me to Paris in January for my twenty-eighth birthday. We're having this fight in our wide-lawn house in Hancock Park with Chris's Tesla out front. I didn't grow up with money, and having it was never particularly important to me. It is, however, a side effect of having your work printed in thirty-five languages.

Chris looks uncomfortable, for once. "I'm not joking," he says. "I made some investments assuming you'd get over this writer's block."

This is news to me. In the years since we moved in together, we've discussed our finances. We even share a financial planner. We have *not* combined my earnings with his, which means he could not have lost my money—so when he says *we need the money*, he means *he* needs the money. His confession is enough to bring me back toward the couch.

"Chris . . ." I say, knowing neither of us will enjoy what's coming. "If you need, I could . . . write you a check."

"Jesus, Katrina," he snaps, right on cue. "I'm not a fucking charity case. I'm a literary agent who just needs to *sell a book.*"

"And that's *my* problem?" While I'm concerned exactly what investments he's made, right now, I'm pissed he's putting the blame on what he's calling my *writer's block.*

"We're getting married," he replies. *On the twelfth of never*, I want to say. He continues. "It's both our problem."

I don't bother confirming it's definitely more his problem for frittering his money on his investments. "We'll look at your finances. We can figure something out."

Chris heaves a sigh. When he does, it's like he releases his combativeness and poise. His next words come out almost understanding. Almost. "I know you don't want to write anymore, but Katrina, this isn't just your career. *My* career could be on the line. The agency expects me to make another huge sale, and they know you're my fiancée. They think it should've been easy. I can't keep coming back to them empty-handed."

It's clear it hurts him to admit this. Chris isn't a man used to falling short. "You would really help me," he continues, louder. "Can't we just discuss it? Get on the phone with Liz? I've already spoken with Nathan's agent. He's in if you are."

My head jerks up. He not only called Liz, but he's reached out to *Nathan*? I feel betrayed. Worse, I feel put in the exact position Chris wants me in. It's becoming increasingly clear everything about this conversation was orchestrated, designed for me to have zero say.

"I. Don't. Write. Anymore," I say, putting space between each word. "Find a new client."

My remark has the intended effect, I note half guiltily. His face reddens—he's obviously remembering Vincent Blake's fresh rejection. He's silent for a long moment, and I start to leave.

"How about a new wife?"

I whip to face him. The floor feels unsteady. The sunlight streaming in our wide windows is harsh, dizzying. My face heats with shock and hurt. "*What?*"

Chris, to his credit, looks pained. "Shit. I—I didn't mean that. It's just— You know I love you. I love everything about you, and part of you is a writer. I guess I miss that part."

I have to give him credit for the line. It hurts in every single way. I know I shouldn't be admiring my fiancé's dialogue when he's suggesting he'll leave me—I guess it's the writer part of me.

Refusing to let my eyes water, I walk from the room.

4

Nathan

I'M STUCK. On my screen, the cursor waits insistently, mocking me. I've been sitting in front of my computer for two hours, and I'm in the exact same place in my manuscript I was when I started this morning.

Ordinarily, an empty hotel room would present ideal writing conditions. I roam my eyes over its features for the hundredth time, hoping I'll find inspiration hiding in the heavy curtains, the crimson carpet, the distraction-free white sheets of the bed. Since my meeting with Jen, I haven't been able to write a single word. The idea of working with Katrina is messing with my head.

Not that it'll ever happen. Jen will call tomorrow and say Katrina refused, and we'll find another way to sell my next book.

Which is why I don't understand why I can't write. I can write no matter what's going on in my life. The night I was hospitalized with the flu, I wrote. The night my dad died, I wrote. The night Melissa and I decided to get divorced, I wrote. It's like breathing. Right now, I'm choking.

The idea of Katrina saying no isn't what paralyzes me. It's the idea of her saying yes. I can't even imagine it. Even while editing *Only Once*, we were only exchanging perfunctory emails every few days. When the book was released, we didn't even do one promotional event together. It probably contributed to the book's success, honestly. After the *New York Times* piece on the end of our partnership, everyone wanted to hunt the novel for clues of what happened between us. As if the truth could've been in those pages.

I close my computer, defeated. The clap of the screen is harsh in the quiet hotel room. I pull out my phone, contemplating calling my ex-wife and quickly deciding it's not a good idea. Conversations with Melissa only leave each of us renewed in our respective resentments. Instead, I call a number I haven't dialed in years.

Harriet's voice picks up on the fourth ring. "Nathan Van Huysen. An honor," she says sarcastically, just the way I'd remembered.

"It's been a while, Harriet."

"Four years," she replies, in light singsong.

I smile. It's how Harriet Soong is. She enjoys ribbing her friends, colleagues, even instructors almost as much as she loves immersing herself in the Southern Gothic mysteries of the novels she writes.

"Yeah, um," I say. "How've you been?"

"Shit, sure." I practically hear her shrug over the phone. "Let's catch up, like it's not a completely fucking weird thing to do right now. I read your new book. *Refraction*," she says dramatically. She pauses, and I find I'm still grinning, even knowing what's coming. "Your worst yet," Harriet informs me.

"Well, I've set the bar high," I shoot back.

Harriet laughs, and it's fortunately not scornful. I half expected she'd just call me a selfish asshole and hang up. I mean, she still might—I'm just glad she hasn't yet. "You haven't changed," she says.

"Parthenon wants me and Katrina to write another book." The words fall out of my mouth, like I can't hold them in any longer.

There's a pause on the other end of the line. "So you're calling *me*, when we haven't so much as emailed in years." I hear her voice shift into seriousness.

"You were there. For . . . all of it."

I've known Harriet as long as I've known Katrina. The three of us met at the New York Resident Writers' Program. She'd often join us on writing retreats—we'd find Airbnbs in unusual locales, hole up with days' worth of wine and frozen food, and attempt to write obscene amounts of words. She moderated our book launch for *Connecting Flights*, which was unsurprisingly perfect, what with her insight and wry humor. When we wrote *Only Once*, Katrina and I rented a house in the Florida Keys just fifteen minutes from Harriet's home, using the money we had from our debut novel. With the wet heat keeping us indoors, we finished *Only Once* in a matter of months.

My ex-wife had not loved the writing retreats. Nevertheless, Melissa understood. It's one of her greatest virtues. She understood. We'd fallen in love our senior year of college and moved in together when we graduated from Dartmouth, her into social work, where every day she heard her clients' struggles with child custody or financial problems, and she understood. It exercises the same muscles writing does, self-imagination and empathy and hypothetical reasoning, and Melissa excelled at it. *Excels.* She's working in the same position in Seattle now. She's dating a radiologist.

When I said I wanted to write *Only Once* with Katrina in Florida, Melissa resisted, not unreasonably. I was married, proposing living in the same house for a few months with a young woman who was *not* my wife, working on our next novel. Most of *Connecting Flights* was written in cafés or our apartments, with one or two weekend or weeklong retreats. What we were proposing with *Only Once* was different—months, uninterrupted. What's more, I understood innately there were new pressures involved in asking my wife for allowances on one book as opposed to a potential career of them.

Nevertheless, when I explained the practice of long retreats was not uncommon, and plenty of cowriters married to other people did it for efficiency and the collaborative process, she reluctantly understood. I don't know, she probably felt like she had no choice. You kind of don't, in your marriage, in the instances when your partner's comfortable just saying how it's going to be—which I'm sure I did too much of.

Melissa would just promise she understood, the way she did with the *Only Once* retreat. Once she consented, she never fought me on the plan. On the day I flew out of New York for Florida, she smiled from the opposite end of the JFK terminal and waved when I went through security.

I knew what she was ignoring, then and for months before. Pretending she didn't notice signs other women would have. My distraction, the casual ease I brought to every conversation. I pretended I didn't notice them, either, even while I felt the pieces of me pulling in different directions and realized Melissa wasn't the biggest piece. Nevertheless, I tried. I called from Florida often. I made her laugh with inside jokes and made plans for what we would do when I was home. I pretended I was in love with her.

Until our conversation in the kitchen one night, three weeks after I got home from writing *Only Once* with Katrina.

Then, she understood.

We were divorced within the year.

"Was there a specific question you had for me?" Harriet asks. Over the line, there's the clatter of a screen door falling shut. I remember the porch in front of Harriet's house, the ocean in view. She's probably watching the sunset in a way we don't see it in Manhattan, or from my condo in Chicago.

"Is this a terrible idea?" I intend the question sarcastically. It comes out searching.

She replies immediately. "Yes."

I huff a laugh and start to pace my hotel room in my socks. "I don't have a choice."

"Okay," Harriet says. "Then why'd you call me? You want me to lie and tell you you'll work everything out? That you'll have the perfect partnership you used to?"

I deflate. Harriet's always been uncanny when it comes to finding the heart of things. In the weeks of the New York Resident Writers' Program—dinners of Chinese or pub food in the small neighborhood where we were staying—and on our retreats, she would often rib Katrina and me about having hidden romantic feelings for each other until, one day, she suddenly stopped.

"Are you ready to grovel?" she asks.

"*Me?*" Groveling to Katrina is the second-most preposterous idea I've heard today, and it's close. "Come on. You know what she did."

"Then you took your *New Yorker* interview. The one where you said writing *Only Once* was the worst time in your life, and you don't think even Katrina Freeling's genius is worth the torture."

I grimace, toeing the carpet. It's not a direct quote. It is, however, close enough for discomfort. I remember the interview fairly vividly, the sterile modernity of the restaurant where I met the middle-aged journalist, the sound of my criticism of Katrina leaving my lips. It stung the second I said it.

The *New Yorker* interview was the end. The formal end, anyway. Truthfully, it was over the day we turned in the draft, but after the interview, Katrina had Chris call and inform me, sounding stiffly professional, that she was retired.

"You want my advice?" Harriet asks when I don't reply. I wait for her to admonish me, to instruct me to grow up and work with my collaborator like a reasonable adult. "Stay the hell away from each other," she says decisively. "If you can't, then write this book as fast as humanly possible."

I nod to myself. It's refreshing, if sobering. "Thanks for your honesty," I say.

I hear the screen door open and shut again. "Have a good night, Nathan."

"Hey, Harriet," I say before she can hang up. "I read your book. It was incredible."

There's silence over the line for a long moment. "Thanks," she says, her voice warming like stone in sunlight. "Really." I don't have the opportunity to expand on the compliment. Harriet hangs up.

In the quiet of my room, I'm left only with her advice. I feel worse, which I wouldn't have imagined possible. I look over, finding my computer on the drab hotel desk, hoping ideas spring from the machine fully formed. They don't, of course. The only thing occupying my head is Katrina.

Working with her *would* be torture. But the undeniable truth is, there's a part of me eager for the torture. The woman is brilliant. I've loved everything she's ever written. Just knowing she's going to write again, it's inspiring. The writer in me can't wait.

The problem is, it's not just the writer who'll have to work with her. It's Nathan Van Huysen she can't stand, and who can't be in the same room with her.

Instead of reopening my computer, I reach into my suitcase.

I pull out my copy of *Only Once*, which I'm hardly ever without. The pages are folded in places, the hardcover edges misshapen. Katrina's name hangs above mine on the front cover. I open to the first chapter, dropping onto the edge of the hotel comforter, and read. There's no truth to these pages, but the trick of fiction is to make you think there is.

I let myself fall for it as often as I can.

5

Katrina

I'M IN MY office that evening, pages and pages in front of me on my desk. They're not pages of prose, though. They're financial statements, records of payments and royalties occupying the wood surface everywhere it's not piled with books. I ran out of bookshelf space years ago and resorted to double-shelving, then putting them in stacks on the floor and in boxes in the closet, then finally giving up every semblance of organization and depositing them wherever there's room.

After talking to Chris, I spent the rest of the day on the phone with our financial adviser. She emailed over the documents in front of me now, which I pored over, unraveling the numbers. It's a myth writers have no faculty for math. I understood Chris's position quickly, and it wasn't good. Earnings from my books and from his other clients, vacations in Europe, the failing investment portfolio on which he's overspent. Then there's the house. I had no idea when we moved out to LA that Chris couldn't afford what he'd put into our four-million-dollar home.

Add in a two-hundred-thousand-dollar renovation and the fucking Tesla, and he's in over his head.

I feel stupid. I should've been conscious of how his finances measured up to mine, but I wasn't. Honestly, I'd been too depressed to focus on much.

I cap my pen and rub my palms on my pants, working to unwind my nerves. James Joyce, who was curled on the rug in the center of the room, gets up on noiseless cat paws and slips out of the crack in the door, perhaps intuiting my mood.

I wouldn't mind selling our house, downscaling our lifestyle. Chris . . . would. It's not just the money, either. Chris likes being attached to a famous author. Every day I don't write, don't publish, I disappoint him—I let him fall a little more out of love with me.

I don't want him to fall out of love with me. Not only for the promise of our engagement but for the Chris I know he can be. For the Chris who would wrap me in huge hugs with sparkling eyes when he'd sell new manuscripts, or who would hold my hand in museums we'd visit on vacation and request I show him my very favorite painting in the gallery.

The idea of losing him and us is exhaustingly painful, which is why I chose to ignore it until now. With our financials in front of me—documenting our life like photographs or love letters—I feel like I'm finally viewing honestly what Chris and I have, weighed down by the baggage of success. Of whatever Chris inherited from his frustrating family. Of me and Nathan, if I was honest. Except "baggage" shouldn't be the metaphor for this sort of thing, because you can put baggage down. When you're weary or your hand hurts, you can say "wait up" and drop the baggage to the ground until you're ready to carry on.

I don't think you ever get to put these kinds of problems down.

They're less like unwieldy luggage and more like the ugly furniture gifted by your in-laws you have to keep in view because they might come over and check. While you grow used to the puce leather chair and the lamp inherited from Grandma's old home, you wish deep down they were gone and know they never will be.

Chris and I have ugly furniture with each other. Years of it.

There's one thing that would fix this. All I need to do is write one book. Well, one book with Nathan. Nevertheless, just one book. I could do it in two months, if I pushed myself.

Two months to save my relationship.

I'm contemplating the passage of time when there's gentle knocking on the door behind me. I turn to find Chris entering. He's holding the bookstore bag I realize I left in the living room, and flowers. White roses. Chris understands the value of a cliché. He lingers near the doorway, looking sculpted out of clay instead of stone, his imposing form soft instead of uncompromising.

"I'm really sorry, Katrina," he says. "I didn't mean what I said. You don't have to write if you don't want to."

He hands me the flowers and places the bag on my desk.

His voice is reluctantly reassuring when he continues, like it's not easy for him to say his next words. "I'll call Liz and tell her it's not happening."

I look up, meeting his eyes. There's contrition in them, effort he's making for Katrina his fiancée, not Katrina the writer. I wonder how long it'll last.

Still, it's real. Just the fact he's offering to call Liz and rescind something he desperately wants on my behalf shows he genuinely loves me.

And without Chris, what does my life even look like? He was by my side when I had nothing. The night we first slept together was the day *Only Once* was released. He kept me grounded, helped me navigate the stratospheric path from published author to household name. The truth is, his fraternity-president features hide streaks of uncommon patience and gentle care, though I haven't felt them lately. He even managed to make good days out of the hardest time of my life. In the post–*Only Once* year, I remember weeks when I felt guilty for doing nothing the entire day except read or nap. Those nights, Chris would spend dinner discussing every detail of whatever I was reading with such focus I couldn't help looking forward to reading more, and telling him more the next night.

He's been good to me. He's been there for me. We might have some ugly furniture, but the house we're building still feels like it could be home.

What's more, I've invested in our relationship, the way Chris has in his flagging financial portfolio. I never expected I would pin so much hope to getting married, but in the years since Chris proposed to me, it's what I've had. Without wanting to publish my writing, the life I'm building with Chris has become the shining milestone I'm pushing for, the north on my compass.

If I give two months—two wretched months, but just two months—I'd be pointed north again.

"No," I say softly.

The decision is made in my mind. The hard part is saying it. Chris watches me, waiting.

"I'll do it," I get out.

His expression shifts immediately. In it I see joy I haven't in months. "You're sure?" his voice wavers.

"I'm sure."

I feel everything but.

He drops to his knees in front of me. Even on the ground, with me in my desk chair, he's exactly my height. He kisses me in a way I hardly recognize, his lips rushing to meet mine, his hair brushing my temple. I drink in the smell of him deeper even than I'm consciously intending to. The feeling is heady. His kiss is not perfunctory, not even desirously expectant. It's immediate. Intimate. And heartbreaking. The reminder of how he never kisses me this way is faint, yet insistent. I push it away, because this is how it'll be now that I'm writing the book.

"You won't regret this," he whispers, withdrawing. "You're a writer, Katrina. You just need to get back to the page."

I nod, overwhelmed. "What about you? Are you sure?"

He studies me, searching. "Of course," he says, sounding confused.

"You don't . . ." I hesitate. I hate even introducing this into the conversation. But I know what's coming, and I want him to be prepared. "You don't care about the rumors about me and Nathan?"

Chris pauses, then laughs, short and unbothered. I feel the warmth left on my lips fading. I don't know what reaction I wanted him to have, but it's not this. "You mean am I worried you had an affair and you'll pick it up again?"

"It's what everyone will say when this gets announced," I explain. I wonder why I even need to. Why he needs me to walk him through what would worry the average man in his position.

His face hasn't changed, incomprehension and humor playing a discordant duet. "I don't care what people say. Whether you and he had a fling in the past, it's not for me to object to. We weren't together. As for this book, I trust you," he says reassuringly.

The floor feels firmer under me. If this wasn't the reaction I wanted, why not? He's being mature, non-territorial, respectful of my professional relationships and romantic history.

"Besides," he continues, "I understand writing a book with someone is intense."

His eyes have an indicative flicker. I'm not following.

"You two will share a lot." He speaks slowly, deliberately. "I don't . . . have a problem with that. You'll do what you have to do. Finishing the book is what's important."

What was indicative in his eyes has hardened into meaning. In one dizzying moment, I understand what he's implying. I was giving him *credit* moments ago, admiring his reserve and respect for me. It's a little less laudable, him not minding if I have an affair in the name of writing one more goddamn novel.

I almost want to question him on it, clarify he wouldn't actually "not have a problem" if I fucked Nathan Van Huysen. But I think I wouldn't like the answer.

He kisses me once more, which I hollowly reciprocate, and gets up. From the door he grins, clearly not noticing how dazed I am.

"Hey, over dinner," he says, "why don't you show me some of those wedding venues?"

I hardly process the invitation, one I would have welcomed enthusiastically yesterday or this morning or whenever. Not now.

I nod, wanting to cry. I wonder if being cheated on feels like being given license to cheat. Chris smiles once more, noticing none of this, then shuts the door behind him.

Mechanically, I cross the room. I pick up the bookstore bag and pull out the copy of *Refraction*, watching my fingers run over the raised lettering of Nathan's name.

Then I open the back flap, where I find his author photo. It's not the one from *Only Once*, and he's visibly three years older. The changes are subtle, but I take in every one of them. The narrowing of his face, the definition of the edges and angles, the reservation in his eyes.

He's looking into the camera. Looking right at me. It's the expression I've seen a hundred times, when he's listening to my ideas, drawing them in, improving them.

I close the cover and walk over to the boxes of books in the closet, where I place the new purchase on top of the copy of *Refraction* I already owned.

6

Nathan

It's minutes until the conference call, and I'm expecting an email from Jen informing me Katrina's called the whole thing off. Of course, I've been expecting that email for the past two days. The morning after I met with Jen, while I walked through LaGuardia to my gate, she wrote me confirming Katrina was in. The next day, a conference call was scheduled with Parthenon.

The fact that I haven't heard from Katrina herself even once is what has me doubting this will ever happen. The point of this call is ostensibly to discuss ideas, yet the coauthors haven't communicated enough to pick a genre. Granted, I haven't exactly reached out, either. I fed myself bullshit reasons whenever I considered contacting her. *She could've gotten a new cell number. She could've changed her email.* For a fiction writer, I came up with pretty unconvincing excuses.

The email doesn't come. I'm on my couch in my condo in Chicago, the white room quiet. It's undecorated and impersonal, except for the books everywhere. Floor-to-ceiling shelves holding my collection of fiction, memoirs, history. They, and the complete absence of anything else noteworthy in my apartment, are reminders of how this—writing—is everything I am. When I found my craft, I clung and clung and clung to it, until it clung to me, intertwined with who I was. And now I have no way of existing outside of it.

Not even Melissa became part of me this way. I've asked myself why I couldn't combine my soul with hers the way I could with writing, the way I knew others could with their spouses. I couldn't. It didn't matter that I genuinely cared for her. I just couldn't. It's taken me too long to recognize what I couldn't have known when I proposed to her, what I didn't even completely understand when we finalized our divorce—I'd mistaken companionship, even chemistry, for love. I found Melissa's work and work ethic inspiring. She had constructive, kind systems for everything in our life, like how we would trade off each night's choice of TV, one of her documentaries for one of my HBO dramas. She was funny in her text messages. She was good in bed and a wonderful friend.

Yet if someone had told me love wasn't just the sum of those parts, but rather the exponent on the end of the equation, I don't think I would have understood what they meant. Which has left me with nothing but pages and pages in my empty, empty home.

Checking the clock on my phone, I see the time I've been counting down to. I dial in to the conference call, putting in the code when the robotic voice instructs me to. I speak into the empty fuzz on the line. "Hello?" I hate this part of conference calls. I feel like I'm shouting into a well, hoping voices respond from the darkness.

"Hi. Jen here," my agent says. "We're just waiting on Chris and Katrina."

"Nathan, hello." I recognize my editor's voice. Elizabeth Quirk, publisher of Parthenon Books, plays the eccentric New York editor to perfection. She wears thick plastic glasses and elaborate shawls, and cups of coffee cover her desk. It's an act, or half the picture. She is ruthlessly entrepreneurial, and I respect her despite my frustration that she's rejected my solo proposal, which has landed me in this position with Katrina. "Have you recovered from your tour?" she inquires.

"You know me," I respond shortly. "Always eager to start the next book."

"Indeed. We love that," Liz replies magnanimously. I know she won't bring up the book Parthenon passed on. We're just going to pretend there's no bad blood between any of us. Not between me and Liz, and certainly not between me and Katrina. "Well," Liz continues, "I can't tell you how excited everyone is in-house about this project."

Right on cue, the line beeps. The voice I hear next is Chris's. "Chris and Katrina here," he says. I hate how he strings their names together like it's second nature. I hate how he says his first. Hearing him reminds me of phone calls four years ago where he'd give us half-assed ideas, and Katrina and I would only need to exchange one look to know we were going to ignore him.

I wait for Katrina's voice.

Everyone does, for a second. When it doesn't come, Liz chimes in. "Katrina! I was just telling Nathan and Jen how excited everyone is for this. It'll be the literary event of the year." I have to roll my eyes. Even if we might be the literary event of the year, publishers love to promise you everything. No one ever really knows until the book is on shelves.

Chris laughs, and it's gratingly evident he's having the exact opposite reaction. He sounds self-congratulatory, presumptuous. I find my mind straying to my now-shelved thriller manuscript. In it there's this supporting character, this fumbling douchebag of an FBI agent who interferes in the central pair's life. I've named him Dean, but character names are easy to change. "Glad to hear it," Chris says. "We all know Nathan and Katrina will deliver something fantastic."

Once again, his fiancée's name second. When we were both his clients, it invariably went the opposite way. Katrina was the one he showered with praise, with special interest. Even then, it was unmistakable why. I guess it worked in the end.

Jen interjects now. If Liz's voice is syrup, Jen's is something stiffer and more refreshing. "I'd love to discuss the timeline. What's Parthenon want for deadlines and publication?" Thank god for my agent. Of everyone on this call, she's the only one I trust.

"For a book this big? I see no reason to delay," Liz says. "So let me turn that question around to the authors."

The line falls silent. I find myself waiting, expecting. Wondering when Katrina will speak up. The combination of hope and dread makes me drum my pen on the pages of my leather-bound journal. Katrina's voice never comes.

The pause expands, and I recognize it's not only Katrina holding out. I could chime in right now. Why I haven't is complex. It's part competition, not wanting to look like the more compliant, eager one in this unhappy reunion. Underneath my petty resistance, though, there's a detestable current of fear. If I speak, I'm pushing through choking curtains of things unsaid four bitter years in the past.

It was four years ago, I remind myself. *Grow up, Nathan.* I won't throw away my career because I don't want to talk to Kat.

"Well"—I bluster in what I hope comes off confident—"we wrote the first draft of *Only Once* in three months." There. I spoke first. Surely Katrina will take her victory and deign to join the discussion.

She doesn't.

"Three months," Liz repeats. I hear the impatient undercurrent in her voice. She's wondering the same thing. Where the hell is Katrina? "Then build in time for revisions, copyedits, promo. Honestly, I'll bump another title and we could have this on our list for next year. But I certainly don't want to rush you."

"Katrina would like to do this quickly as well," Chris interjects. "Two months is the goal."

It wreaks havoc on my blood pressure. Is Katrina even *on* this call? What if Chris speaks for her throughout the entire process? It would be unbearably tedious, not to mention personally unpleasant. If I have to draft this entire book through Chris, I might finally discover the cure for my love of writing. I could become the investment banker my father wanted me to be.

"Well, we're on the same page, then," Liz confirms, the flint in her voice echoing my own misgivings. "I'd love to hear what Katrina and Nathan are thinking for the book's premise."

I pause—this would be the point for Katrina finally to enter the conversation. I give her a second. When once more she's silent, something in me snaps. Clearly Katrina doesn't care about this. Why she's even doing the book is a mystery, but an unimportant one. I *do* care. Fuck investment banking. If Katrina won't participate, I'll lead. I'll do the whole thing if I have to.

"Before *Only Once* came out, we were working on an idea centered on a young couple going through a divorce," I say. It was one of the proposals Katrina and I put together for our follow-up to *Only Once* before our partnership imploded. It was a good pitch, despite being weirdly prophetic. I never expected to be divorced by twenty-eight. Melissa certainly didn't.

"Yes, I remember," Liz says. "Bringing divorce out of the midlife crisis. I liked it. I think we need more, though."

I nod to myself. I'd thought the same. "Of course. *We'll*"—I emphasis the word for one person, and one person only—"need to develop it. But I like the juxtaposition of young love, the honeymoon phase, with everything falling to pieces."

"Liz—"

I sit up sharply. It's the voice I was waiting for. Katrina sounds confident, urgent, the way she does when she's grabbed hold of one of her genius ideas, or it's grabbed hold of her.

It's kind of perverse how Pavlovian my response is. I don't react combatively, nor defensively. Instantly, I feel my mind wake up. I'm energized, hungry to put her ideas and mine together.

"I'd like to play with a formal device. Something with timelines, where we compare their early relationship to the present. What we expect to be juxtaposition will turn out to be similarity by the end."

I process her words. I love the idea, obviously. Katrina's incredibly gifted with conceptual frameworks.

Then I process the way she proposed it. Obviously, it's a comment for me to consider, yet she said it . . . to Liz. It feels like the first move in some sort of chess game.

I immediately jot *timeline framework* into my journal. "Yeah, *Liz*," I say pointedly. I'll play. "We'll interrogate the marriage of fact and fiction, the elements of each in every love story." I feel the idea start to excite me, despite my irritation with Katrina.

"Liz, what do you think of the idea that breaking up is itself passionate, just like falling in love?" Katrina poses the question like it's innocent.

"I think it's fascinating—Liz," I reply, catching myself. "I—I want you, Liz, to know that I think that."

There's wince-inducing quiet on the other end of the line. Liz undoubtedly understands exactly what's going on. She hears her prodigal coauthors acting like children. "Well, you two certainly still work well together," she finally says. I'm not sure how much of her comment is sarcasm. On the one hand, Katrina and I haven't technically spoken to each other. On the other, I can acknowledge how instantaneously we're sparking ideas off each other. "I like this, but you want to keep your readership in mind," she adds.

I frown, not following. "We wrote an affair in *Only Once*. Now we're doing a divorce. I don't imagine readers will struggle with the jump."

"Of course," Liz replies easily. "You know why your readers loved *Only Once,* though. You write romance."

I don't reply, not wanting to encourage the idea. I proposed a *break-up* book. Then Katrina inserted a very good idea involving very minimal romance. The more Liz says, the more I see my break-up book filling up with stolen glances, brushing hands, tender embraces. Kissing.

"Even if the ending is bleak," Liz continues. "It's not like you gave your characters a happily-ever-after in *Only Once.* The story was full of longing, though. In this book, emphasize this passion you're proposing. Find the romance."

Find the romance. Find the romance with Katrina. Yes, I'll just climb Mount Everest when I'm done.

"Right," Chris speaks up. "Definitely. We have to deliver on the brand."

I'm silent. So is Katrina. I'm not going to be the one to object, not if she won't.

Jen jumps in, sparing us. "I think the most productive thing right now is to let Nathan and Katrina begin their process. Once they have more to work with, we'll get back on the phone and figure out next steps."

"Yes, of course," Liz replies immediately. "Have you two planned your writing retreat yet? Where's it going to be?"

I decide to hold the line right here. I'm not saying a damn thing. It's on Katrina to field this horrifying question. The silence stretches, the phone line crackling with more than static. Finally, I win. "We haven't discussed it," Katrina says, her voice wire-sharp.

"I know you'll have a wonderful time," Liz says, and for the first time I wonder if my editor is not that bright. "Call whenever."

"Thanks," I reply.

"Bye, Liz," Katrina says.

We hang up. It feels like retreating. I'm reeling from the conversation—Katrina and I just pitched the book we're writing together without exchanging one word with each other. We haven't even discussed *how* we're writing the book. It hits me, we said we would finish the first draft in two months. While the difficulty of my working relationship with Katrina is very real, our deadline is very real, too.

I do the only thing I can think to do. I call Jen.

"Hey," she says when she picks up, sounding upbeat. "I think that went great, don't you?"

I ignore the question. It's for the best. "Can you call Chris and find out Katrina's schedule? When does she want to do this?"

"You don't want to call her yourself?" I hear Jen judging me.

"Not particularly."

"Nathan, you're going to have to speak to her while you write this book."

"This isn't writing," I point out. "It's scheduling. Can you just tell her I'll meet her wherever, whenever?" It won't make a difference. Katrina could want to write this book on the pearly sands of Aruba or in line at the DMV. I'd have an awful time regardless.

Jen sighs, loud and laborious. "I'll talk to Chris. But I will not babysit you while you refuse to communicate with your coauthor. You *will* go on this retreat, and you *will* be professional."

"I understand," I say earnestly. "Thanks, Jen." I hang up.

Walking upstairs, I replay the conversation in my head. Liz's parting words echo in my ears. *I know you'll have a wonderful time.* Despite myself, they make me laugh.

7

Katrina

BEING IN THIS house feels like having a fever. The warm Florida light outside is too bright, the humidity too heavy. Every detail of the place is vaguely unpleasant—the teal-painted hardwood floors, the wicker furniture, the shutters cutting up the view from every window. Even the fish in the painting in the hall watches me from its frame like it's dissatisfied.

It's been two weeks since the phone call with Nathan, our editor, and our agents. Two weeks since Chris and Jen worked out the timing for this retreat. No one wanted to delay, not even me. Arrangements were made, flights booked, the house prepared. The whole time Nathan and I exchanged not one single email.

I'm in the living room now, computer on the white coffee table, trying to brainstorm. It's a funny word, *brainstorming*. When creativity's going well, it feels intuitive, easy. Not today. The storm in my thoughts is part of the problem. It's shaping up into a hurricane, Nathan and Chris and this dreaded book and the next two months in Key Largo threatening to whip the doors from the hinges in my mind.

Of course, it's not only personal problems getting in my way. I'm out of practice. I haven't written fiction in over three years. The instincts feel dull, sluggish with disuse. I don't have time for sluggish. I refuse to spend even one unnecessary minute in this house.

But I made this choice, I remind myself. Even here, fingertips on the keys, Nathan mere minutes away, it's hard to remember exactly *why* my relationship is worth this. I have to hold my resolve. I take a deep breath, close my eyes. Ideas, burry and indistinct, shift into focus, sending signals down my arms, to my hands, ready for the blank page.

I type one letter and the doorbell rings.

Closing my computer, I iron out the waver in my fingers, embarrassingly relieved to have staved off writing. I rise to my feet, turning with trepidation toward the door. In the windows, shuttered in shocking sky blue, I can see the shape of Nathan. His suitcase next to him on the porch. It feels unreal, having this person who, for four years, I've only seen in memories and side-by-side photos in book reviews stand in the flesh ten feet from me.

I walk slowly into the front room. With a deep breath, I open the door.

• FOUR YEARS EARLIER •

ON THE FRONT porch, the sunlight warms my skin wonderfully. It's sweaty in Key Largo, but not in the ways I mind. Not the sweat of walking in the city in your heaviest coat, or of elevators in summer. Florida's is like after-sex sweat.

My flight got in before Nathan's, and I went to the rental house early to check the place out and claim my bedroom. In the small Italian villa we rented last year, Nathan grabbed the master bedroom for himself, and I was left with the twin bed and the lime-green wallpaper. I couldn't object, not when Nathan paid for that trip on his own. I tried to thank him for it, and he just looked at me and frowned. "What else would I spend it on?" he asked. I thought it was a ridiculous question. He had a wife, who probably would have loved a trip to Italy. But I didn't press. How Nathan managed his marriage was his business.

He's not paying for this trip, though. Pride swells in my chest at the thought. We've made actual money from our first book. Not life-changing money, which is fine. Florida-retreat money is exciting enough.

While I wait, ideas whirl in my head. I'm itching to get started, but I don't. Not without Nathan. The last time I wrote without discussing the direction with him, he read the pages and came up with an inspired improvement in fifteen minutes. I had to start over from scratch. Instead, I'm reading one of the books I found in the house's library. It's historical romance, and I'm loving it, unsurprisingly.

Finally, Nathan's ridiculous rental car rolls up in the driveway. It's a Porsche, per usual. He has the top down, his hair wind-tousled. I watch dryly while he leaps out. "Reading already?" he calls up to the porch, eyeing me. It's a running joke of ours—in every spare moment I have, I'm reading whatever's in reach. Even if it's a stack of moldy newspapers from 1995 I found in the attic.

"Would you rather I'd started writing without you?" I reply.

He grabs his luggage from the trunk, two suitcases and the leather shoulder bag I know carries his laptop. "What, cheat on me?" He smiles like he knows I never would. "Of course not. Though it would be rather thematic."

"Life imitating art," I say.

He hauls his luggage up the porch steps, eyes flitting over the white wooden columns, the sky-blue shutters, the bougainvillea. "I've had some thoughts on the flight on how to move up the first act ending," he comments casually.

"I'm shocked."

"It drags," he insists.

"It doesn't. Give readers some credit."

"Oh, not this again." Nathan looks impatient, but I know he enjoys the back-and-forth. We both do.

I shut my book and stand up in front of him. "Emotions need time to simmer," I say firmly.

Nathan watches me, and I know he's not convinced. "Let's at least wait until we're inside before we start arguing."

I shrug. "You brought it up."

He sets one suitcase down and reaches forward, kissing my cheek in greeting. The gesture is instinctual, something he inherited from his wealthy family. Still, it's sweet, especially when he smiles. "Good to see you, Kat," he says softly.

"You, too." I follow him inside—stepping one foot over the threshold onto the teal hardwood floor. "Like I was saying, I want fifty pages before the act end. No fewer."

Nathan laughs, his voice echoing in the empty house.

• PRESENT DAY •

WHEN I OPEN the front door, I feel like time has reversed. Nathan waits on the porch, looking exactly the same. Same perfect posture, same shoulder bag, even the same Porsche parked in the same driveway. If I were in the mood for humor, I would find the contrast with my rental car—the first dented Hyundai they rolled off the lot—somewhat comical. But I'm not.

The only differences I notice are how he no longer wears a wedding ring and that he looks absolutely miserable. He's scowling, and past his mirrored sunglasses, I don't know if he's meeting my eyes.

"You made it," I say neutrally.

"Disappointed?" While it was jarring hearing his voice on the phone, it's a whole new level of disorienting in person. I've replayed so many conversations we had. To be having new ones is unexpected. I'm certain I'll hear nothing but this combative edge in the coming weeks. The Nathans I knew when we wrote—the playful Nathan, the inquisitive Nathan, the charming Nathan—won't be coming back.

I hold the door open, then turn, heading into the house without waiting to see if he's following. "Your room's ready. Let me know if you need anything and I'll have it brought over."

When I face him again, I find him halted in the entryway. His eyes roam the house, and I know what he's seeing within the white walls. Memories. I see them, too. Some of the best of my life. When we forgot we put dinner in the oven and wound up so engrossed in writing we set off the smoke alarm. When we kept challenging each other to writing sprints and ended up finishing twenty pages each in one exhausting day. When I walked in the door wet with seawater and rain, my skin remembering where sand had clung to my face.

Some of the worst memories of my life, too.

"I was surprised when Jen said you'd rented the *Only Once* house," Nathan says, his demeanor unchanged.

"I didn't rent it," I say. "I own this house. Chris bought it for me for our first anniversary." I include the final detail deliberately. I don't want Nathan imagining I'd personally purchased the graveyard of our partnership. Chris meant the gift to be thoughtful. He didn't know everything that'd happened here. But of course, nothing with Chris comes without a degree of pressure. *Here's your house. Write your next bestselling novel in it.* I've visited as infrequently as possible, choosing instead to rent the place out to MFA students.

The mention of Chris sours Nathan's expression further, impossibly. "How nice of him," he says, scowling again. "Now we'll write another book here. You always were a master of irony. Shall we pick up right where we left off?"

In my head I hear doors slamming, tires howling on the driveway. Where we left off is the last place I want to start. "Us writing here was Chris's idea. I couldn't very well object." I stare him down, hoping he'll challenge me. I want to break open the rib cage of this conversation and examine the wounded heart underneath. I know we never will. It would require honesty, and the only place Nathan's ever honest is on the page. "Everyone wants to bottle lightning. Re-create the circumstances of success," I go on when Nathan, as expected, says nothing.

"Oh, I get it now." He removes his sunglasses, his eyes flashing.

"What?"

"Will Chris be writing with us as well? Conference him in? Fly him down every weekend?" he says spitefully. While he's joking, it's a grim vision. Me and Nathan in this house is bad. Chris and Nathan in this house would be worse. Between Chris's resentment toward Nathan for firing him and Nathan's resentment toward Chris for various other reasons, it'd be less Jonathan Franzen and more Truman Capote in here.

"Don't be ridiculous," I reply.

Nathan shakes his head and walks toward the stairs. "I'm going to shower. Then we'll decide how we're going to do this."

He passes me in the hallway without pausing.

"Good to see you, Kat," he says bitterly, before disappearing upstairs.

8

Nathan

I SOAK IN the steam for what's surely the longest shower of my life. Only when I close my eyes does this bathroom not feel like the prison in which I'm stuck for the next couple of months. I use my imagination to conjure up other showers I'd rather be in. Danielle, the social media strategist whom friends introduced me to in Chicago and in whose bed I found myself weekly before my book tour, had this stone shower with plenty of room for two.

We weren't serious—I haven't been serious with anyone since the end of my marriage. Resetting my life following my divorce wasn't easy. Returning to the single life, I often felt like I was watching reruns of a show I hadn't enjoyed very much on the first run. Leaving New York helped. In Chicago, I reconnected with college friends, forced myself to find new restaurants and new coffeehouses—and, of course, threw myself into work, first on several discarded ideas and finally on *Refraction*.

Every day was routinized, until one morning I woke up and found those routines resembled a life. I got closer with my father, weirdly, or he wanted to. If we would never have working for Goldman Sachs in common, we now had divorce. My mom had left him for some photographer she'd met on the charity gala circuit. Edward Van Huysen had continued to date decades below him, women he would mention to me like I knew them, "Josie" or "Samantha," and who would be gone from his life by Thanksgiving. I got disjointed texts from him with oddly specific words of "wisdom," which eventually turned into requests for book recommendations and, even unlikelier, congratulations on selling *Refraction*, until he died a year ago.

Through everything, writing was my nourishment. It helped me feel human, the way it had when I discovered the craft in high school. It made me feel like myself. If I no longer had something larger I was living for, the comforting context of my life with Melissa, I had enough to keep me living. The earnings from *Only Once*, and each empty page in front of me.

Everything eventually returned—except dating, which happened only in fits and starts, noncommittal and evanescent. Danielle, blonde and dimpled, knew this going into our whatever-it-was. We're over now.

Still, memories of her are the perfect distraction to keep me from facing Katrina downstairs.

Chris. Of course Chris is behind Katrina's willingness to collaborate. It explains everything. The only reason Katrina would return to writing is if her fiancé pushed her to. I know Chris well from when he represented me—he's not a very good man. He's not a very good fiancé or agent, either, if he's pushing his wife-to-be and client into this collaboration. Her dream is writing, not writing with me.

I rub my eyes and open them, the tiles taunting me. If I really want this prison sentence to be only two months, I can't keep hiding in the shower. Plus, I feel my stomach growling. I turn off the water and walk into the bedroom in my towel, the humidity keeping me from drying off. Every inch of the room is hatefully familiar. The ubiquitous white shutters, the bed in the center with the blue comforter, the cream-colored wardrobe. I figure Chris bought the furniture with the house to keep everything the way Katrina remembered, and Katrina, having no interest in this place, never bothered to change it.

Pulling clothes from my suitcase, I dress quickly. While I do, I counsel myself in my head. Working with Katrina will be difficult. But writing? Writing is like breathing. I can put down three thousand words in a day when I need to. Right now, I need to. Which means there's only one thing to do.

Keep breathing.

These thoughts push me out of my bedroom with some semblance of vigor. When I walk downstairs, I ignore memories of the last time my footsteps thudded down them. I ignore the glimpse I get of the fireplace in the living room, its ominous mouth open like it's mocking me.

Entering the kitchen, I catch the scent of seawater from the open sliding doors. The back of the house opens onto the deck with the swimming pool and then, past it, the ocean, the grass of the yard ceding unevenly to sand and surf. I remember looking up from our computers, watching the moonlight shimmering on the waves. It's nighttime now, and the moon is nowhere to be found, obstructed underneath clouds. There's only the endless inky roll of the water.

Katrina's sitting at the bar, her back to me. She's eating frozen pizza she must've heated up while I stalled in the shower. It's the kind we shared dozens of times on the nights while we wrote *Only Once.*

Something in the simple, solitary meal is disarmingly human. She's not the figure I've shaped in my head to near-mythic proportions, the knot snarling the strands of my life. She's just Katrina, having dinner. Her hair unruly in the humidity, her blouse untucked from her white shorts.

Hearing my footsteps, she waves in the direction of the pizza on top of the stove. "Help yourself," she says.

I remember the cupboard that holds the dishes. Which is vexing. I've lived in my condo for two years and still I find myself opening the wrong drawers on occasion. Here, every detail is inscribed into instinct. I pull down one of the ceramic plates with the blue trim, serve myself two slices of pizza, then turn, leaning on the far counter to face Katrina. The kitchen island is the breaker in the ocean between us.

I say nothing, waiting for her to speak.

Finally, she does. "Let's get the planning out of the way." Her face is expressionless. She's got remarkable eyebrows, perfect dark curves prone to twitching up when she's joking or bunching when she's thinking. Right now, they do neither. They're unmoving, just like the round, bee-stung lips she's pursing while her brown eyes watch me. "I assume your writing process hasn't changed?"

"No," I reply. "Yours? I heard you were retired." I can't help the judgmental emphasis on the final word. It pissed me off when I learned she'd retired. Quitting writing with me was one thing. While I didn't like it, I understood it. Quitting writing entirely infuriated me. It felt dishonest. It felt like Katrina had woken up one day and decided not to be herself, not to dream her dreams.

Her freckled cheeks don't flicker. She's like ceramic. "Well, I heard I was torture to write with," she says. I'm genuinely surprised to hear the edge in her voice.

I figured it was coming, I just didn't expect we'd have this discussion on our very first night. Regardless, I have no response—or none I want to say out loud. Instead of the truth, I settle for the easy rejoinder. "Remains to be seen."

I watch this frustrate Katrina. She shifts in her seat like she's unconsciously trying to escape her fury. "I've heard a lot of things in the past four years," she starts, her tone light, like this is just conversation. I know it's not. Nothing is ever *just* conversation with Katrina, no word wasted. Everything's the setup to some ending she's been crafting since the beginning, perfect yet unpredictable. I brace myself when she continues. "I've heard I'm a whore who repeatedly tried to seduce you, then quit writing when I couldn't get you to leave your wife."

I flinch. Not figuratively. I literally feel my face flinch. It's an ugly rumor, and it hurt when I first read it for numerous reasons. Whatever our present situation, I respect Katrina. I used to call her a friend. It's not just repulsive, it's wrong. Nobody who knew her could ever say she tried to seduce me.

Nevertheless, I can handle Kat's retorts. I wrote with her. I know exactly how to parry them. "Funny, because I heard my wife walked in on us fucking, which is why I'm divorced," I say. "You know what my favorite is, though?"

It's Katrina's turn to say nothing.

"I heard I had an affair with you because I wanted to be a better writer. To write infidelity from"—I draw out the word—*"experience."*

Katrina's neck reddens. I understand her visceral reaction. I really do hate this rumor in particular. The idea that I could discard Melissa in service of some artistic bullshit is stomach-turning. I know I made mistakes in my marriage. But Melissa was a human being to me, one I loved. Just not well enough.

"I heard you left your wife because you were in love with me." Katrina's on her feet, her plate clenched in her hand. I'm unprepared for the blow. It's a painful punch to a tender part of me.

"I heard you slept with Chris to hurt me."

The words fly out of my mouth. Katrina's chest heaves under her shirt. I feel my own breath racing sharp and shallow. Whatever this fight was, it's just split like a lightning-struck tree. The damage is fast, irreversible. I wish I'd said nothing. Catastrophe like this is better left for my writing.

Katrina, unmoving where she stands, exhales a short laugh. Now I prepare myself. Years of writing with Kat have left me with a catalogue of everything I know about her. I know she's persistent, unwilling to give up when she feels she's in the right. I know she's incredibly smart and capable of using her smarts like a surgeon's scalpel or a heavy instrument depending on what the situation requires. Right now, I know I'm going to be on the wrong end of one or the other.

"Of course, none of it's true," she says, her tone goading, like she wants to hear me disagree with her.

"Of course," I reply.

We watch each other from the ends of the kitchen.

"Look." The softest note of concession enters Katrina's voice. "Neither of us wants to be here. There's no use discussing it. We just have to write the book," she finishes.

I nod. It's what I told myself upstairs. We just have to write the book. Katrina's eyes shift from me, and in her expression, I see mirrored my own sudden weariness of this conversation.

She goes on. "So, unfortunately, we'll have to outline the story together. Then we can write from the comfort of completely separate rooms"—I nearly permit myself to smile, until she continues—"and trade pages."

I won't tolerate the suggestion. *"No."*

"What do you mean, no?" Her eyebrows do their bunching thing.

"I'm not trading pages with you." I pin her eyes with an unwavering stare. I know she reads the dare in mine. *I won't say it. Will you?* Katrina's the only person who knows there's a damn good reason we shouldn't trade pages. She knows where it led us. I practically smell charred paper, and I imagine Katrina's mind is in the exact same place.

"What else would we do, Nathan?" She sighs, frustrated. "Write everything together? Or perhaps I'll write the first half and you'll write the second, and we'll put them together without reading the other's. *That'd* turn out well."

"I don't care," I reply. "We're not trading pages."

The waves crash in the distance, the rush and roar carrying in through our doors. Katrina pauses, her expression inscrutable. "Fine," she says, her voice returning to the practiced evenness it had when I first arrived. "We'll write every word together."

The idea thrills me a little, though I don't want to rationalize why. I'm surprised it's the option she chose. It means the quality of the book is important to her. What's more, not pressing me on trading pages is the closest she's come to acknowledging what she did. It's both what I want and exactly what I don't. If this were fiction, I could craft the ending I wanted. In life, it offers an equal chance of destroying me.

"But we'll skip the outline," Katrina says suddenly.

I straighten. "You're not serious."

"We'll break the story while we write," Katrina explains. Her sharp shoulders have lost their tension out of what I'm guessing is exhaustion.

"We've never done it that way." We've published two books together, started several more. Each time, we outlined in the same room, then traded pages we'd written separately. It hurts remembering how fun it was, the small smiles we'd exchange when handing off something we were particularly proud of, the game I'd play in my head predicting what comments she'd have. It was exhilarating, until it wasn't. The process we're proposing now will break everything.

"I think we both know writing this book won't look like writing our others," Katrina says. "We'll write a rough draft working from the proposal we did four years ago, then separate while we edit. It'll shorten the time we're together."

"Do I even have a choice?" The question comes out sarcastic, though it's not like I have a better idea.

The resentment in Katrina's eyes dims. "Of course you have a choice," she says. Vulnerability has replaced the venom in her voice. "You can bow out. Cancel the book." It's not a challenge. Not an ultimatum. She's pleading.

Four years ago, I would've cared. But it's not four years ago. "If you want out, call your fiancé," I say.

Katrina's expression stiffens. I practically hear her holding in her anger. The enjoyment I get out of watching her is guilty, but I savor it, anyway. She made this bed for herself. I'm going to indulge in the sight of her lying in it.

She puts her dish in the sink then starts to walk out of the room. "I'll see you tomorrow morning for page one," she says.

9

Katrina

OUR DRINKS HAVE gone cold. The foam on Nathan's cappuccino has collapsed into milky beige, and the only thing left in my mug is the soggiest of tea bags. I hate the obvious metaphor in them. Once the cups were warm, caffeinated, full of the promise of the morning. Now they're sad and empty, and we've gotten nowhere.

Nathan and I sit two feet from each other on the dining table bench, my computer open between us. It is not a companionable two feet. Not the two feet of people relaxing on the couch in front of the TV or waking up together in a queen bed. It's the two feet of students taking college exams next to one another, quiet and competitive, or of patients in the urgent care waiting room not wanting to catch whatever horrible disease the other has.

We're quiet. The only noise in the expansive dining room is the echoing rustle of the ocean and the whir of the overhead fan fighting the humidity. We came down here to write. One coffee, one tea, two bagels, and three hours later, the only thing we've done is format our document.

Nathan clears his throat.

I shift in my place, the skin peeking out of my shorts unsticking painfully from the painted wood. I wait for him to say something, not sure I'd prefer hearing him speak to this tortured silence. Finally, I force a sentence out. It feels like exercising sore limbs, stiff and stinging. "Were you going to say something?"

Nathan glances over, looking very *who, me?* Yes, Nathan, you. The only other person confined in this pastel prison with me.

"Oh," he says, sounding somehow indignant. "No."

I say nothing. Silence reclaims us, stretching wider and wider. Obviously, a huge part of the problem is our inherit discomfort with each other. Every word is a battle to even speak when I'd rather scream or hop on a plane to somewhere far from Nathan Van Huysen. Sitting here, just feet from him, feels viscerally wrong.

But I'd be lying if I told myself our fractious partnership was the entire problem. Part of it doesn't even reach Nathan. It's the nervous turbine humming to life within me, the fear of knowing I'll be putting down words destined for print and for readers probably worldwide. My words. Words that might not compare to *Only Once.* The feeling burrows into my chest, tightening my breath. When sweat springs to my fingers, I bury my hands in my lap so Nathan won't notice.

The ringing of my phone saves us.

I reach with unhidden desperation for the black plastic case vibrating on the wood. With immediate and aching relief, I see Chris's name on my screen. My fiancé. The person who knows how to help me.

"Hi," I say, sounding strangled.

"Hey, babe." Chris's voice is unwavering. The opposite of mine. "How's it going?" Nathan's scowl is reflected in the computer screen, black now from disuse. With how quiet the room is, I have no doubt he can hear every word from Chris.

"Oh, it's . . ." I want to get up, walk out of the room, tell Chris it's horrible, it was a mistake and I feel sick and I'm a fraud and no one should ever want another book from me. Then I think of returning home, of Chris's quiet disappointment, of the widening chasm dividing us. "Good," I say. "Great, actually. We're really getting somewhere."

Nathan's eyebrows rise. He's no longer feigning discretion, his gaze glued to me. I turn away, facing the wall and the potted fern.

"*Fantas*tic." Chris pronounces the first two syllables emphatically. I'm reminded of politicians or football sportscasters. "I knew you could do it. You're talented, Katrina. You're goddamn talented."

I wish I could tell him his confidence just makes me more uneasy. I run a damp hand down my shorts. Making matters worse, Nathan shifts in his seat. I have the feeling he's reminding me he's listening.

"Is there anything you need from me?" Chris asks.

"No. Nothing."

"Well, then I won't keep you," Chris replies unhesitatingly. "Don't want to interrupt the creative process."

I laugh. It's a laugh that shares more with the jerk of my knee under a doctor's mallet than with genuine joy or humor. I regret it immediately. Chris, however, doesn't notice. "Right," I say.

"Love you."

"Love you," I repeat.

I hang up. When I face forward, Nathan is staring, not even making the faintest effort to hide his scorn. It's the first time he's looked me in the face today. I'm caught off guard once more, remembering he's actually here with me, within arms' reach, not in a photo online. The familiarity in his features is jarring. The way stubble shadows his face like it's doing him a favor, the way his blue eyes glitter like the ocean outside. The brooding edge of his brow.

Then he smiles. "You lie to your fiancé often?" he asks.

I want to shove the question back at him, ask him how often he lied to Melissa. Unlike Nathan, however, I have a modicum of discretion. If I let myself fight with him—if I let this discussion spiral out of control, it would leave me nowhere I want to be. "My relationship is none of your business," I say instead, curt and clipped. A conversational CAUTION—WET FLOOR sign.

Which I should've known Nathan couldn't resist. "Of course. I'm just curious," he says, pontificating like fucking Socrates, "why did he push you to do this? He has to know you don't want to. What's in it for him? I mean, money, obviously," he answers himself. "But I doubt even Chris is that selfish, and you certainly wouldn't accept for that reason."

He falls silent, mulling the question over. I hate him for it. I hate how close he's coming to the truth.

"I honestly don't know why you'd agree," he says, "unless it's to make him happy. Oh, Katrina." He looks up, mock mortification in his eyes. "Tell me it isn't that."

My modicum of discretion flies furiously out the window. "Didn't you ever do anything to make your wife—sorry, *ex-wife*—happy?"

The point lands. Nathan's expression storm-clouds over. His jaw clenches, and he stares past me, cheeks flushing. It is enormously satisfying. Nevertheless, wounding him feels a little wrong. I know I'm only reacting out of my old instincts to not hurt Nathan or pry into his personal life. It's not the relationship we have now. The memory is just hard to shake.

Suddenly, with the speed of inspiration, Nathan reaches forward. He seizes my computer without my having the chance to stop him.

The next instant he's typing—a flurry of fingers and keys. I lean over his shoulder to read whatever's possessed him, ignoring our new proximity. If his font size weren't eleven, I wouldn't have to leave only millimeters between my chest and the flat plane of his upper arm.

Nathan's writing from the perspective of Evelyn, our main character. On her way home, she's pulled over to the side of the road. Cars fly past her. It's late at night. She's just blown a tire, and she's waiting for roadside assistance. She's nervous, hands in her—

Hands in her lap, slick with sweat.

It hits me with the force of the cars hurtling past Evelyn what Nathan's doing. He noticed me hiding *my* hands, and he's chosen to write my discomfort into our first official page.

He keeps going. Evelyn's phone rings in her hand. Her husband's name displays on the screen. *Michael.* She laughs to herself—she hadn't even thought to call him.

When Michael speaks, I know what he's going to say.

"Hey, babe. How's it going?"

I watch, helpless, while Nathan renders the conversation in excruciating detail. While the words are Chris's and mine, the voice is Nathan's. He's good, horribly good. He writes with psychological insight and literary intensity, and I feel naked from how perfectly he portrays exactly how I felt in every moment. Evelyn deciding not to tell her husband what she's dealing with, keeping her fears to herself, realizing she doesn't want to share everything with him.

He nears the end of the conversation. Michael asks Evelyn if she needs anything from him, once again echoing Chris word for word. I hold my breath while Nathan writes.

Instead of, "*No. Nothing,*" like I said, Nathan deviates.

The night no longer felt unruly when Evelyn looked out her window. It felt welcoming, the anonymity of the empty sky almost comforting. Evelyn had the impression it was inviting her gently to do what she knew she had wanted to for a while. Into the quiet of the car she spoke four little words.

"I want a divorce."

Nathan stops typing.

He turns the computer toward me, like I wasn't reading over his shoulder. "It's an improvement, right?" he asks, his voice like a loaded gun.

I don't flinch. I don't flush. My face is empty of expression. I wish I could say it's because I'm impassive enough, self-possessed enough for Nathan's provocations not to reach me. It's not, though. I'm simply too shocked for emotion. Shocked he's *starting out* this invasive, messing with me in pages we're meant to produce together. From grade school, I remember the moment a pliant rubber dodgeball hit me in the face on the playground. It's how I feel now.

But Nathan doesn't get to write my relationship.

I hold on to this truth. I nurture it. I stoke the small fire it sets in me. It is, I realize, what infuriates Nathan. He could imagine Chris and me splitting dozens of times on the page. In reality, it would change nothing.

I grab the computer. Knowing he's watching me, I carve into his prose, changing, rearranging, embellishing. On the empty canvas of Evelyn's husband, Michael, I draw Nathan. I have Evelyn describe him as the kind of narcissist only generations of wealth and elite education can breed.

I give him a Porsche. I give him a dimple.

Finally, I face what I've done in Nathan's direction and watch him read it. I relish the small flickers in his expression. Unlike me, his face shows . . . everything. He doesn't miss a single stinging reminder it's him I'm writing in. When I figure he's close to finishing. I ready myself for criticism, arguments, remarks about Chris.

Instead, he leans back from the screen and, smugly, he smiles.

"Now that's a start," he says, his eyes locked on mine.

10

Nathan

• FOUR YEARS EARLIER •

IT FEELS LIKE it's five hundred degrees in here. Even with every fan on, the day just won't cool down, heat emanating from every surface in the house like we're writing inside our own private sauna. I've changed my shirt once, and I'm starting to sweat through my new one. Katrina's faring no better, sitting with her legs crossed on the floor, moisture glistening on her shoulders and the end of her nose. She's pulled her hair up into a rare ponytail.

She speaks without lifting her eyes from her computer screen. "Did you make the change we discussed to chapter two?" Her voice holds the faintest hint of condemnation, like she's ready for me to admit I got swept up in another idea and haven't done it yet. It's not unreasonable—there have been times I've neglected some minor edit in favor of chasing inspiration forward.

Nevertheless, the presumption gets under my skin, leaving me itchy, my muscles tensed. Some small rational part of me knows I shouldn't give in to irritation. "I said I would do it, and I did," I say instead, matching her spite for spite.

Katrina looks up.

I meet her gaze. Undoubtedly, she caught the bite in my tone. She narrows her eyes.

The heat is getting to us, warping our rapport into unpleasant shapes. There's something combustible in the room. Our responses have grown clipped, irritation creeping into every glance shared over the computer. It happens from time to time, when we're feeling deadline pressure, or when something's not working in the book, or even just when one of us hasn't slept well. There are a hundred little reasons that can add up to tension like this. Combined with living every minute of every day with each other, it's a test some marriages can't pass. Which, ultimately, isn't a bad comparison. What Katrina and I have is not far off from a marriage. Cooped up in this hot house, we're starting to sound like squabbling spouses.

I try to refocus on my screen. It doesn't work. Irritated, I unstick my shirt from the sweat of my back, hating the sensation. In moments like this, even mundane irritations—the sensation of damp fabric, the clock innocently displaying 3:29 P.M. in the corner of my screen—become monstrously frustrating.

I know the effect my words will have before I say them. I can't help myself, though. I've heard people compare fights to fire. It's the wrong metaphor. Flames flourish with space, openness, room to breathe, kindling to feed them. Fights come from the opposite—from pressure, restraint, deprivation. What I need is to open a release valve and vent some of this pressure.

"I did want to make one more change, though," I say.

Katrina's eyes swivel to me, suspicious. Rightly so, with how I didn't even try to sound casual. Katrina and I write layered dialogue every day. She knows subtext when she hears it. "Oh?" she shoots back.

"I cut the opening conversation."

Her hands fall from her laptop, her expression slackening with displeasure. "You're joking," she says humorlessly.

I'm morbidly glad to have caused this reaction. There's something grimly fulfilling in pushing us in exactly the wrong direction. I rarely feel this way with Melissa—it's hard to imagine how I could, when our infrequent "fights" consist pretty much only of spats over who loaded the dishwasher the wrong way or who forgot to buy more milk. It's something to be grateful for, I know. "It's dragging," I insist, prodding Katrina on purpose. "I told you already."

To paraphrase Tolstoy, every writing partnership clashes in its own way. One of Katrina's and my persistent disagreements is on pace. While my cowriter likes to paint in the details of life, I prefer to begin where things really begin. In reopening the discussion, I'm playing hopscotch in a minefield.

Kat shifts her laptop to the floor. The glare she sends me is deadly. "And *we* discussed keeping it if we made other changes. We *agreed.* What the hell was our entire conversation for yesterday if you can just change your mind?"

Distantly, I know her point isn't unreasonable. I just know I'm right, which fuels me past whatever remorse I might feel for overriding our decision. Now, while we're on edge with each other, is as good an opportunity as any to have this out.

"It doesn't work," I say. "I'm sorry, Katrina. We're cutting it."

"You're not sorry," she snaps. "You didn't even ask. You just made the decision on your own, *again,* and I'm supposed to, what? Accept it? I have opinions, too, you know."

"Oh, I know." The comment slips out of me. It's uselessly unkind enough to make me pause, recomposing myself. "Can we please cut it?" I ask, gentler.

Her eyes linger on me a moment longer, her mouth hard set. Finally, she shakes her head. "Whatever. Whatever you want, Nathan," she says. She picks up her computer, but I know we're far from finished.

Moments pass, the temperature in the room shifting up a degree. I never know which is worse, war or a stalemate. Right now, I can't distract myself from the unpleasantries we haven't yet said. I can only wait, reading the same lines on my computer over and over.

It's perverse relief when Katrina speaks. "By the way"—her voice is cold—"your metaphor at the bottom of twenty-five is forced."

I hide how the remark hurts me. Criticism from her stings in a way no other reader's ever does. It's payback, of course. My metaphor for her opening conversation. Not quite eye for an eye but close enough. "Delete it, then," I say.

"Already did."

The lightness in her voice is like footsteps over hot coals. We're entering the most dangerous part of every fight. The part where the conflict could die out or, pushed further, erupt into something much worse. We've had screaming matches before. Katrina's stormed out of rooms, her face flushed. I once slammed the door of my home office hard enough that the handle wobbled off. They're ugly memories, scars we keep out of sight on other days. We've always come through them, always moved forward.

Marriage really isn't the worst comparison. You can't write with someone you're afraid to fight with, and you can only fight fearlessly because you know at the end of the day, no matter what you've said, nothing can break you up. Still, fights pick up fuel from every conceivable source, drawing upon old grievances, misremembered slights, pet peeves that amount to nothing. I prepare myself for whatever is coming now.

Katrina opens her mouth. I'm ready to rise to whatever vitriol she has for me.

Right then, instead, all the fans in the room click off.

In the quiet absence of their hum, I look over my shoulder, checking the clock on the microwave. It's dark. Power outage. "Well, balls," I say. The fans were our lifeline. Without them, the heat is stifling. I face Katrina, expecting war, and I'm surprised when I find her smiling.

Just like that, I smile back.

I can't help myself. My anger slips through my fingers like sand.

"*Balls?*" Kat repeats incredulously.

I laugh. "Yes, Katrina. Balls."

Her grin cracks into a giggle, and the sound brightens the whole room. Standing, she sets her computer on the coffee table. "Time for a very frigid shower," she says enthusiastically.

"Good thinking," I reply.

She shoots me another small smile before heading for the stairs, all her anger forgotten. I could leave it there, sweep the fight under the rug like it never happened.

I don't, though. I'm a married man, and in ways I've learned to treat Katrina like I would my wife. "Katrina." She stills, turning to me. "Sorry for cutting the conversation," I say. "If it's important to you, we'll put it back."

Katrina softens, and I feel a weight lifted from my chest. "Apology accepted," she says. "It's fine. You can cut it."

"Thanks," I reply.

The pressure is gone. Despite the heat, the room feels like it's opened up, offering room for fire to kindle. As my cowriter reaches the top of the stairs, she calls down to me. "When I'm out, let's eat all our ice cream before it melts."

"I love that plan," I call back immediately. Returning to my computer, I smile. We'll have many more fights before this book is finished, and each time, we'll find our way through. Back to each other.

11

Nathan

• PRESENT DAY •

FOR THE NEXT few days, our fights fuel our writing. Or really, the fights we're not having. We give them to our characters, letting our own endless discord feed what Michael and Evelyn fling at each other. We put everything onto the page.

I don't object to the method writing. It's been my process pretty much forever. When I first started writing, I would craft my stories out of the stuff of prep-school stress, parental dissatisfactions, girls I couldn't date, how the liveliness and liberation of college would feel. I just kind of went from there, writing my hopes and fears into fiction. Not only did it make for relatable prose, I knew deep down it helped me process. It was easier to channel my feelings into writing. Safer.

It was a lesson I learned early in life—speaking out when my father pressured me to be an investment banker only led to hours-long arguments that ended with him and me like bloodied boxers in our respective corners without a winner. Even with friends, saying the perfect stinging comeback out loud just felt mean. In writing, though? Perfection.

While perhaps not psychologically healthy, the process is productive. Katrina and I pour page after page of the book into our laptops, making remarkable progress even for us. We've produced thirty pages in the past three days.

We lead strangely luxuryless lives for people holed up in a gorgeous Florida cottage. We wake on the far ends of the house, listening—or I know I do—with embarrassing intensity for the sounds of each other rustling bedsheets, opening bathroom doors, turning on showers. There's intimacy we no longer permit in seeing each other unshowered. We used to, on our retreats. I don't let myself miss seeing Katrina's pillow-creased cheeks, sleepy eyes, and the unruly shock of her hair spilling over her neck.

In the kitchen, we crunch down toasted bagels, unspeaking. Then we write for eight hours. The dining room is the war room. In the evenings, I pound frustration into the pavement on nightly runs through the quiet, palm-treed streets of Key Largo. It's my only respite from Katrina, from overthinking the plot points and dialogue we've thrown at each other like barbs.

There's only one potential problem with our new working routine, one Katrina and I have chosen to ignore. We don't write the flashback romantic scenes. It's an unspoken agreement. Whenever we reach one, we move right on to the next scene instead. While I know we have to write them eventually, I'm daunted by the prospect. If we're drawing from our relationship in the scenes where the characters argue, what will we draw from in the scenes of their romance?

I'm contemplating the question while I read the vitriolic passage in front of me, open on Katrina's rose-gold MacBook. Katrina watches me, her eyes hawkish, sitting with one foot curled under her the way she does. Her expression neutral, she's pretending she's impassively waiting for my reaction. I know better. I notice her gaze hasn't left me.

"The parallels to me are a little heavy-handed," I finally say.

Katrina is writing Michael to be selfish, full of himself, and rash. In fairness, I've written Evelyn petty and fearful. I know exactly what I'm doing. Katrina obviously does, too.

She shrugs. "Only someone who knows you like I do would notice."

It's a surprisingly intimate statement. While it's not untrue, it reflects a closeness neither of us is comfortable with. The room goes quiet, except for the unchanging overture of the ceiling fan and the restless ocean. For the first time since she passed the computer over, Katrina's eyes flit from mine.

I'm spared having to reply by someone knocking on the door.

Katrina stands up and starts for the entryway, her brow furrowed. "Did you order takeout?"

In the heat of the day's writing, I've lost track of time. Katrina's guess is reasonable. The past three nights we've ordered from various restaurants in town, eating our dinners out of plastic containers while we read what we've written. Not tonight, however. "No," I say. "It's—"

Katrina opens the door. "Harriet," she says.

I hear Harriet's voice, flippantly easygoing like usual. "Katrina. So nice of you to invite me over for dinner after not speaking to me in years."

She walks in the door, holding a bottle of the pinot noir the three of us used to drink on our retreats. Her heavy-soled boots thud on the floorboards.

Harriet is cool. There's no other way to describe her. Even when we were young writers coming up in New York, I was conscious of her being cool in ways I could never learn or master. Nothing's changed about her.

She's dressed in shades of black and gray and wearing an oversized floppy hat.

"I didn't invite you," Katrina says slowly, frowning at me.

I blink. Katrina is . . . pissed. I thought she and Harriet had kept in touch—honestly, when our partnership collapsed, I presumed Harriet had taken Katrina's side. Evidently, I was wrong. Why Katrina dropped Harriet is hard for me to fathom, though.

"Nathan did," Harriet replies, walking into the dining room, unperturbed by Katrina's frosty welcome. She examines the walls with the fascinated eyes of tourists visiting famous battlefields. "I figured he told you, which I'm now realizing was a supremely stupid assumption. How's the writing going?"

Katrina's reentered the room. From the opposite end of the dining table, she stares me down, squaring her shoulders. "You didn't think to mention we'd be having company?"

I know I could calmly explain what happened. While I have in the past few days said things, written things, even done things to spite Katrina—turning off the fan when I know she prefers it on, using words starting with "un" in our writing when I know she finds them weak and repetitive—this was not one of those things. Harriet texted me, and I genuinely thought Katrina would want to see our old friend. I thought she'd even appreciate the buffer between us. Every night we've eaten our meals in silence, practically racing to be the first one locked safe in our bedrooms for the night. I just forgot to mention I'd invited Harriet.

This, of course, is not what I say. "*We* don't have company," I reply. "*I* do. Last I checked, I don't need to run my plans by you. We're not a couple."

Past her wire-frame glasses, Harriet's eyes widen. "Wow, this is even worse than I thought." She moves to the barstools, where she sits to spectate, helping herself to the tortilla chips Katrina left out from her lunch.

I watch the familiar flush rise from Katrina's collarbone, up her neck, into her cheeks. She's furious. I hold her gaze, positive she could light paper on fire with the vicious heat in her eyes. Conflicting impulses have collided in her, I realize. She *hates* when I make decisions without our having agreed on them. But she can't refuse me without explaining herself—something Katrina's been loath to do for over four years.

Right now, I'm making her choose.

Harriet crunches a chip.

Still looking at me, Katrina grinds out her next words. "Harriet, would you like to stay for dinner?"

Harriet doesn't hesitate. "Oh, fuck yes."

12

Katrina

THE FIRST HALF hour of the dinner is really hard. Despite Nathan's glib comment—*We're not a couple*, I keep hearing in his Connecticut voice—I know *he* knows courtesy would have dictated mentioning he'd invited Harriet over, and I'm frustrated he didn't. I wonder what game he's playing. I don't even entertain the idea there's no stratagem here, no subversion. Every one of our interactions is layers on layers on layers of subtext and hidden conflict.

It's not just Nathan I'm angry with, either. While we fall into old roles and old routines in the kitchen, Harriet dumping pasta in the pot on the stove while Nathan and I work on the garlic bread, I find Harriet's easy humor grating. There's a reason we haven't spoken in years. Harriet crossed some lines in our friendship, and I still haven't forgiven her for it. Having her here, acting like nothing happened, is irritating.

The minutes drag. I start to imagine how the night will go. It's one of the curses of writing for a living, my mind's irrepressible instinct to write the scene of whatever's happening in my real life. And there's one thing every writer knows—nothing is as stressful as dinner scenes. Ours would play out in painful fashion, me glaring silently while Nathan rubs in his coziness with Harriet, knowing how it frustrates me. Maybe, if the powers that be were feeling provocative, we'd have it out. Yell, slam doors. It sounds difficult and depressing, and lately, my days haven't been much else.

So while Nathan's putting the pan of garlic bread into the oven, I make a decision. Writing every minute is hard, and doing it with Nathan Van Huysen is exhausting. I'll unravel if I have to stay mad at these two people the entire night. I have to let my resentment for one of them go.

I pick Harriet.

The night flows easier from there. The sun has set by the time we're ladling pasta onto plates, and the whole house smells like warmth and herbs. We sit down, and Harriet catches us up on the seminar she taught last year. One of her students was Ted Chapman, who was a co-resident from the New York Resident Writers' Program where we met, and whom we all hated. I let myself laugh, let Nathan pour me more wine. And if while we enjoy one another's company it feels like nothing has changed, I know it's just a fiction maintained in the moment.

Without my noticing, hours pass. While I'm loading the dishwasher and Nathan's taking out the trash, Harriet sits at the table, finishing the end of the pinot. I face her, prepared to say I'm glad she's in the neighborhood. It's not exactly an invitation but not a closed door, either.

My words vanish when I find she's pulled over my laptop and is reading from the open screen. "Don't read that," I say, the sentence flying out of me sharply.

Harriet ignores me. My resolve snaps, every ounce of the equanimity I counseled myself into gone in a flash. Furious, I rush over to her and slam the screen shut, my heart rate jumpy.

Harriet looks up in undisguised surprise. "It's just—" I stammer, realizing my reaction was disproportionate. "It's such a rough draft."

Harriet stares, scrutinizing my expression. "I've read half-assed ideas you scrawled in your Notes app at four in the morning. I think I can handle a rough draft."

I hear the kitchen door crack open. Nathan comes inside. He surveys the scene in front of him, me standing over Harriet. I know the tension is obvious. "She was reading our pages," I say, hearing how childish I sound.

Nathan shrugs. "How were they?" he addresses Harriet.

The question feels like betrayal. I recognize it's unfounded—I've always known Nathan loves having his work read, which is his right. Besides, why would I expect him to have my back on anything these days? Once, he would have. I've heard him defend creative choices I've made in pitches and interviews when privately I knew he disagreed with them.

We were partners then. *Were.*

We wait for Harriet's reply. Wordlessly, she finishes her wine in one swallow.

"You're not going to tell us," Nathan says.

Harriet waves in my direction. "She doesn't want my opinion."

"It's not *you,*" I struggle to say. "It's . . ."

"It's what?" Harriet's voice flares. "Care to explain why you forgot I existed for four years?"

Compared with the veiled war Nathan and I have waged recently, Harriet's characteristic directness is almost comforting. I sit down heavily. I have an answer, just not one I want to say in present company. When Harriet and I last spoke, the night was uncannily like this one, except without Nathan. We were in the living room, fifteen feet from here. I was pacing the hardwood while Harriet sat with her feet up. When she walked out of the house after, I shut the door on her in more ways than one.

"She's nervous about having people read her writing." I lift my head when Nathan speaks. Something strange has entered his voice, something strangled and conflicted. Is he . . . helping me? He won't meet my eyes.

"Funny how *you* don't count," Harriet replies to Nathan immediately.

I inhale and exhale, fighting the itch to leave the room. "No, I should work on it," I force out. "What did you think of the pages?"

Harriet studies me. "They're not bad," she says hesitantly.

"But?" Nathan prompts.

Harriet stands. She picks up her bag and pulls out yellowed pages paper-clipped together. I catch sight of a printed sentence and know instantly what Harriet's holding.

It's an early draft of a scene from *Only Once*. The product of Nathan's and my old process was hundreds, even thousands of draft pages we worked and reworked together—a paper trail of us pushing each other for endless tiring, wonderful hours.

The presence of those pages hits me like a punch to the chest. Handwriting dances over them. Nathan's, straight and slim. Mine, long and slanted. They're letters from old, practically forgotten versions of ourselves.

I glance involuntarily at Nathan, who looks as wrecked as I feel.

Harriet drops the pages on the table. "Here's my opinion," she says. "You two have been assholes to me and to each other for too long. Unsurprisingly, your characters are also assholes. Generally, that's fine, except it's impossible to imagine they were ever in love." She looks between us. "Sure, they're getting divorced, they hate each other, et cetera. Still, we need to believe there was ever love in their relationship. We need to see it in glimpses. Otherwise, there's no anguish to this divorce and the story collapses."

She shoulders her bag and heads for the door. I follow her, hating what I'm hearing and needing to hear more.

"I know you won't want to," Harriet goes on, "but I encourage you to look at those pages. You might find them inspiring. Or something." She pauses, hand on the door. "Or, consider some, like, *serious* therapy. The way you two are working through your shit is, frankly, weird. Well, this was a blast," she says, smiling. "Let's do it again in four years. Sooner, if you're done being dicks."

She swings the door wide and leaves into the night.

Processing, I can do nothing but return to the kitchen. I find Nathan hasn't moved nor have the incriminating pages in the center of the table. We say nothing, eyes fixed not on each other. Finally, Nathan heads for the stairs.

"I'm too tired for reading," he says over his shoulder.

13

Nathan

I'VE HAD NO difficulty sleeping the past few nights. I expected I would, what with living for the month in the house my estranged co-writer's fiancée purchased for her to celebrate the most calamitous occasion in my private and professional life. Instead, sleep has come easy. I guess it's—oh, I don't know—the exhaustion of writing with Katrina for eight hours, then running six miles. I hit the crisp white sheets, and I'm out.

Not tonight. I'm restless, wide-eyed in the dark. I shift under the comforter, performing my helpless one-person dance of discomfort, pretending I'm searching for the perfect position of knees and elbows when, really, I know exactly what the problem is.

The pages Harriet left are still in the dining room. They're exposed, documents of my deepest secrets for anyone to see. I don't want to look at them, I don't. They're not just pages of prose. The handwritten edits, the notes we left each other—they're direct evidence of the way Katrina and I once worked. The way we drew our ideas together, the passion of the process. It's not *Only Once* I can't stand seeing. It's the *us* in every edited page downstairs.

I destroyed all the drafts I had. I'm certain Katrina did as well.

Knowing something survived, I'm unable to settle myself. The questions plague me. Which scene is it, festering on the dining table? What moment of our lives was preserved?

Head on the pillow, I negotiate with myself. I *have* to know which pages Harriet kept. I won't read them. I swear I won't.

With my deal struck, I swing my legs out of bed. I don't check the clock when my feet hit the floor. I know I wouldn't like the three numbers—I'm certain it's three—staring up into the darkness. Walking lightly downstairs, I wince with each creak of the floorboards. The last thing I want is for Katrina to know this kept me up.

I feel my way into the kitchen, my eyes adjusting to the darkness. When I reach the table, I search for the pages.

There's only smooth wood under my fingertips, cool to the touch.

Instantly, I know. They're gone.

It's calming, I realize. Katrina surely trashed them. I'm oddly comforted, knowing I'll never have to face whatever memories were woven into our handwriting. My chest lighter, I head for the stairs, feeling like I'll finally be able to sleep.

But when I reach my room, I'm forced to a halt. Down the hallway, past my door, there's light under Katrina's.

I feel pulled. Hands of a frustrating force I would hesitate to deem fate drag me down the hallway, putting me in front of her room. With every footstep I war with myself and lose. I wait in front, conscious of the intimacy of standing outside a woman's door in the middle of the night.

After anguished minutes, I fight to draw up my courage. Eventually,

I win, my knuckles rapping on her door. In the ensuing pause, I recognize my victory will be Pyrrhic. What could I hope to gain from a conversation with Kat at one in the morning?

Finally, Katrina opens the door. In the uneven light coming from the only lamp on in her bedroom, I note she's wearing striped shorts and a tank top, which hangs on her lithe frame with grace I wouldn't have imagined possible for pajamas. Her hair is the way I remember from early mornings years ago, the brown waves wound over one shoulder, brushing her collarbone and below. Her eyes are wary, questioning.

Past her, the pages are splayed open on her bed.

"You took them," I say.

It's a stupid observation, the kind I wouldn't permit my characters to speak because it moves nothing forward, reveals nothing. I'm trapped here now, though. Trapped here with my words, trapped here with the woman who can see through them.

"Nathan, it's the middle of the night." While Katrina's putting on impatience, I know she's faking. I hear her guarded hesitance. "Why are you here?" The uncertainty in her eyes changes into realization, and she continues. "You went looking for them."

"I wasn't the only one," I say, matching her feigned confidence syllable for syllable. It's not hard, I find, like an after-hours rehearsal of the performance we put on for each other every day of writing.

Katrina huffs. "Don't bother yourself with them. There's nothing in these pages."

She's lying. I can read her, the flickers in her expression, the way she plays with the ends of her hair. "What scene is it?" The question comes out of me with a breathlessness I know betrays my interest. I don't know what the point of hiding my reaction would be, though. It's not like Katrina can't read me the exact same way.

She looks away. "An unimportant one." She's *definitely* lying. The flickers of indication in her expression leap into flames. Her cheeks redden. She swallows. Her reactions only heighten my furious curiosity. Now I *have* to know.

"You don't want to give them to me," I say, understanding. "Do I need to remind you it's my handwriting you're reading?"

Katrina retreats deeper into her room, positioning herself in front of the bed. There's protectiveness in the gesture, like she's putting herself in my way. "Nathan, they're meaningless. I just wanted to read them to judge what Harriet was saying."

It's nearly a convincing explanation, except why would she need to judge Harriet's feedback in the middle of the night? I walk into her room, highly aware I'm stepping onto dangerous ground. "If they're meaningless," I venture, "why can't I have them? What's in the pages, Katrina?" I'm coming closer, right up to her, while she stays still.

She lifts her chin up subtly, combative. "Nothing real. It's just fiction," she says, practically exhaling. "Fiction." She repeats the word like it carries enormous weight, or like she wishes it did.

I take another step. I'm walking into fire. It consumes me, fears and fantasies of whatever of my writing lies exposed on Katrina's sheets. The stagnant heat of the room is suffocating. It's not just the Florida weather—it's the room, the feet separating me and Katrina turning into inches. The way I know I shouldn't come closer, yet I do. I know I'm not thinking straight. Practically dizzy, I keep walking toward the pages, toward the bed.

"Prove it," I half whisper. "Prove to me it's fiction."

I've lost track of the layers in the conversation. Katrina's right in front of me now. I lean closer to reach for the pages—to reach for her?—nearly bringing us together. We have half a foot's height difference between us, which means when I bend down, our lips are only inches from touching. I don't know if I'm dreaming, if the restless hours of the night have warped hallucinatory imaginings into my waking moments, or if I recognize the same heat I feel in myself rolling off Katrina. Her perfect stillness feels poised, purposeful. Her round, dark eyes look like they're waiting.

Without breaking eye contact, she lowers herself to the bed, staring up at me from the sheets.

I'm definitely dreaming, though this is brazen even for my dreams. While I watch, fixed in place, her body unfurls. One slender forearm slides backward. I follow the motion, my heart pounding, not daring to wonder where this is going.

Her hand clenches on the pages. Before I can react, she shoves them into my chest. The fire in her eyes is not what I thought. It's confrontation.

"Like I said"—her voice is sharp—"there's nothing worth hiding here. There's nothing at all."

14

Katrina

When Nathan leaves the room, his features hard, I collapse onto the bed. The instant he closes the door, I let everything I'm feeling wash over me. It is not refreshing, like the ocean on summer days. It's more like when unexpected waves hit you right in the face—suddenly you're underwater, spinning, currents pummeling you from every direction. Flat on the bed, I'm breathless. I'm confused and hating the confusion. How could Nathan Van Huysen conjure this much uncertainty in me all these years later?

I reach a hand under my pillow. From beneath the cool cloth, I retrieve the one creased piece of paper I'd hidden when Nathan knocked.

It's the only page I knew I couldn't show him. When his knock echoed into my room, I moved with instinct, shoving the page under the pillow. I couldn't bear for him to have it—couldn't bear to lose it, either. I'm not sure where one desire begins and the other ends. I wasn't lying to him, exactly. The scene *is* inconsequential. The characters, Jessamine and Jordan, go out to drinks in Greenwich—Nathan insisted on Greenwich so he could draw from his upbringing and his parents' marriage—and exchange a charged look. It's nothing, five-and-a-half pages of context, except for one handwritten sentence.

I read over and over again everything he's written in the margins. His handwriting is like a third character on the page. He rewrites the description of Jessamine, the onetime artist who's settled for suburbia with the man she loves, or loved. I'm unable even now to resist conceding everything Nathan's done enlivens the passage. He's rendered her hair, her posture, particularly her clothing, with not only precision but devotion.

When I get to the bottom of the page, I know what I'll find. In Nathan's inimitable handwriting, he's scrawled like a casual afterthought, *Sorry to steal your dress. But you look nice.*

Just reading the line, I'm wrenched into the moment when I first held this page, in hands no less wavering. It's uncanny, how we've cycled over the past four years, ending up exactly where we were when we wrote *Only Once.*

The location isn't the only similarity. In so many frustrating ways, what just happened was a hateful reprise of exactly how Nathan and I behaved when we were at our worst four years ago. Always wondering, never speaking except in writing, where we scream at each other from the comfortable distance of prose and characters.

Heat pounds in my head. I don't even know what it is I want. Half of me aches for when everything wasn't fucked-up with Nathan, the happier days when he and I would exchange ideas easily and, god forbid, laugh while writing. The other half wants to do nothing except be furious forever for the damage he did to our partnership. I'm desperate for whatever would cool me off. My writer's imagination flits past everything I'd wish for. Winter weather, iced tea with no sugar, vanilla ice cream.

In the next moment, I'm pulling out my phone. I'm dialing a number I know as well as my own. It rings and rings, and I have a feeling I'm going to voice mail.

Instead, when Chris picks up, his voice is heavy with sleep. "Katrina," he exhales. "What's wrong?"

The words rush out of me. "Come to Florida."

"Come to—" He repeats my words with incredulity. "Katrina"—he rustles like he's checking his phone—"it's midnight. For me. It's *three* for you. Why are you even awake?"

I had no idea, which I don't say. I'd lost track of time. The idea I've been rereading the pages for hours frustrates me. "Just—come," I get out. "Stay with me."

"What? I can't just come to Florida."

"Please." I hate how plaintive I sound, how hungry. How defenseless I feel perching on the edge of my bed. "You can work remotely," I tell him. This is important, I know. He would never consider coming if he's not promised plenty of computer and phone flexibility.

"Katrina." His voice has changed. He's shaken off sleep, and I recognize the firm calm in his words. "You don't need me to come to Florida. You can do this."

"I do. I do need you." My voice is stripped bare. Where Nathan and I can never be honest with each other, I can be with my fiancé. I grasp on to the idea with wild conviction. It's why we're together. It's why I'm here. This whole conversation is strikingly reminiscent of how we fell in love in the first place. I called him needing help and he was there for me. He's always been there for me. He's picked me up every time I've needed him to.

In the long pause over the line, I imagine having Chris here. Yes, his presence would irritate Nathan, but he would temper the hostility that's impossible to escape in this house. Instead of reading and rereading the same page stashed under my pillow, I could retreat into Chris's arms every night.

"I don't think it's a good idea," he replies finally. I know every nuance and inflection of Chris's voice like they're the cross-streets on my drive home, and I recognize when decisiveness has won out over reassurance. "I'd only be a distraction. Why don't we discuss this tomorrow, babe? It's late, and I have a seven A.M. call with a publisher in London."

Unbeknownst to Chris, I crumple, tears of rage filling my eyes. In the slanted shadow my lamp casts, my bedroom has never felt more like a cage. He's not going to come, even after I prostrated myself asking him. I think it's possible for people we love to quietly, even unknowingly, snap some tether holding us together. I wonder if it's what Chris has done now. I want to feel like I'm speaking to the Chris who clasped one hand over my eyes while he walked me into the study in our home in LA, surprising me with towering white bookshelves holding my entire collection. The Chris who watched seasons of cooking shows with me when I got engrossed in them one summer, despite the fact that he couldn't care less.

Somehow, I don't feel like it's the same Chris on the line with me now.

"Sure," I say. "Fine." I hang up, not giving him the chance to say *I love you.* Not caring if he was going to.

Returning my phone to the nightstand, I cast one final glance at the page of *Only Once*, my eyes lingering where they shouldn't.

I give myself one second, two, before I shove the page into my dresser drawer.

15

Katrina

• FOUR YEARS EARLIER •

WE'RE ON HARRIET'S expansive porch. The day is warm with the kind of breeze I could bask in forever, the gentle wind coming off the ocean like a greeting. I'm curled up on the porch swing, one leg folded under me, my sandals on the deck. Harriet's beside me. Nathan's in the Adirondack chair across from us, scribbling on the pages I wrote last night.

I woke him up when I delivered them this morning. He came to the door hair tousled and shirtless and tried to act like he'd already been awake.

"What exactly have you been up to this morning?" I'd asked him.

"Writing," he'd said.

"Writing shirtless now?"

I couldn't help but catch the blush that entered his cheeks. "For your information, I'd write shirtless all the time if I could." He was inventing it on the spot. I knew because for the past couple of weeks, I've watched him for hours a day come up with clever replies and remarks for our characters. I'd recognized his spitballing face immediately and undeniably, even though it didn't usually come with red cheeks.

"What's stopping you?" I'd asked, eyebrow raised.

He'd shifted his shoulders. I hadn't lingered on his chest. If I had, I would have noticed it wasn't writerly in the stereotypical sense. I'd been to his apartment and seen the expansive, modern gym in his building, not to mention worked around his nightly runs for as long as I'd known him.

"Concern for my beloved cowriter, of course," he'd replied with a grin, dimple winking.

The memory makes me smile. I glance over, finding him still deep in his markup of my pages. "Surely what I wrote isn't that bad," I chide, completely free of resentment or sensitivity. I'd be more self-conscious if I didn't completely trust Nathan. It's like we're one voice sometimes, one mind. I wouldn't feel self-conscious reading my own writing. Nathan reading my writing hardly feels different.

Nathan looks up. "It's great," he says, and I know he means it. I feel warmth illuminating every inch of me, and it's not the sun. It never ceases to surprise me how easily Nathan gives his praise. He could view others with the indifference privilege usually provokes. Instead, it's like the generosity of his circumstances has instilled generosity in him. He compliments me daily, and whenever I look into his eyes the way I am now, it is impossible to doubt he's genuine.

"Then what are you making so many changes to?" I crane my neck playfully.

"I want it more obvious how bewitched Jordan is with Jessamine," Nathan says. "I know they just met, but he should feel like it's . . ." Nathan pauses like he's choosing his words carefully. He looks out over the yard, over the technicolor green of the grass and upturned fuchsia faces of the hibiscus. "Like his eyes, his mind, are drawn to her in every unconscious moment," he finishes.

It's disarming when Nathan says things like this. It makes me feel like Melissa is a lucky woman. I've only met Nathan's wife a few times, which I figure is because Nathan is hesitant to cross his personal and professional lives. Over those few dinners—one where Nathan cooked in his apartment, one at the cozy Thai place near mine—I wondered if Melissa would be cagey or judgmental of her husband's female collaborator, sizing me up. Instead, on top of her stylish blond hair and perfect makeup, she was nothing but warm, funny, and generous. She's probably on the receiving end of plenty of Nathan's poetic devotions. Of course, I'm lucky, too—because they end up in our books.

"If it'll help you write faster, feel free to remove your shirt," I offer.

He barks out a laugh, and I know we're both remembering the moment we shared this morning.

"Excuse me," Harriet says indignantly from beside me. "I do not consent to seeing Nathan shirtless. Take that shit back to your bedroom."

"Bedroom*s*!" I reply immediately, emphasizing the plural.

Harriet rolls her eyes. I check Nathan's reaction furtively, wanting to know if he's bothered by Harriet's comment. He's already returned to writing in the margins of my pages, lost in thought. Shaking off the question, I return to my screen. It's just how Harriet is, I remind myself. She makes innuendos about me and Nathan every now and then, just a running joke. Nothing more. If there were even the hint of feelings between me and Nathan, they'd never progress past hidden unanswered questions. Nathan is married, which I respect—or I would if his marital status was even relevant to me. Which it is not.

I force myself to focus. Rereading my previous lines, I continue working on the scene I was writing until I feel Nathan's eyes on me. When I look up, he's staring. He smiles sheepishly when I catch him. His gaze returns to his page, mine to my computer. Yet, fingers on the keys, I can't think of what to write. Nothing comes. Minutes pass, and once again I feel Nathan's eyes on me. This time, I don't look up.

Finally, Nathan stands. "Done," he says. "Swap?" I nod eagerly, and he walks over with the pages he was working on. When he holds them out, I grab them with curiosity I don't hide, passing over my computer in exchange without complaint. He returns to his chair, and with the immediate ease of years of writing every day and years of writing with me, he picks up the scene where I left off.

I feast my eyes on what he's written for me. His scrawl is everywhere, lively, insistent, leaping from line to line with unmistakable passion.

What he's done with the scene steals my breath. There's new yearning in Jordan's perception of Jessamine. Nathan's colored his every description of her like he's drinking in the details.

Yet it's not Nathan's prose I find breathtaking, not this time. It's how he's written Jessamine sitting just like I am, one leg folded beneath her, wearing exactly what I'm wearing. Desperately, I rationalize his choices. It's just easier to describe something you're looking at rather than inventing it. It doesn't mean anything more than that.

As for what he's written at the bottom of the page, I don't have a convenient rationalization. Nathan praises me all the time. My word choices, my dialogue, my poise and professionalism. The pair of short sentences he's written shouldn't surprise me. Never, though, has Nathan's praise looked like this.

Sorry to steal your dress, he's scrawled. *But you look nice.*

16

Nathan

• PRESENT DAY •

When Katrina slams open my door, the sun is shining. I wake, disoriented, realizing it's morning. It is the only information I know with certainty.

I feel horrendous. Checking the clock on the nightstand near my pillow, I read 7:12 A.M. The early hour explains why I feel hungover, emotionally and physically, my head a painful lump of chewing gum and my eyes stinging. When I last looked at the clock, I recall it displaying almost four A.M. I rustle self-consciously in my sheets, shifting onto my elbows. I'm shirtless, I remember, and I'm sure the state of my hair is criminal.

Katrina does not look hungover. She's freshly showered, her eyes shining with morning-person energy. In her slender hands, she holds a mug, steam rising invitingly from the mouth. She walks into the room, her posture sharp.

"What are you doing?" I ask, honestly unable to understand what the fuck is happening right now. *Katrina is in my room.* She's voluntarily putting herself within fifteen feet of me. With—

"Made your favorite." She holds up the mug.

The smell hits me. My hangover cure of choice, whether alcoholically or emotionally inflicted. The spicy, woodsy scent of coffee fills my room, and momentarily I forget it's Katrina Freeling holding the cup. I know without knowing she's made it exactly right. No cream, no sugar, using the French press downstairs. Which she learned to use for me. Katrina hates coffee herself.

She gestures to the nightstand. Warily, I nod.

While she approaches, I find myself making mental notes of her appearance, her demeanor, filing away details I'll later spin into prose. The way she's pushed her damp hair behind her ear, the gentle curve of her eyebrows. Her lips, a shade past pink and shy of magenta. I don't make a habit of drawing inspiration from real people's physical characteristics. Katrina is the exception. I can't help reaching for her hands, her eyes, her smile when writing.

She puts the coffee down.

"Is it poisoned?" I ask.

Her lips quirk in what couldn't have been a smile. I feel a flash of victory then chasten myself. Smiles from Katrina are points in a game I no longer follow. Without prelude or explanation, she sits on the foot of the bed, her hand resting just inches from my leg, still under the cover. I shift slightly, reestablishing distance. We used to hang out this way, easy early mornings of discussing the day's pages or where we would walk for lunch. I don't know how I ever managed being this close to her on a daily basis.

"I'd like to propose a truce," she says.

I straighten up, not even pretending the suggestion doesn't shock me. The movement is unconscious, and I don't realize until it's happened the comforter has slid six inches farther down my shirtless chest. Katrina notices. I catch the split-second dip her eyes make. When she lifts her hand, I feel how hard she's working not to stand up and resume our stiff separation. She doesn't budge.

"What would a truce look like?" My voice comes out skeptical.

"Neither of us wants to be here," Katrina explains calmly. "But here we are. There's no escape except a finished book. Every day for the next month you and I will be creating fiction together. So let's embrace it. Let's live a fiction."

It's a clever speech, one I have the feeling she's prewritten, crafting dialogue for herself the way she would for our characters. However, Katrina is nothing if not skillful. I have to concede I'm intrigued. I sip my drink, Katrina's white flag of black coffee. Even over the scent, I can smell her hand cream.

"And which fiction would that be, exactly?" I permit myself to ask.

"The one where we're reconciled writing partners eager to collaborate again." Katrina's voice doesn't waver. "For two months, we can tell ourselves this story."

"You want to pretend we're enjoying this?" I'm incredulous.

"Essentially, yes," Katrina confirms.

I pause over my next swallow of coffee. It is its own reminder of the tense, efficient mornings we've spent lately, Katrina staring silently out the kitchen window while I slowly push the French press's plunger. I take the next few seconds to imagine the coming weeks the way she's describing them.

"We won't argue or hurl accusations?" I venture finally. "We won't dredge up the past?"

Katrina doesn't drop her gaze. "It'll make this process . . . easier," she says delicately. It's ironic how forced the word *easier* sounds passing her lips, which I now notice have light indentations in them, like she's chewed them recently.

I say nothing. Considering the idea feels daring. Is it even possible for me and Katrina? What would it mean if it is?

I place my mug carefully on the nightstand, contemplating the answers to these questions. Either we're skillful at living a lie, or deep down, we're weary of the endless conflict between us. I feel it every time I look at her and remember I have to resent her. It isn't natural. I don't know what natural would look like for us, but fueling this hatred is exhausting. It's feeding a fire out in a storm, fighting wind and rain to keep the embers from going out.

"I agree," I hear myself say.

The first hint of surprise flashes in Katrina's huge eyes. "You do?"

"On one condition."

Her brows flatten.

"I'm tired of bagels. Let's go out for breakfast."

I watch it happen. Like I knew she had been—Katrina chews her lip. "You want to . . . get breakfast," she repeats.

"Yes," I confirm.

"And eat it together?"

"Yes, Katrina." I raise an eyebrow. It's obvious what my invitation really is. The first challenge. How much does she mean this truce?

She stands up, looking like every muscle in her body is sore. I'm ready to shake my head, finish the coffee I left on the nightstand, maybe head out on a run. Forget this conversation ever happened.

Then Katrina plasters on a smile, the first one she's given me in four years.

"I'll wait for you downstairs," she says.

17

Nathan

I HAVEN'T RELAXED since Katrina barged into my bedroom this morning. It's not easy to stay stressed on the patio of The Cottage, the restaurant where Katrina and I had brunch every weekend while writing *Only Once.* The place is idyllic, a white picket fence enclosing the tiled terrace, with pastel blue-and-white-striped umbrellas. Waiters dressed in navy sweep past with precarious platters of powdered French toast and colorful frittatas. Chatter and sunlight surround us.

"How is it?" Katrina nods to my eggs Benedict. She's sitting across from me wearing gold-rimmed sunglasses, her sunhat flopping lazily over her hair. Delicately, she sips her grapefruit juice.

"Excellent," I say. "And yours?"

She carves off a bite of her banana chocolate-chip pancakes. "Great," she replies.

This is the problem. It's how it's been the whole morning. Incessant emptiness.

Like beachcombers scouring the sands with metal detectors, we've probed our surroundings for points of interest, finding nothing but the smallest of small talk. The weather, how the neighborhood has changed, the restaurant's juice selection. They had guava, which got three complete sentences out of us.

For two people who make their livings writing dialogue, our conversation is painfully stilted. I'm not giving up, though. If we're going to act like we don't hate each other while writing, we should certainly be able to handle conversation over pancakes. It's practice, the way we would rewrite our own work in the styles of different authors in a creative writing course I took in college. Practice.

Which is why I decide to push a little further. "I have to say," I start, swallowing my swill of coffee, "I'm curious why you agreed to write with me again." It's a risky subject, one closely connected to others we don't want to discuss yet. I'm dipping one careful foot into the water, feeling out the depths, deciding whether I'm ready for the plunge.

Katrina pauses, taking her time while she chews. Instantly, I'm desperate to know what's going on in her head. I repress the fearsome conviction I've gone where I shouldn't have. Practicing cordiality was *Katrina's* idea. She'll understand what I'm doing.

"I guess I was bored," she says finally, her voice calmly neutral.

I frown. Katrina doesn't get *bored.* It's not how her mind works. She's intensely curious and intently observant, capable of sweeping herself up in examining and understanding whatever catches her interest. It's one of her greatest writerly gifts, the authenticity her prose has from the intuition-level understanding she's developed of the world and of people in it.

I pick up my knife. "So it really had nothing to do with Chris?"

Katrina's face hardens for a half second. She sips her drink, and when she sets it down, I can see she's decided something. "No, it did," she says. "I'm doing the book because Chris needs the money." Her voice has shed the practiced nothingness it's held this morning. The change is subtle—she's not wry or emotional. She just sounds matter-of-fact.

I can tell there's more she's not saying, truths too fundamental to ignore. It's not on Katrina to earn Chris money. The reality is, Chris is taking advantage of their personal relationship to better their professional one. She's obviously uncomfortable with the position she's in, and rightfully so.

I stomp out the flicker of pleasure the news of their discord lights in me. We're pretending we're friends, and people don't gloat over proof their friends got engaged to manipulative, money-hungry assholes. Still, for every speculation I'd had—and I'd had many—I never imagined Katrina's return to writing had sprung from so much selfishness on Chris's part.

"Why did *you* agree?" She sounds like she's fighting to keep the question cordial. I find myself grateful for her effort. Where our writing is combat, if productive combat, we're collaborating for once. Collaborating on one respectful, normal conversation. We're in the same lifeboat, our eyes fixed on the same horizon.

Her honesty inspires candor of my own. "My book sales without you are . . . not great," I admit. "Publishers, and apparently readers, only want Nathan Van Huysen when he's writing with you. I can't blame them, either."

Katrina's expression doesn't change. I fight gamely to figure out what's going on behind her sunglasses. I've seen her non-expression on plenty of occasions in the past—I used to watch her read, in sunlight or lamplight in the rooms of houses we'd rent, and I would try to guess what she was thinking. When she'd close the cover, I could never predict whether she was going to look up, eyes luminous, and want to spend the next hour discussing everything she'd loved, or shake her head, frustrated by everything she felt the writer should've improved. I never knew how she did it. How she contained so much and revealed so little.

"I read *Refraction*," she says.

Instantly, every part of me leans in, wanting to hear whatever she'll say next. It's the moment every author hates—the *I read your book*, followed either by praise or by damning nothing. In general, it's a conversation I prefer not to have. With Katrina, I have to know.

"I . . . loved it," she concludes.

The relief would weaken me in the knees if I were standing. I do my impression of Katrina's reserve. "I'm surprised you read it at all," I say genuinely.

"I'll always read everything you write," Katrina replies. Again, honesty. I can hear it in the way her voice goes soft, how easily her words come.

We return to our food, the silence less stilted. I find I'm finally . . . comfortable, or close. I'm ready to take the plunge, fully acclimated to the water. "I should have congratulated you when you got engaged," I say.

I remember when I found out. It wasn't like Katrina emailed me the news, obviously. It was fucking Facebook, the carousel of baby photos and new houses I wish I could get off, connecting me to people with whom I no longer needed connection. People like Chris Calloway, who of course was the one to post, not his new fiancée, smiling with her eyes shut, his hands clasped in hers with her ring finger small in view while he kissed her cheek. I'm sure she approved of the photo. It was so Katrina, so understated and human, nothing showy. Every day I've had the size of the princess-cut diamond on her finger under my nose as we write, and while I cannot be said to respect Chris's taste, in this I understand how Chris wanted to post it for the world to see.

They were on some balcony somewhere. The photo was from New Year's Eve. I found the post the following morning, so hungover even the white fabric of the couch in my living room hurt my eyes. I studied their expressions—Katrina's smile—with the resentful half disbelief reserved for cruelties you knew fate might deal you but hoped it wouldn't, then I locked my phone. My pounding headache wouldn't be the only reason I would be unproductive that New Year's Day.

Closing Facebook wasn't enough, though. My phone wouldn't stop buzzing afterward. Everyone who knew us both had to text me. Had to read in to my pauses and my punctuation, determining for themselves how I felt. I decided the cure for my hangover was another drink, alone this time.

Over the past four years, the moments Katrina's existence has intruded on mine have felt like interludes. They're lost days. I write, of course, but the content is functional, unenthusiastic, the prose equivalent of ground beef. Because every word wasn't written out of passion or intent but out of resistance. Resistance to the terrible gravity of the question I don't want to contemplate—whether Katrina was my real life, and everything else the interlude.

Katrina flushes pink. "It wasn't necessary. It's not like we were speaking," she says, recovering her composure.

We're perilously close to the subjects we've danced around in every spiteful comment and pained look. The thing is, if Katrina's honestly happy engaged to Christopher Calloway, I'm happy for her. If noticing the ring on her finger fills her heart with light, I want nothing else. I just know what I know about Chris, and I know what I know about Katrina.

She takes off her sunglasses, folding them carefully in her hands. "I was . . . sorry to hear about you and Melissa," she goes on. I can see in her eyes she's doing exactly what I am. Testing herself. Finding out if we can really fake this. I imagine her receiving the same texts I did, telling her the news of my divorce. I wonder how she replied.

"Thank you. I have . . . more regrets than I care to admit," I say haltingly. This confession is doubly difficult to make. Not only to Katrina, but to myself. There's no easy way to break off your marriage, like there's no easy way to break your leg, but if I could change the past, I'd still be divorced from Melissa, though there's plenty I'd do differently. Our divorce was comedically painful, like some ugly joke the universe was playing. There were times when I almost wished one of us *had* cheated, just so we could push our marriage to the safe distance of hatred. I know with certainty it would've been preferable to watching my ex-wife sign her divorce papers, then burst into big, broken tears.

Katrina nods. She stares into the distance. "Chris doesn't want me unless I'm a writer," she says after a moment.

The admission pulls me forcefully from memories of Melissa. It's unexpectedly heartbreaking. I feel an instinct I thought I no longer had to comfort her, reassure her. "Katrina . . ." I start.

She looks at me. "It's fine. I mean, it's not, but you don't have to say anything." Putting on her glasses, she flags down the waiter. "Can we get the bill?" she asks with a smile. It's fake, but what she said was real. Everything we've said was real.

It's ironic, I realize. In our pretense, we've somehow stumbled into honesty. We've let ourselves share things we wouldn't when we were our combative selves, entrenched in our present life.

I wonder where it leaves us, because this fake friendship is starting to feel unnervingly real.

18

Katrina

WE'RE ON THE couch, where we've wordlessly agreed we're working today instead of the dining room. Brunch left me feeling off. I don't know why I confessed to Nathan things I hardly concede to myself, truths whose faces I only glimpse when I'm turning over in bed every night. Hearing them out loud, they sounded ridiculous. But the way Nathan listened told me they weren't.

I might've preferred feeling ridiculous.

When we got home, I pushed those insecurities to the side, knowing what scene lay ahead of us. If discussing our lives over pancakes was the warm-up, writing romance together feels like stepping into a boxing arena. We've avoided it long enough, though.

We drifted into the living room, Nathan carrying his computer, and eased onto the couch in front of the porch windows. It's warm, not hot. The cushions sink welcomingly beneath me. The room is cozy, and completely incongruent with what we have to do. Nathan, next to me, is sitting legs crossed with his ankle propped on his knee.

While we write, I feel his eyes move from the screen to my hands folded in my lap. I know what he's noticing, not for the first time. Just like I recognized Nathan was so strikingly similar to how I remembered him, he would've done the same. He would have seen how little I've changed from the Katrina he knew, despite the enormity of the upheavals in our relationship. My hair is long, my skin pale from my indoor workdays.

Except for the ring.

The engagement ring I've worn for two years now is the one outward sign of what's changed in the years Nathan and I have spent pretending each other didn't exist. To be honest, the ring is not the one I would have chosen for myself. But it's very Chris, for which, I have reminded myself, I'm grateful in other ways. It's princess-cut, with strands of diamond and platinum sweeping up the sides of the square stone. Which is huge. I have small hands—comes with being five foot four—and I remember how weird typing was with the noticeable extra weight on one finger. With time, I've gotten used to the feeling.

Chris proposed to me on New Year's Eve. He'd told me we could celebrate at one of our favorite hotel bars, and he'd booked us a suite in the hotel for the night. We went. We had fun. It was predictable fun, uncomplicated. I remember feeling grateful for this. Everything in my life for too long had been hard. Working with Nathan, fretting over *Only Once*, escaping my subconscious in a maze I sometimes suspected had no ending. I wanted something comfortable, ordinary, comprehensible. Enjoying music and drinks with my boyfriend in the company of strangers was perfect.

With minutes until midnight, Chris gently insisted we head up from the crowded bar to check out the room. He walked me to the balcony, the night stretching lavishly below us. Chris handles his liquor well—though there was some pink in his cheeks, his eyes were bright and intense and his speech emotional and clear when he asked me to marry him.

It was easy saying yes. Chris kissed me, drawing my face to his. While he snapped a photo of us, I closed my eyes for some reason. We had sex. I remember feeling happy getting into bed next to him past midnight on what was officially New Year's Day. I was loved. I was okay. I was moving forward. The future in front of me was welcoming and sure.

Maybe Chris wasn't the love story I'd imagined for myself. Our romance wasn't pining and fanfare and fated flourishes. But it was better because it was real. I didn't need to be in a love story—I only needed to be in love.

In general, I couldn't care less what Nathan feels when he sees my engagement ring. Right now, however, I doubt it's helping our progress into the day's scene. The first page is finished—we've written the opening without incident. It's a flashback, one where Evelyn and Michael have just returned home, exhausted from the long day they spent driving down the coast. A spark between them leaps into flame.

It's as far as we've gotten. They exchange one heated look, and now we can't push the cursor forward.

"What if we just don't do the flashbacks?" Nathan proposes, his voice halfway to pleading.

"The book doesn't work without them," I say gently. "We have to show the height of their passion."

Nathan unfolds his leg, putting his other foot on the floor. "Okay, well, what if the height of their passion is . . . gardening, or making pasta? Why does it have to be sex?"

I smother a laugh. *Pasta?* "Are you listening to yourself right now?" I ask. If Nathan Van Huysen is suggesting something so obviously counterproductive to the book's interests, then he's as uncomfortable as I am.

I don't examine the reasons because they're not worth examining.

When we first started working together, writing physical romance was awkward. Writing anything is vulnerable. It's stripping yourself bare for your reader even when your content has nothing to do with sex. Nathan and I blushed and averted our eyes and covered over our discomfort with laughter in those early days. Getting to know each other better didn't make it easier. It made it worse. I didn't want to think about how my friend liked to undress a woman or how he liked to be touched. I didn't want him to know what I liked, either. It doesn't even matter if the things I write don't reflect my personal preferences. *I've* chosen them, which means enough.

Of course, back then, we were trading pages. It was the only thing that made the process bearable. Now, we're both forced to perform under the watchful gaze of a partner. It's the difference between whispering something in your lover's ear beneath the sheets and saying it out loud in the middle of the afternoon. Nathan and I could never have the intimacy that would make this endurable.

Nathan, whose ears have reddened, has the good grace to smile. "Fine," he says, his voice strangled with surrender. He dumps the computer in my lap. "Care to get things started?" Hearing his own word choice, he winces.

Nathan's laptop resting on my thighs, I promptly panic. When I stare down, the screen stares up, like it's planning on swallowing me and every creative skill I have. "How, um, descriptive should we get?" I stammer out. "Like, body parts, or—"

"Not descriptive," Nathan replies decisively. Or desperately.

"Says the guy who labored on one whole page of setting description yesterday."

I swear he nearly laughs. Instead, he sits up straighter. "Katrina," he says with new formality. "You're a bestselling author. I trust you to make this choice. I'll follow your lead."

I roll my eyes. Placing my fingers on the MacBook's flat keys, I start to type. I lead us into Michael and Evelyn's first embrace—writing faster and faster, not letting savage self-consciousness slow me down. I pretend I'm in a bedroom, that I'm writing this for someone else. Anyone else. I finish a passage and pause, certain my cheeks have gone fire-engine red, and we haven't even made it to the bed yet.

Nathan reads over my shoulder. He inhales deeply, and I watch his discomfort war with whatever idea he's having. Finally, he reaches over my hands to add more.

He lends new imagery and new passion, his words spilling onto the crisp white background. In a couple of sentences, he makes me feel Michael's wonder at how much he could want this woman he spends every day with. How he could never have enough of her. While I read, Nathan finishes and leans away from the computer.

I crack my knuckles and start undressing Michael. We're in a rhythm now, Nathan and me. I describe each place their skin touches, each searing kiss. The computer is hot in my lap. When I finish the paragraph, I slant the screen in Nathan's direction.

He clears his throat. "I . . . have nothing to add to that," he grinds out.

I keep going, fingers flying over the keys. I reach the point where Evelyn and Michael slip naked into the sheets. Then . . . I stop. Not even inspiration or every learned instinct I have can help me now. I can't write this. Not with Nathan one foot away. "Can we *please* write this part separately?" I ask.

Nathan's demeanor darkens. "And what? Trade pages?"

"Just for this one chapter," I push.

"No." His reply is immediate.

I knew it would be. I don't even blame him. I can't deny there's an intimacy in trading chapters back and forth. Of course, it's not like what we're doing right now isn't intimate. But writing pages and pages with a single reader in mind changes things. Whole chapters read like letters delivered directly to your door. When the content of those chapters is romantic . . . I've been there before, and I'm not ready to return. I don't know if I'll ever be ready.

"We can do this," Nathan says. I glance over, surprised by how encouraging his voice has become. "We have to. Remember what we'd say on *Only Once*?"

I nod. "It's the characters' thoughts, their feelings. Not ours." I repeat the familiar mantra, feeling like I've pulled the pin out of a grenade and am holding it tight. Charging on, I sketch out the love scene. I write Michael's hand under the covers, running up the inside of Evelyn's thigh. I write her move her leg unconsciously in response, her shuddering sigh when he touches her. "Do you like that?" I ask Nathan in a voice I don't mean to come out low.

He puts his hand in his pocket. "Christ, Katrina."

I realize how the question sounded. "I didn't mean—"

"I know what you meant."

Exasperated, he lifts the computer off my lap and onto his. He writes in the things only someone who's had sex with a woman could, the desperate need Michael has for Evelyn, the way his eyes linger on her lips fluttering open, how he wishes he could feel the soft curves and tender points of her chest every second until forever.

Then he draws the details only Nathan Van Huysen could—the lyricism in their movements, the emotion beneath every brush of lips.

He hands the computer over, the hot metal shocking my thighs. I know what needs to come next. I layer in the same language used in Evelyn and Michael's fights—the clenched fists, the pounding hearts, the furrowed brows—this time with pleasure instead of pain.

"Good," Nathan murmurs. "Yeah."

His words run indecipherable chills down my spine. I finish the scene, racing to the conclusion, where Michael and Evelyn seal the final moment with a kiss. The moment I hit the final period, Nathan stands up.

"Glad that's over," he says.

I close the computer, ignoring my own galloping heartbeat. It's just writing. Writing can get intense. "Want to order takeout for dinner?" I ask cheerfully.

"Works for me." His voice is equally upbeat.

We're pretending everything is normal, like nothing happened. Which . . . nothing did happen. The knowledge does nothing to calm the question lingering in my mind. *If everything is normal, why does normal feel this hard?*

"I'm going to go for my run," Nathan says nonchalantly. His posture looks uncomfortable. "Eat at seven?"

I force a smile. "See you then."

He walks out of the room. I stay on the couch, not sure what I want to do now, only that I don't want to cross his path. It's the characters' scene, I remind myself. Separate from us. I cling to the reassurance like I would a flimsy blanket on a cold, cold night. The line between us and what we write needs to remain firm. If it crumbles, if we let ourselves bleed into our work, we'll have nothing left except a messy confusion of lives and pages.

19

Nathan

• FOUR YEARS EARLIER •

I'M WRITING INTO the night, every light on in my room in defiance of the late hour. My wrists hurt, my vision feels warped, and I don't care. I have to finish the scene of *Only Once* I started hours ago, when Katrina and I went upstairs for the night. We've hit the part I love in the process, where ideas and inspirations outpace my fingers. Everything is fitting into place, and I'm racing to put one more passage down before I sleep.

Katrina and I write constantly now. It's not exhausting—it's exhilarating. It's perpetual motion. This is the point I'm always chasing, where the ending materializes on the horizon, the clouds part, and everything becomes dazzlingly clear. There's nothing like it. Every night when my head hits the pillow, I already can't wait to wake up, meet Katrina in the kitchen, and keep writing.

I check the clock. One A.M. *Shit.* I know I'll need rest if I want to work productively tomorrow.

When I grudgingly stand, I hear a knock on my door.

I smile. Katrina's up late, just like I am. She's pulled forward by the same ineffable momentum driving me. Leaving my computer open, I cross the room to the door. Whatever weariness was drawing on me has disappeared. It's Katrina—she's my second wind. When I open the door, she's standing on the other side holding pages.

"Working late?" I put one hand on the upper door frame, leaning in the entryway.

Kat is flushed. She's put her hair up, which she only ever does when she's writing in a sprint. She looks like she ran one, too. When she speaks, she's not quite shy, not quite casual. "I did a first pass on the . . . dream," she says.

I straighten in the doorway. My eyes flit down to the pages in her hands, and I feel guilty, as if my gaze were following Katrina's low-cut neckline instead. Which it doesn't. The object of my curiosity is paper and ink. But those pages hold the first explicit content in the book—a scene where Jessamine fantasizes about Jordan in a dream.

"I didn't know you were working on that," I say.

"I wasn't planning to," she replies. "I just . . ."

She won't meet my eyes.

"I was inspired," she finishes. Several strands of her hair have fallen loose from her ponytail, framing her face. They caress her cheek when she shifts her posture. In the light from my room, her skin looks soft.

"I can't wait to read it," I say, meaning every word. Katrina notices her runaway hair and pushes it behind her ear. I hold out my hand for the pages.

She doesn't give them over. "Nathan . . ." She pauses like her words have gotten stuck somewhere inside her. "It's a sex dream," she goes on. While she's stating the obvious, her voice wavers. "But it's not *my* sex dream, okay? I need that to be clear. It's the character speaking. Not, you know. Me."

I force a laugh, even though Katrina saying the words *sex dream* elicit in me decidedly nonhumorous reactions. "I know," I say. She fixes me with a long look. "I won't mistake what's in these pages for your personal preferences," I promise her.

She nods. "Good," she replies, sounding more certain than she looks. My hand is still outstretched, and finally, she passes over the pages. "I'm not cut out for this kind of writing," she goes on with an uneasy laugh.

The errant urge catches hold of me to reach out for her, make some gentle gesture, caress her shoulder or squeeze her hand. The idea flees from my mind as quickly as it came. "This is why we have each other, right?" I say instead.

"Right." She stands there for a moment longer, framed in the dark of the hallway, like she wants to say more. "Have, um, fun with it," she says.

"Interesting choice of words."

Katrina laughs. It relieves some of the stiffness of the conversation. "Good *night*, Nathan," she says half sarcastically.

I shake my head, smiling with her. "Night, Kat." When she heads down the hallway, her bare feet noiseless on the hardwood, I shut my door. Crossing the room, I close my computer on the unfinished paragraph I was working on. The pen I pick up is the one I use whenever I'm revising. It was my father's college graduation gift to me, and while I know he wanted me to use it to sign contracts or patient charts, the pen was still the closest he'd come to implicit endorsement of my career choice. Uncapping the silver Montblanc, I climb into bed.

The scene Katrina's written ignites immediately. It's bold, getting right into the heat of the characters' passion without hesitating. I'm sucked in.

Katrina was wrong. She's very, *very* cut out for this.

Her writing is sensory and charged, wrapped up in conflicting emotions. Jessamine desires a man she can't want, except here, ensconced in her unconscious. The freedom exhilarates her, and the pages run with naked passion. Katrina labors over the feelings, pushing them to their tipping points.

It's not just wonderful writing captivating me, I know. Every word, every description is infused with perfect Katrinaness. It's impossible not to see her fingerprints everywhere. She warned me this wasn't *her* fantasy. *Of course not*, I remind myself.

But in the middle of the night, lying in my bed, with her words of yearned-for pleasures and forbidden embraces filling my head, I do what I know I shouldn't. I invite the line between author and character to blur. I hear everything in Katrina's voice, and it sets me on fire.

Working the waver out of my fingers, I put pen to paper. I read everything twice, three times. By the third, I'm complimenting what I like, contributing where I can. I feel it happening while I do—this fantasy is no longer just in her voice. It's in ours. We've built it together. The opportunity dizzies me. Like a dream, these pages let my thoughts run wild, let me indulge in everything I shouldn't.

Only when I finish do I wrestle down my wayward mind. I tell myself what I do whenever Jessamine and Jordan fall further in love. Getting swept up in their feelings is easy. It's what good writing does. But it's only *their* feelings. This isn't my fantasy. It's not a fantasy at all.

It's fiction.

20

Katrina

• PRESENT DAY •

OUR TRUCE IS working. Writing comes easier for Nathan and me over the next couple of days. It's not the psychological roughhousing I've grown used to over the past weeks, either. Nathan and I don't disgorge our grudges onto the page. We're civil, even easygoing, pointing out questions with candor and understanding. It's far from the morning we spent in Florence writing *Connecting Flights* where Nathan put ridiculous dialogue ideas into our characters' voices while I laughed so hard my stomach hurt, but it's something.

On Saturday, we decide we need to get out of the house. We used to be frequent café writers. When we weren't on retreats, we'd hole up in the coffee shops of New York instead of working in each other's living rooms. I found the rhythms of the background music and conversation invigorating, while Nathan—I think, though I never spoke my suspicions—got uncomfortable when Melissa could hear his creative process. Now that we're not fighting constantly while we figure out each scene, I'm confident—well, more confident—we can write in public without disrupting our fellow patrons or embarrassing ourselves.

Nathan suggests inviting Harriet. Hiding my reluctance, I agree. Despite our temporary truce when she came over for dinner, there's still too much bad history between us, more than we can ignore for long and more than I want to confront right now. Which I don't want to explain to Nathan, especially since I've developed a distressing habit of saying more to him than I mean to.

The house isn't far from town. We follow side streets heavy with greenery, palm fronds and high-canopied trees stretching far above the power lines, until we reach the café Harriet suggested. I grudgingly find myself glad we are here, in Florida. It's the faintest echo of how Nathan and I felt on our other retreats, as if travel—unfamiliar streets, the ring of novelty in every rustle of trees, sidewalk conversation, or the scrape of shoes on pavement—was pushing open the gates of inspiration.

When we walk up to the café, the converted bungalow's teal porch and pointed white roof stand out on the street. Inside, the place is perfect. They have everything conducive to daylong writing—wide windows, a large tea selection, lots of outlets. I sit next to Nathan while Harriet sits across from us, stealing inquisitive glances she thinks I don't notice.

The afternoon has been jarringly pleasant. Harriet's asked our advice on a syllabus she's preparing, and I've managed to make conversation with the two people who months ago I never would've chosen to be in the same room with. Over his shoulder, I'm watching Nathan write. He's in the middle of a sentence when I interject. "Wait, you need to—"

"Shit, you're right," he says.

He deletes.

"What about . . ." He refocuses the sentence.

"Yeah," I say. "Just don't forget to reference—"

He writes exactly what I was going to say.

Lifting his fingers from the keys, he smiles. "Not bad, right?" I roll my eyes and pull the computer in front of me.

"Wow," Harriet says. I stop typing. When I look up, she's staring, no longer hiding her interest. I realize she hasn't worked on her syllabus for the past few minutes.

"What?" Nathan sounds uncomfortable, like he knows where Harriet's comment is going.

"You two are . . . really getting along," she replies. Her voice holds surprise verging on suspicion.

I feel Nathan stiffen next to me. "We're trying," I say, not knowing why my reply comes out defensive.

"Trying? Shit, you're succeeding," Harriet says. She narrows her eyes. "How?"

Nathan's quicker to respond. "Does it matter?"

"I mean, no," Harriet replies. "It doesn't matter like world peace or feeding the hungry *matters*. I'm just desperately curious. You're doing the thing where you read each other's minds. Worse, you look like you're having *fun*."

When the cappuccino machine hisses, I flinch, startled. "We're not having fun," I clarify decisively. Nathan's head turns slightly, but he says nothing.

"I figured you invited me today to be your buffer or something," Harriet says. "I guess I was wrong."

"I invited you because we're friends," Nathan says easily. Harriet eyes him a moment longer, understanding what I do. It's a half response, direct yet incomplete, evading the real subject of the conversation.

Harriet lets him. Uncapping her pen, she returns to her syllabus.

I keep typing, my ears buzzing. I should feel proud we've fooled Harriet. Proud we're finally working cohesively. It's a *good* thing, I tell myself. But then why do I feel like I've broken the rules?

"No," Nathan interrupts my writing. "'Always.' Not 'forever.'"

He means word choice. I reread the sentence. *Evelyn remembered those first private seconds right after they'd said "I do," when they'd laughed with relief at surviving the hard part and all that was left was dinner and dancing and the love they'd feel forever. Had any of that changed?* I grimace, knowing exactly where Nathan's comment is going.

"'Love they'd feel always.'" He emphasizes the final word, confirming my fears.

"Forever," I reply patiently. "For the alliteration."

Nathan's voice remains light. "You have this grudge against the word *always*. You *always* have." He flashes me his dimple.

I ignore the dimple, which was unfair. "Not true." It was partly true. I can't explain my hatred of the word, but I resent that he's calling me on it.

"Katrina." He puts his elbows on the table, pleading his case. "It completely changes the connotation. 'Forever' is about . . ." He grows contemplative, grasping for the distinction. "Forever is about reaching into the future, into years far away and unknowable. 'Always' is about every second of every day. It's as far-reaching as 'forever,' it just starts sooner." His eyes have fixed on mine. "The word is immediate and immortal. And better."

No way. I'm not letting him off with some evocative Nathan Van Huysen speech. "Forever hits you instantly with its hugeness," I fire back.

Nathan says nothing, studying me. Then he turns to Harriet.

"Not a chance," she says, eyebrows rising. "I refuse to get involved. Work this out yourselves." I swear I see a pleased gleam in her eyes. When I frown, she just shrugs.

I face Nathan. "Rock paper scissors?" I offer hopefully.

Nathan eyes my dryly. We have, on occasion, used the playground game to settle writing disputes. Right now, however, Nathan doesn't put his fist forward.

Instead, he stands up. "I have a better idea."

I watch uncomprehendingly, dread filling my chest. The feeling heightens when, without hesitation, he stands up on his chair.

"Oh my god," I say. "Get down from there."

He flashes me the dimple again. "Excuse me, everyone," he says loudly to the room, surveying the café. I stuff my hands in my lap, knowing I won't like whatever he's going to do. "I need your help settling a score."

Heads swivel in his direction. I hear whispering, undoubtedly people wondering why this strange man is standing on a chair. Nathan doesn't look bothered.

"We're writing a book. Raise your hand for the sentence you prefer." He's exuding his characteristic charm, and I can see some of the skeptical cafégoers drawn in. "'The love they'd feel always,' or 'the love they'd feel forever.' Show of hands for 'always.'"

He waits, expectant. No one raises their hand.

"Come on," he implores the crowd, his voice enticing. "My partner and I can't agree, and we have to go home together tonight. Don't make us fight about this over dinner."

A laugh escapes me, and I immediately clap a hand over my mouth, earning glances from Nathan's audience. A man in a fishing vest raises his hand, followed by the two teenagers in the back. Seeing them, Nathan jumps a little in excitement and nearly falls, his chair wobbling under him. I laugh louder now, not hiding it.

Nathan notices. His eyes flash to me, his lips forming half a smile. "Show of hands for 'forever'?" he requests, his gaze still on me.

More hands rise. With surging satisfaction, I look around at my new constituents. The elderly couple near the coffee counter appear fully committed. Both the baristas prefer "forever." The thirtysomething woman working on her computer is raising her hand without looking up from her screen. I've won. Nathan hangs his head dejectedly.

"I'll accept the judgment, though I do not like it. Thanks, everyone," he says, stepping down from his chair. When he sits next to me once more, he looks exhilarated.

"Wait, seriously?" I say. "You're going to do my word just because four people in this café raised their hands?"

"I said I would, and so I shall," he replies with mock gravitas. His eyes sparkle.

I laugh again, unable to help myself. "You're ridiculous."

"This surprises you?" he returns immediately.

I only shake my head, chiding, and return to the computer. The hint of my smile lingers on my lips. Focus fails me—I reread our last sentence over and over until I feel Harriet's eyes on me. When I look up, she's staring. There's no mistaking what she's thinking, and now, I have no defense. This time, I didn't just look like I was having fun. I was.

21

Nathan

WE LEAVE THE café around sunset. Harriet headed out an hour ago, shaking her head while Katrina and I discussed the scene we were working on.

It was a good day, in every way I measure a day. Katrina and I finished the scene we had scheduled, and what we wrote was excellent. What's more, we enjoyed ourselves. Harriet wasn't wrong—when Katrina and I collaborate well, finishing each other's sentences isn't the half of our synchrony. We finish each other's phrases, motifs, nuances. My uncle, who rowed for Harvard, would describe the feeling of the whole crew finding their collective rhythm, gliding over the water with flawless force. It's how I feel on Katrina's and my good days.

We walk home, enjoying the first cool of the evening. I wish I could bask in the orange and pink sky or the pride in what we wrote. Instead, my stomach is knotted. The day was *too* pleasant. It scares me. I know where patterns of days like today lead, and I won't return there.

Katrina walks next to me, the hem of her white cotton dress fluttering in the breeze, revealing glimpses of her calves. She looks contentedly down the road, her eyes drifting like she's lost in her imagination, her lips half open. The silence is comfortable, which is why I need to ruin it.

"Why are you marrying him?"

I know immediately I've shattered our growing camaraderie. It eases the tension in my stomach. Katrina's eyes slant to me. She doesn't slow her steps, her sandals crunching on the sandy pavement.

"I love him." Her voice is frigid.

Good. I need to remember this is here, always under the surface of our performed friendship. I can fake it however long I need if I don't forget what's real. It's not like I believe her, of course, which I don't say. It's reassuring, the idea we might lie to each other again.

Because she *is* lying. Some people wear relationships like cozy sweaters. Others wear them like chains, others like armor. Katrina wears hers like a heavy coat, restrictive, even uncomfortable, if protective from the cold outside world. It's not quite love, even though it's not quite the lack thereof.

Pursing her lips, she doesn't let me respond. "Why'd you get divorced?" she asks, clearly wanting to level the playing field. "Did Melissa leave you because of the rumors?"

She doesn't specify which rumors she means. There's no need. "No," I reply curtly, enjoying the combativeness. "She didn't leave me. I ended it."

Katrina is silent. For a reckless second, I want her to ask why. I want the question dangling in front of me like a garish piñata. I want the chance to give in to every impulse, to completely wreck everything between us, to destroy even the possibility of finishing this book. To quit pretending we could ever be friends.

She doesn't ask why. She doesn't say anything the rest of the way, and neither do I.

22

Katrina

SINCE OUR WALK home from the café, it's been five figurative degrees colder in the house. I know what Nathan was doing, and furthermore, I get it. I'd fallen into old feelings, old emotional cracks I thought I'd paved over. Watching him up on his chair, I felt like I was watching the Nathan who lit up our festival panel events or made our workshop friends laugh. I won't pretend I'm not a little grateful he pushed us apart.

I'm hopelessly conflicted—I don't want to be here, writing with Nathan in our house, and I do want to, because returning home would mean facing Chris's and my poor financial picture and the probable ruin of my relationship.

I have so much practice wanting and not wanting at once.

On Sunday, we give ourselves the day off from writing, the way we used to. We've always insisted we need the time to rest and do research. In the past, that looked like outings to the beach, but neither of us broached that possibility today.

While I was reading on the porch in the morning, Nathan had jogged out in running shorts, hardly pausing long enough to wave goodbye before starting off down the block. I tried to settle back into reading, but I couldn't. I didn't want to be cooped up in this house, waiting for Nathan to return. I grabbed my bag, and I started walking.

Harriet's house is fifteen minutes from ours. When I march up the front steps, I'm sweating from the humidity. I knock on the white wood and wait. I would have texted, except I deleted Harriet's number in a rage years ago, and if I'd asked Nathan for it, I would've had to endure his prying questions on why I no longer had it.

Right when I'm starting to turn around, Harriet answers the door.

"I was wondering when you'd turn up," she greets me. Her ebony hair is down, falling over her black Cocteau Twins shirt.

"Have a minute to talk?" I ask.

From behind the screen, Harriet studies me for a moment. Finally, she swings open the door. I walk in, noticing immediately she's remodeled the place. It looks less Florida-quirky, more simplistic. Gone is the retro leafy wallpaper, in its place white walls, dark wood furniture, and marble sculptures. It's a reminder that not everything has stayed the same in four years.

The other reminder is how Harriet crosses her arms and frowns at me. "No Nathan today?" she inquires. It is not a cheerful or casual question.

I don't bother answering. "You were out of line," I say instead. I'm not talking about the café, and she knows it.

Harriet's eyebrows rise. "Really? Isn't this conversation a little late?"

"If you don't want to have it, I'll walk out right now," I reply. I give her a look that says the rest. *And we'll never move past this.*

Harriet sighs, long and drawn-out. Not exasperation. Resignation. "Fine," she says. "Let's do this. You think I was out of line? I was your friend. I was trying to *help* you."

"How exactly? By ruining my partnership? My career?" I don't hesitate in replying. I've had half a dozen versions of this fight in my head in the shower. While I never thought I'd have them in person, I hadn't considered returning here, being in proximity with more pieces of my past than only Nathan Van Huysen.

Her mouth flat, Harriet looks unconvinced. "Come on. You were ruining your partnership on your own. You're just mad because I said something you didn't want to hear."

I shake my head. Does she know how obvious her retorts sound? How uninformed? "I'm mad because you didn't respect me," I say.

"How was I not respecting you?" Her eyes have gone wide with mocking incredulity.

"What you said—" I start.

She cuts me off. "Enough euphemisms. I told you you were in love with Nathan and you couldn't handle it." She looks me square in the eye. "Because it was true."

For the first time in the conversation, I'm off-balance, groping for words in response to ones I didn't expect. Facing each other from the ends of the room, we're like prizefighters dancing around the ring, and she's just dealt me a stinging, head-spinning shot.

Finally, my counter comes to me. "He was *married*."

"Yeah, he was," Harriet replies levelly. "And if I thought you two had fucked, our conversation would have been *very* different."

My face feels hot. I haven't yet found my composure, Harriet's words ringing in my ears. *Because it was true.* I hadn't wanted to face them four years ago, either. I hadn't wanted to face any of it. I was in the darkest period of my life. It didn't matter that Harriet and I had fallen into friendship with what I recognized was remarkable ease after Nathan introduced us on the second day of the New York Resident Writers' Program. It didn't matter she and Nathan and I had celebrated just the three of us when she sold her first book. Didn't matter she'd been the first friend I told when my cat died. When she'd walked uninvited into the Florida house the day after Nathan had left, I couldn't understand why she just wanted to push and prod and sneer.

I drop onto the dark blue fabric of the chair behind me. "Whether it was true or not wasn't the point. If—if I was . . . what you said"—I can't help dodging the "L" word—"what good would admitting it be? We had a whole career in front of us. We had lives."

I must appear miserable, because Harriet's face softens. "I wasn't trying to be cruel," she says, leaning on the wall closer to me. We look a little less like prizefighters now, more like people who used to be friends. "But Katrina, you can't just pretend feelings that are inconvenient don't exist," she continues. While her voice is not gentle, it's not harsh, either. "I thought you both would be writing together forever, and I just couldn't sit by and watch you fall for him, right at his side but out of reach. I thought . . . if you talked about it, or maybe got some space or something, it would be good for you."

I say nothing, suddenly exhausted. We've split open the years of silence on the subject, and instead of wary, or resentful, or everything I was when Harriet used to cross my mind, I'm only numb. I don't know where Harriet's wrong or where she's right. I only know I did what I had to do to protect me and Nathan both.

Hesitantly, Harriet leans off the wall. She crosses the room and sits in the chair nearest to me.

"Did you ever talk to him about it?" she asks.

I cut her a look. Then immediately, the combative flicker extinguishes in me. I'm tired of fighting everyone and everything. "Of course not," I say softly. "Nathan doesn't . . . do that." Nathan doesn't talk about what's real. He writes it. He uses it to inspire and deepen his art.

"What he said about you in the *New Yorker* interview . . . He was hurting. I know it," Harriet says, her voice reaching for me now instead of pushing me away.

I frown, remembering the interview. The sting of Nathan's words was palpable, physical. It was like emotional food poisoning, worked painfully into my gut, unwilling to let me ignore it. His quotes, cruel and flippant and ever-so-Nathan, were the first I'd heard from him in weeks. "He doesn't need you to defend him," I reply, knowing it's not exactly what Harriet's doing, yet needing to say it nonetheless.

She receives my frustration gracefully. "Right. Well, none of it matters now, does it? You're engaged and, as far as I've heard, this book is the last you'll be writing together."

Her eyes find mine, questioning.

"Definitely," I confirm, dropping my gaze to the floor. "None of it matters now." I try to take comfort in the idea, but it feels hollow. Finally, I look up, finding my friend watching me from her chair. Catching myself thinking of Harriet as my friend is reassuring, even fortifying. She is, or I want her to be. Our fight was never about her—not really, I realize. If I'm honest with myself, any anger I had for her died years ago. I was holding on to the ghost of a feeling, telling myself it was real when it wasn't. "I'm sorry I shut you out," I say. "I . . . should have talked to you years ago."

Harriet pauses, then smiles. "You and Nathan have a lot in common." I laugh a little. I can't even take offense—Harriet's right. I skirted and dodged and evaded this conversation exactly the way Nathan would have, the way he refuses to have conversations off the page. "Friends again?" Harriet asks.

Now I smile. "Thank god," I say, relief fluttering its wings in my chest. "I can't do this alone with him."

She laughs, leaning her elbow on one armrest. Suddenly, seamlessly, our relationship feels whole again, like we haven't missed years of strained distance. "Remember in Italy when you two got in that screaming match at two in the morning about—what was it, even? I just remember coming downstairs and threatening to pour water on your laptops if you didn't shut up."

My smile widens. "He had some metaphor he was fixated on," I say. "After you scolded us, I went to bed and proceeded to send him shouty texts for the next hour."

"I should've figured." Harriet shakes her head, playfully rueful. Then her expression shifts. Sincere, even somber, she speaks softer. "Can I say one thing without you not speaking to me for the next four years?"

I tense. Right when the ground felt solid under my feet, she's reminded me it's still thin ice. "If you insist," I say slowly.

"I don't know what feelings are left between you and Nathan. Maybe it's just resentment. Maybe it's—" When I shoot her a look, she wisely doesn't finish the sentence. "Whatever it is," she goes on, "it will come out in this book you're writing."

"We're professionals," I reply instantly, noticing how rote the words feel. How like a prayer. "We can separate ourselves from our work."

"No," Harriet says. "You can't."

I say nothing. While it's possible Harriet mistakes my silence for stubbornness, I'm guessing she sees my helplessness for what it is.

She stands up. "No one creates from nothing," she goes on. "You *will* put yourselves into your writing. Just . . . be careful."

While I want to object, I don't know how. Isn't it exactly what Nathan and I have been doing? Drawing our animosity into our pages? I cross one leg over the other in a meaningless, uncomfortable gesture.

"It's hot as shit in here," Harriet declares. It's a reprieve, a generously early end to the discussion. A kindness from a friend. "Want to go for a swim? You can borrow a suit."

"Yeah. Sure. That sounds great."

I follow her upstairs, my mind stuck in the living room, snagged like fabric on a sharp corner. The seam starts to open, and I'm left mulling on Harriet's warning. I'm not wondering whether she's right—she is. I'm wondering which parts of myself will end up under Nathan's pen.

23

Nathan

MY RUN WAS punishing, exactly what I needed. I don't prefer running after sundown the way I've had to on this retreat. Our neighborhood has so few streetlights that every passing car is a danger. Today, though, I've had nothing to do except run. I've wrung perverse enjoyment out of tracing my route with the sun pounding down on me, squinting while I navigate the paths I usually do in darkness.

I don't know what Katrina's doing right now. I doubt she's on the phone with Chris, whom I've hardly even seen her texting since we got here. She's probably on the porch, immersed in whatever she's reading, not noticing the tops of her feet have started to sunburn.

Rounding the corner onto our street, I slow my steps. I've been out for over an hour, and sweat is pouring down my back. As I walk, I see a woman struggling to lift a rug. It was obviously delivered to the curb, leaving her to wrestle the heavy roll to her door. I recognize her, sort of. Straight blond hair strangled into a ponytail like she was in a hurry, long legs in spandex. I've seen her several times in the past few days, hauling boxes into the back unit on the lot. From the looks of it, she's just moved in.

Glancing up from the uncooperative rug, she spots me. "Hey," she calls out. I hear something Southern in the one-and-a-half syllables she gives the word. "Mind giving me a hand?"

I hold open my arms, showcasing the sweat dripping off them. "Mind the sweat?"

The woman eyes me. I know the look she's giving me. It's one I've learned to decipher, living my single life in Chicago. She likes what she sees. Her smile spreads flirtatiously.

"No," she says. "Not at all."

I jog over. When I hoist up one end of the rug, she lifts the other.

"I'm Meredith," she says.

"Nathan," I introduce myself. While we head toward her house, Meredith walking backward, we pass a very inviting swimming pool beneath a towering bougainvillea. Papery pink flowers float listlessly on the water. We continue up the short flight of front steps into her living room, where cardboard boxes cover the floor.

"I just moved to town." Her eyes sweep over the boxes. "Obviously. You live nearby, right?" I catch her wince. "I'm not a creep, despite how that sounded. Just trying to learn the neighbors."

I laugh, sympathetic to her self-consciousness. I remember well the rootless feeling of moving out of my home with Melissa and to my new city. I wonder what Meredith's story is, which sounds cliché when the thought runs through my head, but it's why I write fiction and where I find inspiration. "Don't worry about it," I reassure her. "Yeah, I'm staying down the street. The house with the blue shutters."

"Vacationing?"

I shake my head. "Here for work. For the summer."

Her eyebrows rise. I realize it's the answer she was hoping for. When she doesn't reply immediately, I indulge in the opportunity to look a little closer. She's hot, probably in her early thirties, with a volleyball player's frame. Her tan is too perfect to be unintentional, and her black halter top reveals a lean midriff.

She catches me looking, then grins. "Well, Nathan," she says, "thanks for your help." She sounds sure of herself—instead of a woman who needed my help and invited me into her unfinished living room, she's a woman who now knows I was checking her out.

"Good luck with the boxes," I say.

She walks me to the door. "I hope you run by again soon."

On my way out, I flash her the dimple. By the time I reach the street, I've started strategizing how to get Meredith's number. It's a reflex at this point, after weeks on book tour in new cities each night. Opportunities like this one aren't easy to come by. Meredith is attractive, by all indications single, and definitely flirtatious. It's like the universe has delivered me a gift to sustain me through the next months with Katrina.

I wait for the prospect to excite me. It doesn't.

With every passing second, the fire in me doesn't heighten. Why *wouldn't* I want to end stressful days of writing doing whatever Meredith wanted in her new bedroom, our wineglasses half empty on her living room floor? There's no good reason.

Yet my desire only flickers, never quite catching. I'm not uninterested in the possibility, I'm just not enthusiastic. While I walk back to the house with the blue shutters, I wonder why not.

24

Katrina

"THEY STILL LOVE each other," Nathan says.

"But they're not *in* love." We're coming up on twenty minutes of this discussion, the clock in the corner of my screen reminding me how much time has passed without progress. "And they never will be again," I add.

We're sitting at the dining table. It's the point in the day's writing where we would ordinarily either have found our groove or gotten irritable—we've been working for hours, yet with the late afternoon sun glaring marigold through the shutters, we have hours to go. Instead, our conversation on the walk home from the café has coated everything in cool professionalism.

We're patient, even detached, while we discuss the looming question of how the book's going to end. We need to plan out how the plot's going to build, and we can't agree.

"I'm not saying they don't resent their feelings." Nathan's pretense of diplomacy is unwavering. "But you can't deny they're there." His voice is a little hoarse from the day's prolonged discussion.

I clench my jaw. I don't like the direction this conversation has gone or the precise point hanging us up. I want to *keep* things detached. But the debate feels uncomfortably loaded, and I don't enjoy walking the ugly tightrope that is discussing lingering feelings with Nathan Van Huysen. "Are you trying to tell me you don't think Michael and Evelyn will ever move on or fall in love with anyone else?" I ask.

"Of course not," he replies instantly. "You can love two people at once in different ways."

I make the mistake of meeting his eyes. Wishing I hadn't caught the fleeting shadow in them, I look away. Like a character in a ghost story, I pretend I imagined what I saw.

I stand up and start pacing, distancing myself from him. I know I could let the discussion go if Harriet hadn't put the idea in my head that we would write repressed feelings into this book. It's her fault, not ours, that I'm reading into everything Nathan and I say. But with Harriet's warning ringing in my ears, I can't agree with what Nathan's proposing, not if there's a chance this conversation isn't just about our characters.

"They care about each other," I get out. "But their passion has changed form. Love to hate."

Nathan watches me from the dining table. "So you want to end this book with them signing their divorce papers and burning every memory they have of each other?"

I falter, pausing on one end of the room, under the tauntingly tranquil painting of a sailboat on open water. I want to say yes. Nathan is, however, unfortunately right. The ending I've wound up proposing isn't interesting. It lacks nuance.

Which means if I were to push for it, I realize, it would only be out of personal feeling. Because it's the ending *I* want for myself—sending in this book and forgetting every memory Nathan and I have of each other.

If I let that hope become Evelyn and Michael's, I would prove Harriet exactly right. Instead, I have to write with my feelings utterly to the side no matter the ending.

"No," I say.

Nathan slants his head a little, like he's not sure he heard right.

I elaborate, finally seeing with refreshing clarity what the ending should be. "You're right. This book is about how love changes and how it stays the same. Even their parting is itself an act of love. Love to hate, then back to love, less passionate this time, but there. Forever." The final word comes out weighty, making the hair on my neck stand up.

Nathan studies me, undoubtedly trying to parse what I'm feeling from what I'm saying.

I don't give him the chance. I sit back down at the computer. "So we end with them finalizing their divorce *then* telling each other they love each other," I say while I type, pouring ideas into the outline. "Both things, though contradictory, feel equally true to them. The past lives on in the present."

He pulls his gaze from me. "And they kiss with real emotion. One last time."

I blink at the tone in his voice. "Then they part ways for good."

"The end," Nathan says.

We're silent for a moment. Sweat springs to my hands. I ignore the sensation, focusing instead on the flicker of pride I have for the ending we've just formulated. I did it. What's more, I did it with *Nathan*. *We* did it. We can keep our own emotions out of this.

For the first time in weeks, I start feeling steady, even confident. Because I don't just know how the end of the story will look, I realize. I know how the end of writing it with Nathan will look. We'll hold ourselves apart from each other the way we've been doing since the café. We'll deploy unkindness instead of growing dangerously close. We'll write from story structure. Not from feeling.

Nathan's eyes return to me, and I hear him draw in a breath like he's about to say something.

I preempt him, reaching for my phone. It shatters the moment somehow, changing the pressure in the room. Chris has texted me, I find when I illuminate my screen. **Making headlines**, he's sent. The next message is a link, a *Vanity Fair* article.

"Shit," I say.

"What?" Nathan glances over.

I unlock my phone and open the link. In the website's stylish font, I read the headline. "Your Favorite Bestselling Duo Might Be Back Together." My stomach drops. Underneath the headline, there's a picture of us at the café. Nathan's standing on the chair, speaking to the crowd. I'm watching him, entranced and grinning. My eyes catch on my expression in the photo, and I can't drag them through the rest of the story.

Nathan moves closer, reading from my screen. "*Vanity Fair* didn't even review *Refraction*," he says grumpily. "Then they post this shit?" He shakes his head. "Whatever. It doesn't matter. It's not like they confirm the book. Just speculation." Leaning back before I finish scrolling to the end, he pushes his hair from his forehead brusquely.

"Right. Yeah," I say. "It's nothing, really." I scroll up, pausing once more on the photograph. The smile on my lips. The way Nathan is midmotion, like he's about to turn to me.

"Are we having an affair yet?"

Nathan's question yanks my head up. "What?"

He nods to my phone. *Of course.* He means is there online speculation that we're having an affair.

My cheeks redden. "Not yet. It's only a matter of time, though." I mean the online speculation, too. Obviously.

Nathan looks at me a moment too long. "Looking forward to it," he says.

25

Katrina

• FOUR YEARS EARLIER •

NATHAN SCRUTINIZES ME from the armchair while I read. He does not look relaxed, which is unusual. Generally, Nathan lavishes in having his work read—not that he's categorically a narcissist, he's just rightfully proud of his writing, and others enjoying it exhilarates him. Right now is the exception. I'm sprawled on the couch, reading the pages he handed me this morning, fresh from the printer.

It's a sex scene. It's *the* sex scene. The *only once.* Nathan wrote the first pass of what is probably the most momentous scene in the novel, where Jessamine and Jordan give in to their passion. It's the first time we've done this. Nathan and I have never until now collaborated on a sex scene like this one.

Reading it with him nearby is . . . challenging. Especially when he's bouncing his leg and intently watching me flip pages.

"Could you not stare at me, please? It's making this weird," I say, not pulling my eyes from the page.

I don't have to look to know he's rolling his eyes. "Be professional," he replies.

Now I glance over for half a moment. "I am! It's just hard to read while you're . . . fixated on me."

He huffs. I don't know if it's a laugh or a noise of protest. Without further warning, he stands up and crosses the room, sitting down right next to me on the couch. He commences reading over my shoulder.

"How is this better?" Despite my consternation, I can't help smiling a little.

"Katrina, please!" he implores me. "Read the scene and tell me how it is. Put me out of my misery."

I wait hopefully for him to return to his chair. When he doesn't, I realize I have no choice except to comply. "It's . . ." I hesitate, fidgeting with the edge of the page I'm holding. "It's hot," I finish, not dishonestly.

Nathan snorts. Once more I diligently ignore his expression, his inevitable grin.

"I mean, the writing is great, too, of course," I go on.

"Naturally."

I fight the impulse to shake my head scornfully. I won't give him the satisfaction. "But it's—yeah, it's effective." I cross my legs. It's a lot to read about Jessamine's hands on Jordan's body, her mounting pleasure, knowing every word was considered, chosen, and typed by Nathan.

"Effective," Nathan repeats, evaluating. "It's not the worst review a woman could give, although I usually aspire to amazing, even earth-shattering."

Heat pounds in my cheeks. "Well, I don't know what to tell you."

"I welcome constructive criticism," he replies immediately. "What would you prefer?"

I exhale, hoping it's inconspicuous, hoping it hides how the pace of my heartbeat has picked up. The pages in my hands feel like they're waiting for me. I have writing preferences—punctuations, word choice. And I have other preferences. "Me?" I ask. "Or Jessamine?"

He pauses, eyes fixed on me. "You."

The word sounds larger than it is. I want to break our stare. I resist, holding his gaze. When I speak, my voice is steady. "I'd speed things up." I've seen Nathan react with skepticism or disappointment when I've critiqued his writing. What passes over his expression now is something different.

"Not one for savoring it?" His voice is unreadable.

"The second time, yes. If there was one," I say. "The first time . . . after all the waiting, I wouldn't want to wait longer." I swallow. "If I were Jessamine."

Nathan's the one to end our eye contact, clearing his throat. I'm instantly aware of how close we are. His shoulder is pressed into mine. When he breathes, I can feel his chest against my side.

What is this? I feel knocked off-balance, like I'm unsteady on my feet even though I'm sitting down. We've ventured into dangerous territory somehow, ignoring every sign we should stop. The worst part is, I don't even know exactly what territory it is. Who are we talking about? Surely not ourselves. Not while Nathan's *married.*

I reverse, hard. "I'm going to work on the scene where they're caught," I say, standing up.

The sentence douses the heat in the room. I'm indescribably relieved. Heading for the stairs with hasty steps, I'm nearly out of the room when I hear Nathan's voice behind me. "Noted."

I can't help pausing. From the first step, I turn back. He's exactly where he was, on the sofa, the pages sitting untouched next to him.

"What you said," he continues. "It's noted. I understand the feeling of having waited long enough."

I study him for even the faintest indication of what's going on in his head. His expression is restrained, lips closed, jaw set. His posture defensive. Everything about his demeanor is uncharacteristically withdrawn. Yet his gaze is searing.

I walk up the stairs without replying.

26

Nathan

• PRESENT DAY •

I DUNK MY head underwater. The pool is perfect, refreshing on my skin while I float with my eyes closed, weightless in a dark world. Letting the seconds pass, I feel tension drifting out of me.

After arguing over a plot point for forty-five minutes, Katrina and I decided we needed time to cool off. Literally, in my case. Though frustrating, our fight was unexpectedly vintage. Classic Nathan and Katrina. We weren't fighting over yearslong personal resentments or unresolved issues. No, this was just a fearsome, multiple-front campaign over whether to begin a chapter with conflict or more color of the character's life. We each drew blood—Katrina claimed I wasn't confident I could write something good enough to carry the opening, while I contended her idea was just plain boring.

It was obvious things wouldn't improve from there. This fight, even when resolved, wasn't going away. With each new paragraph, it would rear up once more, leaving us squabbling over creative positions neither of us really cared about, endlessly taking revenge for earlier wounds. It would have been unbearable. Worse, it would have been unproductive.

When we called off writing for the next hour, Katrina went up to her room. On my own in the dining room, I gazed out the sliding doors, this plan forming in my head. Neither of us has even dipped a toe in the house's pool this trip, and some space from Katrina would certainly help.

I'm enjoying my solitude. Surfacing from my float, I start swimming short laps in the five-foot-deep pool. The exertion unwinds the pressure in my chest, and the mindless repetition of the exercise is giving me some much-needed mental remove from the fight.

Until I reach the end of the pool on my fourth lap. I lift my head up from the water to find Katrina walking onto the pool deck.

She's wearing only her bathing suit. The blue one-piece hugs her hip bones and chest with hungry, sleek precision. Her hair is up in a casual bun on the top of her head. Sunglasses hide her eyes, which I'm certain haven't landed on me even once.

Book in hand, she slips into the opposite end of the pool.

I exhale, trying to recapture the relaxation I just felt. Katrina flips open her book, which she rests on the concrete edge of the pool. Her back faces me, blue straps stretching an *X* over her shoulder blades like a treasure map, or a warning.

Without acknowledging me, she lifts one wet hand out of the pool to recklessly turn the page.

I dunk myself under once more, pushing off firmly from the pool wall. Not even half a lap in, I start considering bringing my laptop out to *my* end of the pool. I could work on one of my other books. I probably *should* work on one of my other books, in fact. When this is over with Katrina, I'll have to return to my own career.

"Are you planning on splashing the whole time?"

Katrina's voice stops me midstroke. I pause, dropping my feet in the middle of the pool to gaze over at her. She has the gall to come out here while I'm using the pool then insinuate I'm the one interrupting her?

I raise an eyebrow. "Am I distracting you?" I ask facetiously.

"A little," she replies.

I stare, searching for self-consciousness in her tone and finding none. It's almost humorous. The point of this hour, though, was to avoid petty fighting, so I stay silent.

She glances over her bare shoulder at me, which only makes the lines of her shoulder blades sharpen. I can't help following the fabric of her suit under the crystal-clear water to her legs, all the way down to where she stands on pointed toes on the bottom of the pool.

I look away. The fifteen yards of water separating us was not the distance I had in mind. Without splashing, I wade over to the concrete edge, where I haul myself out of the pool. While I'm reaching for the towel I left on one of the deck chairs, Katrina's voice floats to me through the warm humidity.

"I didn't mean you had to get out."

"It's fine," I say. "I just need some space. Besides, there's something I want to do in town."

Katrina, either mollified or silently stewing, doesn't reply. Toweled off, I walk past her. Her eyes remain glued to her book, which I notice is flecked and warped with pool water.

I can't help myself. "Your book is getting wet," I say flatly.

Finally, she glances up, and I'm inexplicably glad to find humor warring with irritation in her expression. She kind of wants to laugh. As I walk inside, I smile. Soon enough, we'll be back to normal, or what passes for normal for us.

I head up to my room, where I change into my clothes. Pausing in the mirror, I slick my wet hair back in a way I'm not too humble to admit looks good, then grab my keys. I make the ten-minute drive to the local independent bookstore, my rented Porsche purring down the quaint streets. When I park, I pull from the glove compartment the pouch of Sharpies I never travel without and stride in.

The bookstore is exactly like I remember from Katrina's and my frequent trips here while we wrote *Only Once*. The scent of pages and wood greets me. The postcard rack, the doormat, everything feels like home.

It's one of my favorite parts of being an author—introducing myself to booksellers and readers. Maybe it makes me vain, although it's not the attention I'm after. Or, not entirely. It's getting the chance to hear from real people who've found themselves in my words. It reminds me of the point of what I'm doing. Writing can feel like a solitary, sometimes lonely profession, even with a coauthor. But it's not. My pages connect me with unseen strings to readers I often never encounter. I love chances to meet them—to pull those strings into the light.

I head deeper into the store, looking for the clerk. I find her shelving in the Young Adult section.

The short, middle-aged woman straightens up when I pause nearby. "Hi," she says. "Looking for something?"

"Actually, I'm an author. I was hoping I could sign some stock." I glance past her, worry flashing in me for a second. I hope they even have *Refraction*. There's an adage in publishing—a signed book is a sold book. Right now, I'm desperate to help *Refraction*'s sales numbers however I can. This is the career I'll return to after Katrina, and signing copies is probably slightly more helpful than carrying my laptop poolside.

"How wonderful. Let me see if we have any of your books in stock right now. If not, I'll order them in for you to sign later." She sounds genuinely enthusiastic. Adjusting her glasses, she studies my faces. "What's your name?"

I stick out my hand, flashing her the dimple. "Nathan Van Huysen."

27

Katrina

I LASTED TEN minutes without Nathan. Standing in the pool on my own quickly felt oppressive, suddenly changing the sunlight from warm and invigorating to muggy and sharp. My mind kept running roughshod over the question of where he'd gone, so casual and decisive, leaving just me in our quiet backyard.

I was jealous—not of him spending time somewhere other than with me, but of him having somewhere else to spend it. I'm starting to feel like my whole life right now revolves around Nathan and writing this book. I have nothing of my own. Reading poolside with my elbows on the concrete was enough temporarily to distract me, until I finished my book. Then, nothing, except the painfully gentle lapping of the water.

Defiantly, I lifted myself onto the patio. I was *not* going to mope in the pool until Nathan returned. If he could go do whatever he was doing, live a life outside our writing, so could I. Finishing my book gave me the perfect way to start.

Fifteen minutes later, I'm dressed, my hair still in a half-wet bun, and parking on the street in Key Largo's small commercial stretch. The day feels bright once more, full of possibility. I focus on the sights, the sounds, the dry grass under my sandals, the palm fronds swishing in the clear sky. I'm not even wondering what Nathan's up to.

Walking toward the neighborhood's only independent bookstore, I start thinking about what new books I might want. Maybe to other people, finding a new novel to read isn't necessarily an entire life, but to me, it's something.

As I'm reaching for the door, it swings open, and a man walks out, nearly colliding with me.

I stumble—and his hand is on my arm, steadying me. Finally, I find my footing.

And then I look up.

"*Nathan?*"

We study each other, motionless, on the small front step. Nathan's hand doesn't leave my elbow, probably just out of surprise. He's slicked back his hair. It does look kind of good.

"This," he says, "is very much the opposite of getting space."

"I—" He's still holding my arm. "How could I have possibly known you were here?" I manage.

Like he's finally remembered himself, Nathan's hand falls to his side. Then his face breaks into half a grin. "Well, this is ironic."

"What are you even doing here?" I ask. I look down, searching for a shopping bag or book in his hands. Nothing.

"Signing *Refraction* stock."

I sigh in frustration, shifting my gaze past him to where the grass meets the highway. "Of course you were," I mutter. It is darkly comedic, how much this models our lives in miniature. Nathan and I somehow keep ending up on collision courses of one form or another.

"I'm . . . sorry?" he says. He doesn't look sorry. He looks amused.

"I'm done now, so feel free to carry on like you never saw me," he continues.

I chew my lip, peering in the store's front window, where hardcover mysteries and cookbooks stand on display. While I don't really want to admit my hesitation, I know Nathan isn't just going to walk away. "Well, I can't now," I say haltingly.

Nathan frowns. "Why not?"

"You probably introduced yourself to the bookseller," I explain. "They just pulled up your catalogue."

"Yes . . . ?" He leans on the step's metal railing, in no hurry. I notice in his pocket the leather pouch in which he carries his signing pens.

I force patience into my voice. "They would've seen your back catalogue, the two books you wrote with a coauthor. If I walk in there right after you—" I gesture for him to fill in what would happen.

Something coy enters Nathan's eyes. It's playfulness with sharp edges, like juggling knives. "It's like she might recognize you. God forbid, we'd have to sign some of our books together."

"*Not* happening." I meet his coyness with warning, which I hope he sees flash in my expression.

If my refusal wounds him, he doesn't show it. In fact, he couldn't look more relaxed, hands curling lightly around the peeling paint of the railing. "Well, I don't know what to tell you," he says.

I linger on the step, saying nothing. My chest feels clenched. I'm pissed. I know it's irrational—Nathan couldn't possibly have known this would be my destination, nor how his presence here would snarl my hopes for the day. Yet, here I stand, snarled. While he smirks with his sunglasses hanging from his shirt collar, the same defiance I felt in the pool seizes me. "I finished the book I was reading," I declare. "I need something new."

His grin hitching, Nathan is silent. Then his brow furrows. "You're not seriously suggesting what I think you're suggesting."

"Please? Just go back in and get one book for me," I implore. "Just one single book."

Nathan breathes out through his nose. "Which book?" he asks flatly.

"Oh, I don't know," I reply.

"Katrina!" He pushes himself up from the railing. Hearing the exasperation in his voice, I have to swallow a laugh.

"Just go in there and tell me what they have," I instruct him politely, starting to enjoy myself now. "I'm looking for something upbeat. Escapist. Romance, probably." When he hesitates, I reach for his arm and pull him to face the entrance, feeling him shake with laughter.

Reluctantly, he disappears inside. I move a couple storefronts away, not wanting to be spotted. Hiding by the chain-link fence of the nearby boat dealership, in the shade of the tree on the street corner, I feel furtive. Secret Agent Katrina in denim shorts and sandals. It's kind of ridiculous, and kind of fun.

After a few minutes, Nathan emerges from the bookstore, looks around for me, then jogs my way.

"So," he begins, endearingly serious. "They have that new release everyone's been talking about. *The Client.* Pink and yellow cover. They also have a new book in that historical romance series you used to read about the bastard princes. Oh, and one I'd never heard of but seems like your thing—a modern take on *Middlemarch.*"

My mouth opens and closes. I knew it would be fun making work for Nathan. What I didn't expect was how good a job he'd do. It's a sorely sweet reminder that Nathan used to be my best friend, the person I discussed books with more than anyone else in the world. Four years later, I thought those ties would have untethered. It means something to realize they haven't, but I'm not sure what.

I'm conscious of his eyes on me, waiting for my pick. Considering each one, I stay silent—not to exasperate him, each one genuinely sounds great.

Picking up on my indecision, he smiles knowingly. "All three it is," he says. I grin, reaching for my wallet. Nathan waves me away. "Don't worry about it." He's gone before I can protest.

While I wait, enjoying the ocean-tinged breeze, I realize our frustration from earlier has disappeared completely despite the distinct lack of space we achieved.

When Nathan returns, he's carrying a brown paper bag, which he hands to me triumphantly. I feel familiar new-book feelings, excitement and instant intrigue. For his part, Nathan looks distinctly proud of himself. "The clerk definitely thought I was buying this for a woman," he informs me.

I stiffen. "What did you tell her?"

"Relax," he scoffs. "I didn't say bestselling author Katrina Freeling is hiding in the bushes outside like a paranoid weirdo." Now a laugh does escape me. Nathan's chest puffs up further. "I told her they were for me," he continues. "There's no reason they couldn't have been."

"Thanks, Nathan. Really," I say. We stand in the shade while the moment stretches, neither of us quite knowing what to do with ourselves. "Well . . . I'll see you at home, I guess."

Nathan peers interestedly into the shopping bag. "You know, I wouldn't mind having something to read myself."

I laugh again. Reaching into the bag, I pull out *The Scoundrel Prince.*

"Just the one I'd hoped for," he says delightedly when I hand the book over. "This series is unfairly addictive."

Tucking *The Scoundrel Prince* under his arm, he waves over his shoulder, leaving me on the grassy street corner. With my new purchases in hand, I return to my car, not fighting my smile. On the drive home, I find I'm actually looking forward to returning to work with him.

28

Nathan

FINGERS KNEADING THE bridge of my nose, I'm wondering if writing was ever easy, or if it's just unending frustration. I know I've enjoyed it in the past, felt confident and competent. Were those only hallucinations? Misremembered distortions, the products of cognitive dissonance?

They weren't, obviously. But it's how I feel, irrationally, when writing is not going well. I'm working with Katrina on the new book's *second* sex scene in the midst of the couple's divorce. While ostensibly its passion is fueled by hate, the point of the scene is to mirror the tenderness of the previous sex scene. It's their "one last time," and while Katrina and I plod through the paragraphs, I can't help thinking of how this book is *our* "one last time."

The comparison is extremely unhelpful, especially combined with how every one of Katrina's and my conversations lately feels like it's occurring on multiple levels. The result? I'm off my game. My writing is bland, forced, joyless.

I knew today was going to be a bad day, though. I knew it the instant I walked downstairs and noticed Katrina had changed her shampoo.

This was calamitous. Not the change in the shampoo, obviously, which was nice. But the fact that I *noticed*. Over the time we've spent here, Katrina's and my writing and personal routine has changed from the intense pace of our first few days into a tentative truce. Now we've found our new rhythm, punctuated by painful reminders of exactly what split us up before.

In the meantime, I became someone who *noticed her shampoo*. For the rest of the morning, I kept noticing, unable to escape my consciousness of her. It was damning, inviting, everywhere. Right now, seated next to her on the dining table bench, I'm noticing it every time she flips her hair over her shoulder.

The café reminded me we could have fun together. Running into her outside the bookstore reminded me we could even be friends. This reminds me why we shouldn't.

"It's not passionate enough," she says, frowning at the screen. Her fingers idly scroll up and down on the MacBook's trackpad. "We need the intensity of the feeling to come through. It's hotter even than the height of their relationship. Infused with the sense of the ending."

I nod, wordless and miserable.

"Hello?" Katrina glances over. "Thoughts? It's like I'm speaking to myself today."

I can't even resent her glib comment. She's completely right. I'm useless. I get up and, for no reason whatsoever, walk my mug to the sink. The light breeze outside rattles the shutters faintly. "No. Sorry. You're right. This is about"—I swallow, digging deep inside myself, forcing ideas forward—"how when you've had something with someone, it's easy for . . . an ember to leap into a flame with the slightest change in the wind."

I stand over the sink, closing my eyes. *The slightest change.*

Like going to sleep after staring at a picture of a girl smiling at you when you weren't looking, then waking up and noticing her fucking shampoo.

Katrina's voice from the dining table sounds small. "No matter what they tell themselves, Michael and Evelyn will always be attracted to each other." I hate myself for wondering if there's anything beneath her words. "But it's purely physical," she adds.

I return to the table, standing behind her while she types those thoughts in. "Which is a lie, of course," I say.

She stiffens. Whether it's at what I said or whether she's startled by my presence, I don't know.

"May I?" I ask. She yields the computer to me, and I stand over her while I type. I force myself to put the tension coursing through me onto the page. The exorcism feels good.

What's more, the writing is good. It's better than anything I've written today. I keep going, everything finally feeling clear, fluid, emotional. It's working. *Because of course it is,* I remind myself. I've long known the best writing comes from truth.

Sliding the computer back to Katrina, I sit. I'm not nervous.

"Not bad," she concedes, skimming the paragraphs.

"It's good, and we both know it."

I'm watching for it now, so I notice when she flattens the smile fighting to curve her lips. She starts typing. The minutes pass, the rhythm returning. When we exchange the computer, our fingers brush. We hardly have to speak while we write, our words joining in a perfect give-and-take. The whole time, I'm remembering how this is something I can never feel on my own. It's part of what makes cowriting wondrous.

In the years I was apart from Katrina, I'd forgotten the feeling, hadn't permitted myself to miss it.

Worse, I know I'll forget it once more when we return to our separate careers, our separate lives.

I watch the pages grow. Not mine, not hers—ours. It's indescribable, even to me.

Katrina speaks the dialogue she's writing for Evelyn. *"I want you, but this isn't love."*

I slide my hands over hers to give Michael his reply. *I could never mistake one for the other. Not with you.*

Michael pulls Evelyn's lips to his, and for the first time, Katrina and I fumble. "The choreography . . . doesn't work," I say, figuring out the problem while I'm speaking. "Michael should stand so he's on her level."

Katrina slants me the look she does whenever she has no patience for my objections. "The choreography works fine. It's sexy."

"It's not sexy—" I start to protest.

Katrina stands up. I watch, not understanding, while she moves to the other side of the table so we're seated opposite each other. Then she climbs up on the bench on her knees, just like Evelyn. "Lean forward, please," she instructs me.

I do, not daring to think about what's happening.

Katrina places one hand on the tabletop for support, then leans herself fully over the table. I ignore the flash of nude bra I glimpse under the collar of her shirt. With her free hand, she cups the back of my neck. We're close now. When her hair falls forward from her shoulder and brushes my face, I'm hit with the scent of her shampoo.

"Sexy, right?" Despite the smolder in her eyes, her voice isn't inviting. It's victorious.

The question opens floodgates in me. Feelings scream forth. I'm struggling under the inchoate rush, from the nearly impossible exertion of not saying everything I want to say. *Please* and *why can't we forget what happened four years ago* and finally *oh god, there are so much harder things than not writing well.*

"Fine," I say, my voice nearly a whisper. "Yeah, it is." The table is digging into my chest, which I don't say. It could not possibly be relevant.

Heart hammering, I suddenly want to forget everything I know about cowriting with her. I want to forget every friendly moment we've ever had, to banish every memory—because I *know*, with fucking certainty, this waits behind every good day with Katrina. This crush of feelings I can't have. It's exactly why I wrecked whatever friendship we were building on the way back from the café. Why I should be glad for our *one last time*. Because I would risk dying of thirst to save myself from drowning.

Her lips twitch. This time, she doesn't hide her smile. It takes every ounce of strength in me to keep my hands flat on the table in front of me. I can think of too many places they'd rather be.

Like she's realized she's still touching my neck, just inches from me, her expression goes bashful. She leans back, swallowing.

I want to grab her hand and pull her to me. Then, I don't know.

I don't get the chance. Between us, my phone vibrates on the table, humming loudly on the wood. When I glance down, Jen's name is illuminated on the screen. Instinctually, my eyes flit up to Katrina's. She looks desperate for me to pick up. So I do. "Hey, Jen," I say, sounding the farthest thing from casual. "What's up?"

"Nathan. Hi. I have an opportunity here," Jen says. Right to the point. "Is Katrina nearby?"

"Yeah. She's right here." I put the phone on speaker.

I feel pulled into the past, like nothing's changed, like years haven't gone by. I'm living the replica of every other phone call Katrina and I took just like this one, leaning in with the phone on speaker to hear everything together. Listening to Chris or our publisher while ignoring the uncommon closeness.

"I—" Katrina swallows once more. "I'm here."

"I discussed this with Chris, who liked the idea. He said I could bring it directly to you. There's a journalist with the *New York Times*, Noah Lippman, who reached out to me interested in profiling you both. Your return to cowriting, et cetera, et cetera. He saw the *Vanity Fair* piece. If we position it right, this profile could announce your new book and promote *Refraction*. But of course," she says, "it's up to you both."

I look to Katrina, certain I know how she'll respond.

"Sure," she replies. Her voice holds nothing except cordiality, like the question is insignificant. Like someone's offered her sugar in her tea.

Jen is immediately thrilled, rattling off logistics with which I don't keep up. I'm fixated on Katrina. *Sure?* To the *New York Times* profiling us? I don't understand why she's suddenly willing to go public with me. It's possible it's some vestige of our truce, some part of the façade she insists we're putting on, but part of me wonders if it's because things have changed between us.

I mechanically say yes to dates, times, plans, then hang up. When I do, Katrina only excuses herself from the room. She walks out while I watch uselessly.

I feel the distance. For long minutes after she's gone, I stare at the place where she leaned over the table, the skin on my neck growing hot where her hand was. I remember what I wanted, how she lingered too long, how close I was to reaching out for her. How inescapable the impulse was.

I wrap myself in the only consolation I have. It's just instinct, the volatile side effect of our proximity. Purely physical, like Michael and Evelyn. It doesn't have to be more.

29

Nathan

I PUSH MYSELF hard on my nightly run. I want my body exhausted, wrecked, empty of everything except the pain of exertion. When I hit my sheets, I want to collapse into sleep so hard I won't remember whatever dreams I have about what happened with Katrina. They'll come, I know, the visions seared into my head of her leaning over the dining table, her body low, her scent intoxicating. It's one thing dreams have in common with writing—their tendency to betray me to myself.

The echo of my footsteps is the only sound on the dark street. I've run for hours. Finally, I let myself stop on our corner, lungs on fire, thighs screaming. I bend over with my hands on my knees and gulp for breath.

"You're either training for a race," I hear over my shoulder, "or you're punishing yourself."

It's Meredith. I recognize the Southern lilt in her voice. Straightening up, I find her hefting a garbage bag out to the bin. Her slouchy, open-front sweater falls off one shoulder, exposing a deep V-neck. I know she's joking, even though her words hit uncomfortably close to truth.

"Tough day at work," I say noncommittally.

Meredith pauses for a moment, her gaze lingering on me. "I was just going to pour myself a drink. Want to join me?" she asks, making no effort to hide the implication in her voice. Everything she's offering is out in the open.

I consider it, my chest heaving. If I'm searching for ways to forget everything I want with Katrina, this might be what I need. The night breeze rolls over me while I write the scene in my head. I say yes and she opens the wine and pours us glasses. I skipped dinner with Katrina, so I suggest we have something to eat. We heat up her leftovers or we order in. Either way, she ditches the sweater, and I slide closer to her on the floor, where we're sitting because she doesn't have chairs yet. I give her the chance to pull away. She doesn't. I spend the night with her, working out whatever sexual frustration my run didn't shake.

It's tempting. Suddenly the idea of returning to the house with Katrina, of lying sleepless the whole night, waiting for tomorrow, sounds like hell. Why shouldn't I say yes? I'm single, Meredith understands I'm not a long-term commitment—I'm only here for the summer. This would hurt no one.

"I'd like to," I say. "But I can't."

Meredith looks slightly surprised. If she's hurt, she covers the feeling well. She shrugs it off and smiles. "Well, if you change your mind . . ." She nods to her door. Pulling her sweater up over her shoulder, she heads back inside.

I watch her until her door shuts. While I hate myself for the night I refused, deep down, I know I had to. When my marriage ended, I promised myself I'd never be with someone when I wanted someone else.

On the empty street, I look in the direction of Katrina's house, of the night I've chosen—the one that will go absolutely nowhere, that'll leave me aching and sleepless.

I walk the rest of the way home, feeling the sting of every muscle I pushed too hard.

30

Katrina

WHEN I HEAR his keys in the door, I'm embarrassingly relieved. Settling into the couch cushions, I pick up the book I tried and failed to read—the *Middlemarch* one Nathan bought me. I don't want to look like I was just waiting for him to return, even though I was. Usually he runs and then we have dinner, but tonight he stayed out so long I finished half of the frozen kung pao chicken I picked up from the supermarket on our first day here.

It irritates me how worried I was while I waited. But underneath the worry, I'm shaken, confused. I know we crossed a line while writing. Crossed it into where, though, I don't know.

Nathan walks inside, the rubber soles of his running shoes noisy on the floor. The sound clatters into the house when he closes the front door. He heads for the stairs, hardly giving me a glance.

"I left a plate for you on the counter." I don't know what impulse compels me to call out. If he wants dinner, he's a grown man. He'll figure it out. It's not my responsibility.

He doesn't look over. "Right. Thanks," he says.

He's sweaty, flushed, obviously in a terrible mood. I should let him go upstairs, let everything remain unspoken, undisturbed. I don't. "Nathan." I hate how high my voice comes out. "I owe you an apology."

He pauses. Then he steps off the first stair, facing me, saying nothing.

I continue with effort. "I shouldn't have"—*Oh god, why did I do that?*—"touched you like I did. It was unprofessional. I'm sorry."

What I've said is the closest we've come to discussing what's wrong between us. I could feel what Nathan was thinking when I held the back of his neck, reckless—I could follow him to the place his mind was going, because mine was going there, too. It's like some sort of destructive sun, millions of miles from us and still hot enough to scorch.

I'm dreading his reply. His expression is indecipherable when it comes. "It's fine," he says. "No big deal."

Somehow, it's the least satisfying thing he could have said. I nod, the words not sitting right with me. Shutting my book, I realize a second too late that I've forgotten to put the bookmark in the pages. Nathan notices. I don't give him the opportunity to comment. "I've developed a theory," I begin, my voice carrying confidence I don't feel. "What you write can influence how you feel or what you think. Like write a sad scene, and you might find yourself depressed. Write something with joy and humor, and you might feel happy—for a little while. It's not *real.* That's important. It's just a temporary feeling. Literary transference."

I know the term from psychology classes I took in college. We read about how a person might project feelings or beliefs pertaining to one person onto someone else. I've thought about it for years now in relation to writing. Even when I used to write by myself, I would sink into the headspace of my characters. With Nathan, with any cowriter, it's natural to project feelings that belong on the page onto a person.

Nathan hasn't moved from the stairs. He places one elbow on the railing, his posture relaxing.

His gaze does not. And I wait, because I know what he's about to ask.

"Why are you telling me about *literary transference* right now, Katrina?" I recognize the way his eyes have pinned mine. He knows why. He just wants to hear me say it.

I won't give him the reaction he's hoping for. I don't hesitate. "Writing sexual content would naturally have the effect I'm describing," I say. "Especially when you're writing that content with or near . . . someone else." I manage not to rush the final words even though I want to.

Nathan half smiles. Sweat slides down his face, his neck. I know him well enough to recognize the calculation in his movement when he removes his shirt to wipe his forehead.

I've seen Nathan's chest. Many times. We've swam in oceans on two continents together, sunned in deck chairs in Capri. I wasn't really looking the other day when we went in the pool. In fact, with my back turned, I was consciously not looking.

Now is different. Nathan's in shape, which is no surprise. He has the resources, the time, and the discipline to be. I'm trying to focus objectively on these facts, except I'd forgotten the perfect geometry of him over the past four years. My mouth is dry, my face hot. I can't stop staring, remembering how close we were earlier.

His eyes sparkle, not the sparkle of sunlight over water or stars scattering the sky. There is nothing gentle or inviting in the look he gives me. It's closer to flint sparking steel in the seconds before flame.

"You're telling me writing our sex scene made you feel how, exactly?" he inquires. "I'm quite curious."

I hold my head high. "My *point* is," I say hotly, "it doesn't mean anything."

Nathan laughs. He steps backward up the stairs. "Work hard on that theory?" he asks. "I hope it helps you sleep tonight. You can tell yourself whatever story you want, Katrina. You're a writer." His mirth is dry, devoid of generosity or good nature. Spinning on his heel, he continues up the steps, footfalls heavy on the hardwood.

I slump back on the couch, feeling defeated. I'd meant my apology to Nathan genuinely, no matter the stiff unpleasantness of some of our exchanges since the café. His rejection hurts in ways I don't want to acknowledge, not when they so obviously reveal how uncomfortable I am with everything spoiled between us. What's more, he's grabbed the shield I've used to fend off questions I'm tired of confronting—like where *exactly* my decision to lean over the table had come from—and thrown it into the ocean.

No, I think to myself. I won't give him that satisfaction. I shove my bookmark carelessly into the pages of the book I wasn't reading. Upstairs, I hear the hiss of Nathan's shower. When the images come to my mind of him undressing, stepping into the steam, I let them. I don't care if he smirks or plies me with glib questions. I'm right. This is only the fevered product of our writing. Transference.

It'll fade.

31

Nathan

• FOUR YEARS EARLIER •

IT'S SEVEN IN the morning. I'm sitting grumpily on one of the striped towels we found in the house, squinting out over the ocean. Katrina's next to me, putting on sunscreen. It's humid—muggy, really—threatening the thunderstorms predicted for today. The beach, unsurprisingly, is empty.

My cowriter, having read the weather report, dragged me out of bed at five minutes to six, insisting we spend some time in the water before we're cooped up indoors. I'm sandy wherever I even glancingly touched the beach—the tops of my feet, the edges of my hands. It's everywhere. I don't want to be here, under the clouds folding their ominous blanket over the sun. Even though it's Sunday, I want to be in the house, writing.

We've spent the past two days on the same scene without any forward movement. The lack of progress frustrates me. I don't just dislike writer's block—I don't believe in it. Writer's block is nothing but the point where you've forgotten what your characters really want. The solution isn't sitting on the Florida sand in the wet early morning, it's getting back to work.

Something cold and slimy hits my shoulder, interrupting my rumination. When I look up, I find Katrina standing over me in her black one-piece, holding the sunscreen, which she just squeezed onto me.

Ruefully, I rub it in.

"Seriously? Moping while you're here?" She spins playfully, throwing her arms out with enthusiasm. Stray curls of her hair flutter over her face. "With one of your favorite people," she adds.

"I'm not moping," I reply. "I'm brooding. It's entirely different."

Katrina laughs, her nose scrunching up in delight. Then she plasters on fake sympathy. "Right. So sorry," she says.

Part of me wants to laugh with her, just a little. Instead, I push us stubbornly into the conversation *I* want to have. "What if we move the dinner scene. Maybe that's the problem. It would take weeks of rewriting, but—"

Katrina tosses the sunscreen into my lap. *"Nope,"* she says. "I'm not discussing work with you today. Today, you're not my writing partner, you're . . ."

Her hanging fragment is enough to pull my focus from our scene. I don't know how she's going to finish the sentence. What are we to each other if not writing partners? Our creative collaboration is where our relationship began. We weren't even friends first. I search her face for clues, reading nothing in the gaze she's fixed somewhere past me.

"You're the guy I'm at the beach with," she finishes, smiling. I register my split second of disappointment before she continues. "Don't make me replace you."

Frowning, I gesture to the open sand. "Katrina, there's nobody here *to* replace me. Because it's seven in the morning, and it's about to rain."

Cocking her hip, Katrina pouts. Unhesitatingly, she reaches her hand out for me. "Then I guess I'll have to go in the water with *you*." Now I do smile, if only slightly. Taking her hand, I stand. Our palms touch for hardly long enough for me to notice the feel of her skin before she releases me. The contact is nothing. It's empty, like clicking the stovetop burner without the gas on. "Besides," she says, "maybe inspiration will strike."

"Hopefully before the lightning."

She rolls her eyes. Without warning, she's off, running down the sand and into the water, where she submerges fully. When she comes up, her hair is slicked down her neck.

I'm pulled forward, following the small semicircles her footsteps have left on the wet sand. I walk in slowly, the sea surrounding my feet in cooling contrast to the morning. It's refreshing. I stride in farther, the salty tide rising up my chest while I continue out to Katrina.

She floats on her back, her flat stomach rising and falling while she breathes. Water beads on her eyelashes. "When we first met," she muses quietly, "did you ever imagine we'd be here?"

Knowing there will be no quiet contemplation while Katrina is determined to leave the book behind for the day, I dunk my head. The shock to my system is invigorating. I come up, exhaling hard and pushing my hair up my forehead.

"Yes," I say.

She lifts her head from the water to look at me. Even in the cloudy sun, the flecks in her brown eyes sparkle. "Really?" She's curious to the point of incredulity. "The first night we walked home from dinner, you imagined writing a novel with me in Florida?"

I lift my feet off the soft ocean floor, floating the way she just was. Thinking back to the first days I knew her, I remember going for coffee and coming up with what would become our debut novel. It was seamless. Katrina said something offhand, I suggested it could be a premise and embellished it, she twisted it once more, and I knew we had something. Not just the idea—I knew *we* had something.

"I didn't envision Florida specifically," I say. "But everything else, yeah. It's why I pursued you so tirelessly." I don't hide from the gravity of what I'm saying. Our relationship is strong enough for honesty. "I could see everything we'd have together. Everything we don't have yet, too. We will."

Katrina looks flattered, which makes me happy in ways I can't quite decipher. She moves in the water, lazily pulling herself forward with hands outstretched, her chin barely skimming the surface. "I didn't know what to think when you proposed cowriting together," she informs me.

"Probably that it was some elaborate ploy to sleep with you."

Katrina laughs, her cheeks flushed. "The thought did cross my mind, but then you mentioned being engaged. Seriously, though, a stranger approaches you and wants to write a book together? It seemed . . . unreal." On the final word, her voice sounds delicate, even fragile.

I stop floating and face her. We've drifted deeper out, and I can barely get my feet beneath me. "What convinced you to take me seriously?"

She's quiet, treading water. The current pushes us closer together. "The more I talked to you, I felt something I never had. It was like you could articulate every thought of mine I didn't know how to. Like you were bringing my own self into sharper focus." She smiles self-consciously. "I don't know if that makes sense."

"It does." I meet her eyes over the shimmering water separating us. Something crackles over the inches of space in the seconds-long glance we hold while we float.

Then the sky splits open, pouring water on us. It literally douses the moment. We startle, looking simultaneously to the sky. I hadn't noticed the black clouds closing over us. Katrina shrieks a little.

"Run?" she shouts, blinking water from her eyes. I'm already nodding. When she takes off for the shore, I follow her, feeling like I'm moving in slow motion. Together, we grab our towels and clothes, everything drenched, and sprint to the car.

A few feet in front of me, one of Katrina's sandals slips out of her grasp, falling onto the sand. She doubles back for it, covering her head ineffectually with one hand when the rain gets harder, pelting pockmarks into the beach. I pass her, moving hastily. While I'm unlocking the car, the first boom of thunder rumbles through us.

We climb in, slamming the doors shut. We should have taken Katrina's car, but I don't have a car in New York and the chance to drive the Porsche was my only incentive for agreeing to this plan in the first place. Everything is soaked and covered in sand. I should be furious. I'll have to pay the company a small fortune for this kind of damage to a rental Porsche Carrera—damage I knew would happen if we drove to the beach hours before predicted thunderstorms.

Instead, I start laughing. I don't stop. Katrina joins me, and suddenly I'm in stitches, my eyes watering while Katrina doubles over in the passenger seat. The rain is coming down too hard on the windows to see anything. The water is a curtain, hiding us in our own private world.

I look at Katrina, her hair disheveled, her eyes sparkling, and I find I'm no longer laughing. There's sand on her face, right beneath her eye. The next moment, I feel like I'm watching from somewhere else—I reach out, compelled, and wipe the sand from her skin. She stills under my touch, the only sound the furious pounding of rain on the car.

She holds my gaze, oceans of possibility in her huge eyes. I'm drowning in them, sinking into her. I let my hand linger too long.

I glance down at her lips and feel her breath catch. For the first time, I have the impossible need to pull her face to mine. To kiss her. To hold her close.

The stomach-punch of guilt slams into me. I'm not just disgusted with myself, I'm disoriented. I'm happily married, in love with my beautiful wife. My eyes don't wander. I don't *want* to kiss other women. Nor do I sexualize my female friends and colleagues. Katrina is worth more. Even so, it takes everything in me to remove my hand and face forward.

I focus on forcing the idea from my head. I would never cheat on Melissa—and a stray thought isn't cheating, as long as it remains just that. Which it will.

Katrina says nothing while I start the engine. I have no idea what she's thinking, though I know her well enough to be certain she's thinking something. It's funny how people can sit side by side, separate whirlwinds each self-contained.

When the windshield wipers engage, lightning flashes over the ocean.

32

Katrina

• PRESENT DAY •

THE PREPARATION FOR the *New York Times* profile is immediate and intense. It has everyone whipped up into a media frenzy, a circus where no one knows quite who's the ringleader. Liz fights gamely for the role—the next morning we wake up to an email on which she's copied the entire Parthenon publicity team. They want to "get on a call" this evening. They're four of my least favorite words in the English language. *Get on a call.*

The long list of names who will be listening in unsettles my stomach. It reminds me of the endless conferences with my team in the weeks before the release of *Only Once*. Calls in which everyone would gush about the book, how special it was, how they couldn't wait to share it with the world.

I only heard the pressure. Pressure for the book to perform to their expectations, pressure to deliver the next one quickly and better, pressure to enjoy every promotion and interview because this was my "dream come true." I felt like I was on top of the Empire State Building and at the bottom of the ocean at once.

I'm not unusual in what scares me. What frightens me frightens everyone. I'm scared of being nothing. Not becoming nothing, in the sense of dying. I mean the life-in-death of being no one special. Being nobody's person. Being worth nothing.

When I was young, I felt not very important. I was the middle child of five. I loved my mom, and she loved me, but I was indistinct. I was hopelessly uncoordinated, so sports were out. I was smart in a small town, where smarts earned respectful shrugs and not much more. Sometimes I felt like I couldn't figure out why I existed. Which sounded dark whenever it crossed my mind, but it wasn't, really, not to me. Just confusing.

When I found writing, I realized what it meant to have something where I shone. Where I could be someone.

It scared me. It scared me to have this thing I'd long instinctually felt I was missing, because I knew with cutting clarity how it would feel to lose it. When *Only Once* was coming out, those fears finally caught up to me, and even though I got control of my nerves, it took me months, even years, to recover from what they had done. Emotional episodes like those hit like natural disasters. Everything isn't just repaired once the hurricane or the flood passes. I needed to rebuild.

Which wasn't easy when some days I felt like I was flunking an exam on myself. I would find myself literally unable to decide whether I wanted to read or rewatch old *Gilmore Girls* episodes or run in the park. Some days, I dutifully picked plans and executed them.

Other days, the indecision sent me back to bed.

Dating Chris helped. Moving to LA helped, and eventually, I returned to myself. But I'm still scared every day of returning to those doldrums.

With four minutes until the call, I'm fighting familiar battles within myself. Waiting on one of the barstools in the kitchen, I thumb my phone mindlessly. I don't want to look at the dial-in number or the list of discussion points Liz's assistant sent over.

Noticing my discomfort, Nathan ducks his eyes, looking for mine. He's been the one unexpected reassurance of the day. We'd gone to bed on uncertain terms on the heels of my feeble apology and his taunting response. But something's gotten him out of bed in brighter spirits today. I don't dare imagine it's forgiveness—he's probably just hungry to publicize our new book—but whatever it is, it's welcome.

He's leaning on the edge of the counter perpendicular to me. When he speaks, there's empathy I hardly recognize in his voice. "We don't have to do this, you know. The call, the profile, any of it."

He means the book, too. I don't know how I know he does. I ball my hand in my lap. "I want to." However uncomfortable the publicity process makes me, everything happening now will keep happening. I need to face reality.

Nathan's gaze remains on me. I know he wants to ask why, when I'm obviously forcing myself. Instead, he only types in the conference call number. We wait, saying nothing, until the line beeps. "Katrina and Nathan here," he says, placing the phone on the counter.

"Wonderful!" I wince at the enthusiasm in Liz's voice. "How are you two? How's Florida?"

I remember our last conference call—the one where I refused to speak to Nathan. I couldn't. Everything was moving fast. I felt captive, Chris watching me while I faced the open line into Nathan's world. Like a hostage negotiator responsible for the release of a career I didn't know if I wanted. Now, here Nathan is, leaning on the kitchen counter next to me. There's a part of me wrestling with how this image makes no sense, and another part noticing he hasn't shaved today and dark circles hang under his eyes.

Eyes, I realize, that are focused on me. He wants me to respond. "It's good," I say. "We're . . ." I hold Nathan's gaze. "Making a lot of progress."

"Love to hear it. Well, we're very excited about using this profile to announce you've reunited for another book. Of course"—Liz doesn't pause, for which I give her credit—"because of how the press has speculated about your partnership in the past, we've discussed in-house how best to present you."

I press my palms to my shorts, the motion involuntary. It's washing over me just how often Nathan and I will have to perform, for each other, for everyone else, forever. We'll have to fend off the questions of how our partnership was severed, and how we reunited, *forever.*

The wild thought enters my head to just . . . be honest. I chase it off instantly. It would be impossible. Honest with Nathan is too huge a concept to comprehend.

Jen cuts in. "This reporter is going to be looking for a story." Her voice is delicate, if casually so. "He's definitely going to pry into your split and the rumors around it."

I have to give Nathan credit for how quickly and calmly he responds. "Topics we've navigated in public plenty of times," he points out.

"Yes, but now you're together, and, well . . ."

Liz finishes the sentence. "Frankly, none of us has any idea what that looks like."

Nathan flashes me a smile like we're in on some secret joke. While I haven't quite caught the punch line yet, I notice how the circles under his eyes seem to lighten. Once more, gratitude fills me for this inexplicably giving Nathan. "Now I understand," he says playfully, leaning closer to the phone. "You're calling to make sure we don't scream at each other in front of the reporter."

I watch him, halfway to impressed. His elbows resting on the counter, the posture pulling up the sleeves of his white Bob Dylan T-shirt, he looks comfortable. Hints of the warmth I felt when he climbed onto the chair in the café flicker in me now. I'd honestly forgotten in the past four years how good he was with people.

The line is silent. No one knows if Nathan's joking. Finally, it's Jen who's brave enough to reply. "Kind of, yeah," she says. "We want your book to be the story, not you."

"Although . . ." Liz chimes in, with singsong stretching of the word. "A little peek into your relationship has always sold books."

I understand what she's saying. She's not wrong, either. Signs of tension between Nathan and me would fuel the fire of our notoriety. People would line up for the book, reading for the answer to whether we love each other or hate each other. I don't blame them. If I thought it would help me find out, I'd scour the pages myself.

The next voice who speaks is one I don't recognize. Someone from publicity? I ignore the unpleasant reminder of the lengthy call sheet. "It's about hinting just enough to create mystery. The history of you two is so storied. We don't want to waste it."

The explanation is like a lecture, enough that I'm interrupted in my nervousness to roll my eyes.

Chris jumps in, which is when I realize I haven't heard his voice in days. "Of course. We want whatever will sell copies." He pauses. "Right, Katrina?"

I've noticed how Chris never uses "Kat" on work calls. I'm "Katrina." Generously, I respect the professional veneer he's trying to maintain, but I've never understood it. It's not like everybody doesn't know he's engaged to his bestselling client.

"Yeah. Right," I say, not convinced. *Would* I do whatever will sell copies?

"I'm flying out for the interview," Chris says offhandedly.

I whip to stare into the phone screen, like he's in there somewhere, shaking me in person with this sudden revelation. "What?"

Nathan immediately tenses.

"I don't want you to have to deal with logistics," Chris says calmly. "I'll handle it, and I'll be there if . . . anything comes up."

When my surprise wears off, the hurt seeps in, like my heart's stumbled and skinned its knees. I can't enjoy whatever eagerness I might've felt to see my fiancé. The fact is, when I *begged* him to come to Florida, he wouldn't. Now, feeling the slightest hint of professional obligation, he decides in one day to fly out.

Because it's Katrina he's coming for. Not Kat.

The line is silent. Nathan obviously won't say anything, waiting instead for me to respond. Despite how I'm feeling, I know this call with our whole team, with Nathan, isn't the place to delve into romantic disappointment.

"Is that it, everyone?" It's the best I can do.

My blood is pounding so hard I barely hear what they say. The usual pleasantries, how they're so excited to read the book, early talk of promotions, foreign sales, book festivals. After everyone signs off, Nathan hangs up and drops his phone into his pocket.

"How about we take a walk?" Nathan suggests suddenly.

I look up, not sure I've heard him right.

"We heard everyone else's opinion about how we should approach this interview," he goes on. "I wonder what *we* want out of it."

I study him. Doesn't he want what they do—book sales? Why else would he be writing with me in the first place?

"Unless . . ." He falters, his eyes skirting from me.

Swiftly, I rise from my seat. I'm not shying away from this conversation, not if Nathan's willing to have it. "A walk sounds lovely."

Something crosses his expression, a softness I haven't seen on him in years.

It makes him unbearably handsome.

33

Nathan

WE WALK THROUGH the neighborhood. I'm calm, which I guess I didn't expect, knowing what we're going to be discussing. Even I'm aware of how unlike me proposing this walk was. I just couldn't face spending the night in the shadow of the publicity call.

On our street, the start of sunset casts orange over everything. We catch slices of ocean between the houses, the breeze rolling innocently off the water. It's the hour of prepping for dinner or driving home from the office, and no one is out right now. It's just me and Katrina.

I wonder if she realizes I hardly slept last night. She probably does—the dark circles under my eyes look like boxers' bruises, which is fitting, seeing how much time I've spent in the ring with my subconscious recently. She'd sent me to bed with *literary transference* and the grim gratification of knowing what she was implying—she'd practically confessed to feeling attracted to me, whether founded in our writing or not.

But as the night wore on, I'd felt guiltier for mocking her explanation. I couldn't impeach her motives—she wanted to keep us from treading into treacherous waters or dredging up our past. Which was what I wanted. Furthermore, I reasoned, was her explanation so different from what I'd told myself when the table incident happened? I reconstructed the day—I'd promised myself my reaction was *purely physical* while Katrina had gone upstairs once we got off the phone with Jen.

Which was when I remembered the call today in preparation for the interview. Despite her unusual willingness to do the *Times* piece, I'm fairly certain one thing hasn't changed over the years. Katrina *hates* publicity. Before bookstore events promoting our debut, I would practice panel question responses with her to ease her reluctance. I wrote the majority of our interview responses for blogs or websites because I knew they grated on her. I could only imagine today's call did not have her in the calmest frame of mind.

Feeling remorseful for how I'd handled her transference explanation, I decided—today, I could be Katrina's friend. From there, we would see.

"Was it just me," she starts while we walk, "or did it feel like they wanted us to neither confirm nor deny whether we had an affair?" She speaks casually, like she's wondering what frozen food to heat up, not opening up the question that ruined us.

I cough. "It wasn't just you."

"I get it," Katrina continues easily. "Of course the reporter will ask those questions."

"But we don't have to do what they're suggesting," I cut in. "We can tell the reporter the truth. Our relationship is professional, and we never slept together. Not while we wrote *Only Once*, not ever. We've never even kissed." I'm instantly conscious of what implications might lie under what I've just said. Affairs concern sleeping with other people. The kissing hardly comes into it, so in a way, I've accidentally answered a question no one asked. Except myself.

Katrina laughs. "The truth," she muses.

"It is the truth, Katrina." I'm pressing now, the intensity in my voice incoherent with the tranquility of the Florida evening. But I need this out there if I'm going to hold on to this tentative effort to be friendly toward her.

"I know that," she snaps.

The sudden sting in her tone surprises me. I look over. She's facing forward, her mouth flat. What does she want me to say? Does she want me to confess to how I can't stop thinking about her, how I can't sleep, how I hate the progress we've made on the book because I know once we finish, she'll be gone from me?

There's a bigger reason why the full truth is unwelcome, one she knows. I voice it, anyway. "You're engaged," I say quietly. "Aren't you worried how this could affect your relationship?"

Chris was on the call, I note in my head, and didn't object once. I just don't understand it. Regardless of whatever personal feelings I may have, I won't wish on Katrina what I went through at the end of my marriage. While I don't like Chris, I respect the commitment he and Katrina made. I refuse to break it, not physically and not in insinuation to this reporter or the world.

Katrina gives me a cutting glance out of the corner of her eye. The sun is low now, the light a golden glow on her face. She takes a deep breath.

"Chris gave me permission to fuck you if it meant finishing this book," she says. "So I doubt he'd care about rumors."

I stop walking. That word from Katrina has caught my mind like a sharp corner, ripping a gash in how I expected this night would go.

Sensing I'm not with her, Katrina pauses. She faces me from a few feet ahead on the sidewalk. "I didn't, like, ask if I could, if that's what you're freaking out about," she says.

It wasn't. It hadn't even occurred to me. "Do you . . . have an open relationship?" The question jumps into the space in my head her words emptied. It's not even the most important question. In fact, it feels silly. But for some reason, I need it answered first.

Katrina huffs a laugh. "I guess so." She looks past me, like she'd never contemplated the possibility. "When it'll *sell copies*."

"That's an awful thing to say." There's no malice in my reply. The sadness of what she's said is so huge it eclipses even the fact her fiancé said she could sleep with me. Because this is how it is with Katrina, my subconscious whispers to me. It's not just Kat herself I find irresistible—her laughter, her eyes, her body. It's *this*. It's the impulses so much simpler, so much more innocent, so much more fundamental. To feel her wounds with her. To be there for her. To help her through. Even now, I couldn't fight it if I tried. My first thought is for her.

Her expression closes up. "Yeah, well. It's true." She continues walking, like she's decided this part of the conversation is over.

I follow her, thinking back to last night, when she touched me, when I had to fight down everything I wanted. She's just revealed she has the type of relationship where I could do those things. I should be excited. Yet somehow, I'm not. Not while she's unmistakably unhappy, and furthermore, the idea of sleeping with her, then sending her home to Los Angeles and Chris has me nowhere near excited.

I have to remind myself that while I know Chris's feelings on the matter, I still don't know Katrina's. Surely, if she felt the way I did last night and knew she had permission from her fiancé to act on those feelings, she would have. She didn't, though. I know what it means.

"We shut down the rumors. All of them." I say decisively.

Katrina blinks, surprised. "And the book sales?"

"We're writing a fucking good book," I say. "It doesn't need rumors about us to sell."

She's silent. Finally, she nods. "The truth, then. We tell them nothing ever happened between us." Her voice gathers conviction, momentum. "And we split because . . . ?"

She's right. We can't tell the whole story.

"Because writing a book with someone is hard. We needed space," I say. "That's all." It's not all. But that piece of the truth is for us and no one else. If we're ever going to confront what happened, it won't be in front of a reporter. It won't be to make our publisher happy or promote a book.

Katrina looks over, smiling slightly. "This is really going to piss Chris off."

I don't let myself laugh. "Does it bother you?"

Her smile doesn't change. "No."

34

Katrina

• FOUR YEARS EARLIER •

HIS HAND. HIS fingers near my lips. His eyes.

The thunderstorms haven't subsided. I'm in bed, reading, diligently ignoring the feelings coursing through me. Except when I turn every page, in each split second, my memory transports me to the beach. To Nathan's car. I replay the moment, envisioning every detail. *His hand, gently brushing my cheek. His fingers, featherlight on my skin. His eyes, dipping down to my half-open lips. The way I hold my breath, waiting.*

When he started the car, I was ashamed of my own disappointment. Nathan is *married.* I cannot want to kiss him. Repeating this to myself under the covers, I hardly notice the echoing roll of the thunder outside.

But I'm pulled from my thoughts by the whisper of paper on hardwood, cutting through the pattering rain. I get out of bed and find pages have been slid under my door.

I check the clock. It's nearly two A.M. *Wait, it's nearly two A.M.?* I've flipped pages and fended off memories for three hours? Regardless, the new pages confuse me. Nathan never writes this late into the night—he prefers to start each day well rested. What's more, he never passes pages under the door. He just gives me scenes in the morning. He would've seen my light was on when he dropped these off. *Why didn't he just knock?*

I pick up the strange, secretive packet. They're warm, the edges freshly curled from the printer. It's the best feeling. For a second, I can't resist holding them to me, soaking in the heat.

Then my breath hitches when I realize what I'm holding. I read, lingering in front of my closed door, the words pulling me in. It's the scene where Jessamine and Jordan have their first kiss.

Except in the outline, this scene doesn't come until much further in the story. Nathan's moved the kiss up into the scene we were stuck on. It's an enormous deviation from the outline, which immediately has me wondering why he didn't discuss the change with me first.

When I keep reading, I know.

The scene is set on the beach behind Jessamine's and Jordan's neighboring lake houses, where they're vacationing. It's early in the morning. They've woken up early to watch the sunrise while their spouses choose to sleep in. Returning to my bed, I read on.

> *They ran up from the water, kicking sand and silt as they raced to the dock. Jordan's feet tingled from the shock of the cold water. He didn't know why he'd dared her to run into the lake, or why she'd done it, or why he'd followed. Catching their breath on the dock, they overlooked the water, their backs to the homes where their spouses slept.*
>
> *The fog curtained over the lake, pink in the morning light, hiding the far edge from view. Everything was quiet, their own private world.*

I flip pages, feverish. Because I know what Nathan's describing.

It's our morning, without the thunderstorm. He's captured the quiet, the early sunlight, the breathlessness perfectly.

> *Jordan's eyes wandered from the water, finally finding Jessamine, whose gaze was fixed forward. Her chest rose and fell beneath her bathing suit and the white cover-up she didn't bother to remove before running in. In a few moments, she wouldn't be winded. Neither of them would be.*
>
> *What Jordan wanted fell onto him instantly, like it dropped out of the sky, yet it made him weightless. He knew it was wrong. Nevertheless, he felt pulled. Reaching forward, he placed his hands on Jessamine's hips. She looked up, unsurprised and wanting.*
>
> *Jordan did what he'd imagined doing for so long. What he could have done only under the rosy dust of dawn. He kissed Jessamine, and she kissed him.*

I put the pages down, flushed, head spinning. It's different from how Nathan usually writes. His prose is immediate, personal in a way his studied poeticism usually isn't. I force myself to finish reading what he's written.

> *Jessamine reacted like she'd imagined the kiss the same way he had, her hands rising to his face, running through his hair. Plummeting together into passion, they were joined. The kiss was erasing, engulfing everything surrounding them—the lake, the houses, the day still breaking—into empty ecstasy.*
>
> *They withdrew, more out of breath than when they'd raced to the dock. In the silence, they said nothing. Jordan noticed sand from their sprint under Jessamine's eye.*

Lifting his hand, he swiped it from her cheek, his fingers gentle on her skin.

It's then I know Nathan's not writing our characters.

At the bottom of the last page, he's scrawled a message. *I figured out what he wanted. No other scene could work.*

I reread the pages over and over for the next hour. I don't change a thing.

35

Katrina

• PRESENT DAY •

OVER THE NEXT two weeks, I don't have the chance to worry about the interview, or about how telling Nathan what Chris said had left me crying in the shower the next morning. The writing is exhausting. We're reaching the heart of the novel, where it's easiest to lose momentum. We combat the drag the way we always have—without rest.

The process isn't easy. Disagreements spring up daily, though they're only about sentence structure and metaphors. Nothing personal. We resolve them one by one, though they occasionally end with me slamming a door after we've fought for fifteen minutes over a single word.

Even so, I'm grateful for the hard work. I sleep soundly every night, wrists aching from typing, throat raw from speaking, but with words and ideas between every thought.

When we pass thirty thousand words, almost halfway, after writing all day, we decide to take our dinner out onto the porch.

The sun has set. I sit in the porch swing, a plate of almost-finished bruschetta in my lap, a glass of wine on the floor near my bare toes. I'm perfectly relaxed, my head tipped back as I gently rock the swing with my foot. Nathan sits in the chair nearest me, sipping his wine with the easy, contented expression he gets only when he's pleased with the day's writing.

"Nathan?"

I don't recognize the voice. Turning, I find a woman running by. She slows to jogging in place on the curb. Her golden hair is in a ponytail, her workout clothes neon and flatteringly fitted.

Nathan straightens. "Meredith. Hi."

I watch him, his changed posture, the way he skims his hand through his hair. He's no longer relaxed, for sure. I'm just not certain what exactly has replaced his previous calm. I know desire on Nathan. It's there in his eyes, just not on its own.

"Not running tonight?" Meredith calls. Whatever strange new strain I hear in Nathan's voice, hers matches.

He glances over at me. A hint of embarrassment passes over his features. I meet his eyes, questioning. "Long day of work," he replies stiffly, "so I skipped it."

Meredith's eyes flit to me. I read the curiosity in them.

"Oh, right," Nathan says, evidently noticing what I have. "Meredith, this is my . . . colleague, Katrina. Katrina, you and Meredith are . . . neighbors."

Nathan's explained to me, often half drunkenly, how he didn't find his confidence or charm until the end of high school. On one night he deeply regretted, he even told me he didn't have his first kiss until sophomore year of college. It was hard to imagine—until now. Watching him navigate the places of me and Meredith in this conversation, I'm catching remnants of the old, socially skittish Nathan Van Huysen.

"Lovely to meet you," I say to Meredith genuinely.

She looks between him and me. Understanding lights her eyes. What crosses her face is something like relief, like she's answered leftover questions from some conversation I wasn't part of.

"You, too," she replies. Her voice is warm and a little Southern. "Have a lovely evening." She shoots Nathan a smile, puts in her headphones, and waves in parting before continuing her jog down the street.

Nathan settles back into his seat, looking lightly relieved.

"She seemed nice," I say, smirking.

"I don't really know her," he replies.

I raise an eyebrow, and Nathan honest-to-god blushes.

"It's not—it wasn't like that." He shifts in his seat, the way he does when I point out he's used *exhilarating* three times in one chapter.

"You *have* been taking longer runs," I muse. "Now I know where you've been disappearing to."

"Oh my god," he protests, his voice loud in the humid night. I let myself laugh a little. "I was *running*. Not—whatever you're implying."

I shrug, my laughter having settled into a soft smile. It's weird to joke with him like this, to enjoy his company. This easy humor feels like it used to. Long before *Only Once*, when we were friends.

"I'm serious, Katrina. She's nice, but . . ." He falters. His eyes drop to his lap, his expression newly tender. When he looks up, something is different. The air is sweeter, the night softer, the sound of the waves a gentle whisper. My smile fades, and I feel pleasant heat in my face. The porchlight shines on Nathan's hair, spinning brown into gold.

The moment stretches, then passes, which feels right.

"Need a refill?" I pick up the bottle of wine.

His glass is only half empty. "Sure," he says, holding it out to me.

I pour for him. Relaxing into my seat, I glance at him over my drink. "She *was* cute, though. You could do worse."

Nathan laughs, no longer uncomfortable. "You'll never drop this, will you?"

"Oh, never."

He shakes his head. Quiet comes over us, and I don't fight the realization it brings. I'm not pretending the way I said we would. I don't need to. It's no longer hard working with him, laughing with him, being with him.

I'm happy here.

36

Nathan

I'M IN FRONT of Katrina's door, warm pages in hand. This is probably a terrible idea.

Once we'd finished with dinner and dishes, I returned to my room, showered, and sat down in front of my computer. I felt restless, the same kind of restless I've felt every night I didn't run myself to exhaustion. My fingers itched. My mind was lighting up—not the lightbulb of neatly inspired ideas. More like a house on fire. I wanted to write.

I knew it was my own fault I couldn't. Refusing to trade pages with Katrina had barred me from writing on my own. I don't want to work on stuff for my solo career, either. Not now. This book with Katrina is consuming me, gradually becoming the only thing I want to concentrate on.

It's not like I'd forgotten the reasons not to exchange chapters with her. Everything I'd permitted myself to confess in them before, under cover of literature, led us right to the chasm off of which our relationship had plunged. Still . . . after our dinner, after laughing with Katrina on the porch, sharing unexpected and wonderful moments with the woman who is starting to feel genuinely like a friend again, I wondered if maybe I could permit myself one small step back into what we used to be.

I placed my fingers on the keys lightly, innocuously, like I didn't want to scare myself off.

The thoughts poured out of me. While I wrote, I reminded myself, I didn't *need* to give Katrina the pages I was flying through. I could trash them. My own private transgression into territory I'd forbidden us to enter.

When I finished, though, I knew I'd written something for her to see. The chapter finds Michael hitting the town with a friend, indulging in soon-to-be unmarried life. Yet the whole evening, everything he sees, everything he does, he filters through memories of Evelyn and their marriage. He knows that while they can divide their lives, physically and legally, they'll never be separate from each other.

I wrote with Melissa in mind but also Katrina. Being with her now is proof that you can think you've rebuilt, shored your walls, and yet still a person to whom you've given too much of yourself is a hurricane who can sweep in with a shared smile over a glass of wine in the early evening.

The pages pulled me into the hallway, up to Katrina's door, where they have left me. Hesitating, unsure and certain, confused and clear.

I knock.

Katrina opens the door within moments. She hasn't yet changed for bed. Her narrow shoulders are relaxed, and surprise—maybe even pleasant surprise—livens her expression. When her eyes drop to what I'm holding, I answer her unspoken question.

"We don't have to use them," I say. "You don't even have to read them."

"I want to read them," she says immediately. Her gaze rises to mine. "You're . . . sure?"

I know what she's really asking. Do I really want to go down this road with her again? It's one I've refused out of self-preservation. Flying past the guardrails I've constructed for us could end disastrously.

I hold the pages out to her.

"I had a nice time tonight," I say.

Katrina's expression softens. I have the impulse to look away, like I'm witnessing something secret. I don't. I stare, starting to lose myself in the warm brown of her eyes. "I did, too," she replies.

It's the end of the conversation. "Good night, Kat." The name slips off my tongue with frightening ease. When I see its effect on her, the nearly imperceptible flickers of pleasure I catch lighting her expression, it wrecks me.

"See you in the morning." She shuts her door.

I return to my room, having forgotten each of the contradictions I felt when I walked up to her door. They're covered over now, underneath warm brown eyes and a secret smile. For the first time in weeks, I know I'll sleep soundly.

WHEN I WAKE, I find my pages under the door. I get out of bed hurriedly, nearly knocking my elbow on the wall, ignoring how naked my excitement is. Picking up the pages, I immediately flip through.

Katrina's handwriting is everywhere.

My heart constricts. I love the feeling. Following the lines of her loping penmanship, chasing her thoughts from page to page, I feel like I'm easing into a rhythm I never forgot. It's one of the joys of working with Katrina. I'm never self-conscious reading her revisions. I'm excited by them.

Under the final line of the chapter, she's written a note for me.

Stayed up late working on the next scene, so I went to get tea. Text me if you want coffee.

It's innocuous, and it's everything. What's happening here, in red ink on fresh pages and tossed-off kindnesses, is irreversible. It's the beginning of our lives fitting back together, finding the impressions left when we pulled them apart.

37

Nathan

I PACE THE living room, glancing at the stairs. It's been fifteen minutes since Katrina called down saying she was just putting on her shoes. Fifteen minutes . . . of her putting on shoes. Out of the corner of my eye, I've watched the night darken from periwinkle to navy past our shutters. She's having second thoughts. She has to be.

For two weeks now, we've traded pages every night, passing them under each other's doors like clandestine letters. Which, in many ways, they are. I feel us getting closer. Compliments come easier on paper, confessions, casual thoughts. It's how writing is. It cuts to the core, suffering no obfuscations. It's where the truth is laid bare. I've learned things big and small—how Katrina wants more from her life, how she yearns for and fears the world of writing and publishing, how she hates the smell of basil. She gifts me these secrets, sometimes in the words she slashes, sometimes in the feelings she chooses to elaborate or the feelings she chooses to remove.

With the two of us writing simultaneously, we're making startling progress on the manuscript. When we both took stabs at a scene where the newly separated Evelyn goes to a nightclub, looking for a rebound, Katrina suggested in a comment on the pages we do some setting research.

We're an hour from Miami, she'd written. *Sunday?*

I'd replied beneath her question the next morning. *I'll pick you up at seven.*

It's 7:21. I'm preparing to head up to her room and ask if she wants to call off the plan when I hear her door open and shut.

When she emerges from the hallway, pausing at the top of the stairs, I forget I'm halfway on the first step. I forget everything. I forget I'm Nathan, who went years not exchanging even an email with the person in front of me now. I forget she's Katrina, who fled from everything we had. I only know this woman is breathtaking.

Her dress, the palest pink, drapes over her curves, dipping low in the front. The hem hits high on her thighs. In between the silk and her black heels is a mile of skin I've spent twenty-one minutes and four years waiting for. Her hair drawls loosely down her back, the lipstick kissing her mouth a dark rose. When her eyes meet mine, her long lashes flicker.

"What?" she asks.

I want to say she's gorgeous. Heart-stopping. If I started, I don't know how I would stop. I've worked my entire adult life to marshal the English language into whatever I wanted. But were I to try to capture Katrina with it, it would best even me.

I don't try. "I wondered if you were standing me up," I say instead.

She laughs. It makes my heart pound. "Pretty sure you can't stand up the person you live with." She descends the stairs, stopping in front of me, so I'm looking up while she looks down. I notice she's gripping the bannister, her knuckles white. "I called Chris and told him what we were doing tonight," she says.

Hearing Chris's name stuns me for a second. Katrina never mentions her fiancé without prompting. "What'd he say?" I ask cautiously.

"He just wanted to hear about our progress on the book." She worries the finger and thumb of her other hand. "Then he told me to *have fun*." Her words come out bitter.

I remember what she said on our walk. Chris gave her permission to do whatever she wanted with me. I hear in those two resentful syllables—*have fun*—how it hurts her knowing her fiancé values her writing over her fidelity.

I don't have the opportunity or the right to give her the whole English language. I do have the chance to ease the pain. I hold out my hand to her. "I'm certainly ready to have fun if you are."

She looks down. Then she takes my hand.

"I'm ready," she says, holding my gaze for a long moment.

Together, we walk out into the evening.

38

Katrina

I'M ON THE dance floor, two drinks in. I have no idea where Nathan is. The club is sensory overload within four walls, the electronic beat pounding through crisp metal railings and black velvet booths. Smoke and lasers obscure the DJ conducting the controlled chaos. I lose myself in the music throbbing against my skin.

Half-heartedly, I try to center myself in Evelyn's head, working to internalize details of the room, the sensations. It's why we're here, ostensibly. Method research, like when we spent seven hours sitting in the Venice airport to pick up descriptive texture for *Connecting Flights*.

It's not entirely why *I'm* here, though. Earlier this evening, what I needed from this trip into the city changed. I want the pummeling music, the chaotic lights. I want escape. If I wind up with some sharp descriptors or poignant observations for Evelyn, so much the better.

The drive into Miami was pleasant enough. Nathan, in his dark jacket and white shirt with several buttons open, was quiet but not stiff.

We casually went over the details of the scene we were researching while I gazed out the Porsche's windshield. Miami seemed a likeable, lively composite of other places I know—the clean commercialism of San Diego combined with the old-school relaxation of Italy and the vibrance of Havana. When we reached the club, Nathan and I staked out the bar. He ordered us drinks, and we lingered, observing things we wanted to incorporate.

When he grabbed his Cuba libre and headed for the balcony, I made for the dance floor. I found immersing myself in the crowd easy. With every movement of my sweat-slicked body, I fought to shake off Chris's words from earlier. *Katrina, you don't need to get my permission for each thing you two do. I told you. It's fine. Have fun.*

His voice had been cold, businesslike. An agent keeping his client happy. It'd left me feeling sick, hunched over the toilet for twenty minutes while Nathan waited downstairs. Nothing came up. Finally, I found my composure and, putting one heeled foot in front of the other, I left my room. Chris had told me to have fun. I was determined I would.

The song changes, shifting into something slower, even sensual. Which is when I see Nathan. He's on the edge of the dance floor, not dancing.

Past the crowd, his eyes are fixed on me. His gaze cuts through the fog and the noise, searing me.

I stop dancing.

Breathing hard, I push my hair out of my eyes. The way he's looking at me is loaded with intention. I feel it on my skin, and I don't look away.

While the crowd surrounding me continues to gyrate and sway, Nathan walks toward me. He stops in front of me, the swirling lights casting red shadows on his face. Without questioning myself, I reach out languidly, resting my hand in the crook of his neck and shoulder. I feel his palm on my hip. We both inhale. Then we're moving to the rhythm, together this time.

I'm pressed to him, falling dizzily from moment to moment. Sweat meets with sweat, his skin on mine. I've never been this close to Nathan in the six years I've known him. Heat pounds in me in every place we touch. I indulgently notice every detail of him I've forced myself to ignore, the contours of his chest, the confidence of his fingers on my waist, the gleam in his eyes.

It's clear from farther down he's . . . no less preoccupied. I cut every cord holding me back. With a shimmying movement snaking slowly down the length of me, I press myself to the firm place in the front of his pants. His grip tightens. While we exhale together, he closes his eyes.

The revelation washes over me. Its impact is a tidal wave, overwhelming and leveling everything in me. We were always, always, headed for this. Chris doesn't care. Nathan wants this. I can feel how things have already changed between us. Four years apart and yet we know each other in ways no one else does.

Wasn't this inevitable? We've served the sentence for a crime we never committed. Why shouldn't we commit it now? There are no possible consequences left.

I tilt my head to look at him. Reaching up, I place a hand lightly on his face. His eyes flutter open.

Slowly, I lean forward, pressing my lips to his.

His fingers dig deeper into my skin. But his mouth is a different story. His lips don't move. He's not dancing. He's not kissing me.

Pulling away, I'm a mixture of confusion and hurt. I search his eyes for explanation. He wanted this. We both did. Who's he protecting by refusing? Surely not Chris. But Nathan's eyes are blank pages. While I just watch him, his fingers close over my raised hand. It feels like a caress, until he lifts my hand from his face.

His expression storms, desire colliding with anger. Without a word, he spins and walks off the dance floor.

39

Katrina

I PACE THE floor of my room. The wind outside is restless, an irritating counterpart to my mood. It's half past midnight, forty-five minutes since we returned home from Miami. We drove in utter silence, which didn't surprise me. I know where this discussion will be had.

Sure enough, moments later, pages slide under my door, shoved with such force they fan out on the hardwood.

I collect the pages, which Nathan's eviscerated in his sharp handwriting. It's the scene we'd written where Evelyn goes to a club. He's edited it, adding in the setting descriptions we researched and much, much more. His handwriting is frantic, the pen digging deep grooves into the paper. But his most harried comments come in the conversation Evelyn strikes up with a man standing at the bar.

He's replaced whole paragraphs, slashing what I'd written and inserting lines and lines of his own fervent prose.

It didn't matter who the stranger was. She'd already forgotten his name. What mattered was he wasn't Michael. It was this Evelyn found intoxicating. Only this. Everything he said, every facial expression, was wonderfully foreign to her.

When she let him kiss her, she wasn't thinking of the man holding her. She was thinking of the man he wasn't.

Every comment is the same. Nathan drives his point home with punishing strokes of his pen. Evelyn thinks she's pursuing this fling because she's doing what *she* wants. Instead, it's not about her at all. It's about Michael.

I know what Nathan really means. What he's writing to *me*.

Maybe I was using him a little. It doesn't mean kissing Nathan wouldn't have been more, though.

Which he would have known if he'd spoken one word to me on this subject. In the club, in the car, in the living room when we got home. The flash of rage I feel with this thought is unlike myself, yet I don't hide from it. I don't finish reading the pages. Furiously, I uncap my pen and write a single sentence.

Imagine how different our lives would be if you could speak your feelings instead of only writing them.

My handwriting is shaky, quivering with feeling. He hasn't changed. I was naïve to think finding our friendship once more meant anything else. Nathan can never be anything else. He doesn't have the courage.

With the chapter in my hand, I step into the hallway. I won't indulge in our petty, furtive back-and-forth. It's Nathan's game. Not mine. I place the pages on the hall table. If he wants them, he'll have to leave his room for them. I don't care if he reads them tonight, tomorrow, or never.

40

Nathan

THE DAY BEFORE the *New York Times* interview, we're in the living room with Harriet, who's playing reporter. Katrina is seated far from me, our opposing armchairs facing each other. She's rigid, her posture painfully perfect. Harriet's in the middle, sitting on the couch, giving us practice questions.

"Where did you guys meet?" she asks dutifully.

"Writer's workshop," Katrina says.

"In New York," I add.

Harriet waits. Her pause stretches into speechlessness, then into disappointment. "Seriously, guys? Please," she says sternly. "Try with complete sentences."

I shift the collar of my shirt, chastised. When I steal a glance at Katrina, I catch her looking at me for a split second. Instantly, she faces the window behind Harriet, pretending her eyes were on the gorgeous view the whole while.

When she crosses her arms over her chest, I know the gesture is not idle. It's defensive. We've hardly spoken since Sunday. No whisper of discussion about the club or the pages I gave her. No mention of what I firmly refuse to call a kiss despite our lips meeting. It wasn't a kiss. It was a collision. Now, it's like none of it ever happened.

I received her comment in my edits and understood exactly what she was saying. Katrina loves to pretend that what we communicate in our writing isn't real. It's easier for her, safer, free of guilt or responsibility or other heavy realities. It just couldn't be more wrong. Writing is where our—where everyone's—purest truths lie. On the page, thoughts and feelings can be expressed without interference, without ineloquences or fear or fumbling. There's no room for turning back or losing your nerve. Only one thing remains—what you want to communicate.

Katrina can tell herself things would be different if I spoke my feelings instead of writing them. But it's not true. She knows how I feel. How I felt. I was never unclear. Her choices were her own.

Harriet sighs, returning me to our interview. "Okay," she says. "Something easier, then. What's your new book about?"

"Divorce—" Katrina starts to say.

She's cut off when keys rattle outside. The front door unlocks, and Chris walks in. He's holding a leather duffel I suspect he picked out on Rodeo Drive. The precision with which he's obviously chosen everything he's wearing screams vanity. The linen jacket, the gold-rimmed sunglasses, the soft leather loafers. He looks just like I remember. The visceral dislike I feel is not easy for me to repress, so I don't.

"Chris," Katrina says, startled. Watching her hastily recompose herself, I can only think of every way Katrina's told me he's hurt her. "You didn't tell me you landed. I would've picked you up from the airport," she says.

"It's fine." Chris sounds unbothered. "I had a car drive me."

"Oh," Katrina says, sounding empty.

"Don't let me interrupt." Chris drops his duffel by the stairs, flashing his megawatt smile.

When I first met Chris Calloway, I was giddy with excitement. Every writer in my position has and would have felt the same way. Signing with an agent is where getting published starts, and Chris wasn't just *an* agent. He was the rising star at one of the most prestigious agencies in New York. Katrina and I were overjoyed.

Which was how I knew I wasn't just out of sorts when I swiftly realized I couldn't stand him. Katrina and I had had our introductory call, received our offer of representation, and signed our contract. We met Chris for drinks at O'Neill's, which felt spectacularly professional and real. My enthusiasm wore off with every name-drop, every career accomplishment, every question he directed *only* to my pretty, impossibly polite cowriter. Over the past four years, I've wondered if the Chris I knew was merely youthful and high on success, and if career stability and dating Katrina evened him out.

Looking at him now, I doubt it.

"You're not interrupting," Katrina replies. "We're not writing right now. You remember Harriet?" She gestures to the literal human being I'm pretty sure Chris didn't even notice. "She's helping us prep for the interview."

Chris glances at Harriet. While his smile stays fixed, I doubt I'm the only one who notices how fake it is. "Harriet, of course." He pauses. "I hear you're teaching now?" The judgment in his voice is unmistakable. It doesn't surprise me to know Chris is the kind of guy who considers education to be "flunking out" of publishing.

Harriet plasters on an equally fake smile. "I am."

"That's terrific. Fantastic," he says with ridiculous enthusiasm.

"I hear you got a Peloton," Harriet says.

Chris's eyes narrow. This is why I love Harriet. Instead of letting him stoke his sense of professional superiority, she's left him struggling to work out exactly how he's been insulted. Which is why I can't help myself—I laugh.

His eyes fall on me now. He's dropped every pretense of pleasantry. "Nathan. Great to see you again. How have you been?"

I hold the ugly gaze peering out of his handsome face. "Terrific," I say. "Fantastic. You?"

He walks over to sit on the arm of Katrina's chair, placing a hand on her shoulder. "Couldn't be better. Please"—he waves into the room—"continue."

Is he serious? I can't continue this pretend interview with Chris fucking *watching*. Katrina, who's shrunk in her seat, undoubtedly feels similarly. She looks up, imploring. "You don't want to go up to our room?" she asks him. The reminder they'll share a bed tonight makes me clench my jaw.

"I want to see some of this first," Chris replies firmly.

Either he doesn't notice how his response upsets Katrina, or, likelier, he doesn't care. She faces Harriet, looking frayed. "What was the question?" she forces out.

"The book you're writing now," Harriet prompts, uncharacteristically gentle. She knows there's something unpleasant going on here.

"It's about divorce," I cut in. "Katrina and I have respectively had our fair share of romantic ups and downs." I fire Chris a pointed glance, finding his lips curled in a cold smirk. "We wanted to get personal, delve into some of our experiences in separation and the end of love."

Katrina lets out a featherweight laugh. "It's not *that* negative. It's a love story."

"Of course," I rejoin. "Which is what we're working on now. Finding the love." I let my words hang. "In the story," I add.

Harriet nods, her expression starting to show strain. "And why," she asks reluctantly, "did you return to writing together?"

I preempt Katrina. "Well, Kat did, because her agent—who happens to be her fiancé—forced her to."

Katrina's head whips to me. "Nathan!"

I glare at her. She told me to speak my feelings. Well, here they are. Let's fucking speak them.

"Okay, that's enough for me. I'm going to go," Harriet says, understandably not wanting to witness whatever happens next.

It's a wise decision. It's silent while she slips out the front door. "Sorry," I say. "Although, really, I'm not." I address Chris. "Maybe you want to comment? You'll be in the interview, right? Supervising? Why don't you handle those questions?"

Chris's smile falters. He stands up. "I think I'll go up to our bedroom after all. I worry I'm a distraction."

"Chris, it's not—" Katrina pleads.

Her fiancé cuts her off. "Don't worry about it." He leans down. The unnecessarily long kiss he gives her is, I know, for my benefit. I want to pull my eyes from the cruel display, but I can't, even while my body revolts. I rue the way my writer's eye for detail catches every second of Chris's lips bearing down on Katrina's, the way his hand holds her face possessively.

Katrina pushes him off her, wiping her mouth. Her gaze is fiery.

I stand, sick. Suddenly, I don't just hate Chris, I hate myself for what I just provoked him into doing. Furious, and guilty and disgusted, I walk out of the room before Chris can.

41

Katrina

• FOUR YEARS EARLIER •

I'M HYPERAWARE OF where my arm presses into Nathan's. When he shifts on the couch, his legs spread outward, his knee grazing mine. I don't move away. We've sat this way plenty of times, on countless conference calls. It's purely for convenience. When we sit near each other, we can share the speaker while one of us jots notes on the computer. It's nothing.

After the beach, it doesn't feel like nothing. Not to me. I have no idea where Nathan's head is, no clue what his relaxed posture or his quick smiles mean.

Our agent's voice over the line cuts my concentration. "My dream team," Chris says, like he's calling a football game. "How's Florida?"

I'm not in the mood for the small talk. I'm impatient. Chris has just heard from our editor, Liz, whom we sent our outline and everything we have of the book to request an extension. We're close to finishing. We just don't want to rush the crucial scenes of the ending.

"Inspiring," Nathan replies, clearly also uninterested in chitchat.

"I'll say!" Chris enthuses. "Katrina, having a nice time?"

Nathan rolls his eyes. I smile slightly. It's a joke we share, how often Chris directs personal questions my way. Not that agents and authors can't have friendships, but Chris never extends the same curiosity to Nathan.

I steer the conversation in the direction I want. "It's great. We've rented the house for a couple more weeks so we can finish the book here."

"Well, you don't have to worry about it. Liz approved the extension," Chris informs us. I feel myself exhale softly. Chris goes on. "Guys, I have to tell you, she loves what you've written. *Loves* it. Like, making it a lead title. *The* lead title. This book is going to break you out."

When Nathan looks over, I feel excitement radiating off him. I meet his growing smile with my own. It's beyond whatever we could have possibly hoped to hear. In a private, enormously satisfying way, it's not entirely a surprise. We knew what we were writing was special. Nevertheless, hearing it from Liz is validating.

"I really think this is going to be huge for you," Chris continues. "Life-changing. So just keep doing whatever you're doing."

I don't predict Nathan's reaction. He pulls his arm from where his skin met mine and wraps me in a sideways hug. My own arm curls over his chest. Success is a wonderful feeling. Sharing that success with your closest friend? There's nothing like it. My heart fills with happiness for him, for myself, for us, the joys overlapping and compounding one another until I feel weightless.

Neither of us speaks for a second. It occurs to me Chris has no idea what's happening on our end of the line. It's a private moment, which makes it sweeter. Finally, it's Nathan who replies. "We're thrilled to hear it. We really believe in this story. We put . . . a lot of ourselves into it." On his final words, his eyes flash to me. I don't meet them. *What does he mean by that?*

"Great, well, I'm going to start talking it up to some of my film contacts," Chris declares, speaking quickly. "The bigger we blow this up, the better."

Nervous energy I didn't expect hums in me. "Don't you want to wait until we . . . finish the book? What if we"—I swallow. I want to say, *What if we fuck it up?*—"fumble the ending?" I say instead.

Chris laughs loudly. "You won't," he promises me. It's a uniquely unreassuring reassurance. "Only a few contacts, just to start generating some heat. Trust me." I squirm, feeling pressure I'm not used to. I notice Nathan's eyes on me. He doesn't look skeptical or critical, just genuinely confused. "Hey, and as soon as you have ideas for what you want your next book to be, let's discuss," he continues.

Next book? We're not even done with *this* book. I once went go-karting with my siblings, and I did not enjoy myself—I couldn't understand how others found the careening fun instead of frightening. It's how I feel now.

"We have a couple concepts," Nathan says, watching me. "Nothing we're ready to share yet."

"Fair enough," Chris replies, massaging the words. "The sooner the better, of course. We're going to want to keep this momentum." I hear the new lilt in his voice when he speaks next. "Sound good, Katrina? How are you feeling about this?"

Nathan shakes his head, but he's too pleased with the news to frown.

"I'm . . . a little shocked, honestly," I say.

"I understand. You'll need to adjust to this new period in your life," Chris says. "Don't forget, I'm here for you, Kat."

At this, Nathan's eyebrows rise. I have to admit, it's a little much, even for Chris. "Thanks, Chris," I say with stiff cheer. With nothing else to add, we say our goodbyes.

When I hang up the phone, I find Nathan looking stunned. "Wow," he says, giddy again.

"I know," I say. While I want to let him celebrate, I can't shake my nerves. "We still have to finish the book, though. Who knows what will happen."

"Right, yeah," he says, sounding eager to the point of impatient. His eyes have gone starry. "But lead title? Movie rights? Kat, this is huge."

My stomach knots. I hate how this feeling has taken hold of me, this wiry, jittery creature. But I don't know how to fight it. "Let's just not get ahead of ourselves, okay?" I hear myself say. "When we're done, when the book is out, then we can celebrate."

Nathan studies me. His earlier curiosity has returned, and I know he knows me well enough to have discerned I'm downplaying this on purpose. He only gives me a soft smile, though. "Sure," he says. I would feel horrible for how he's tempering his enthusiasm, except his expression is gentle. "We'll wait until we finish the book. And hey, Katrina?"

I look up.

"Chris is there for you. Whenever you need."

I don't laugh. While Nathan's remark has the timing and irony of a joke, something in his expression and the sharpness of his voice says it's not one, not really. He's looking elsewhere now, his smile wan and mocking. What's more, my pent-up nervous energy doesn't exactly have me in the mood for humor.

"It bothers you, doesn't it?" I ask, matching the edge in his voice. "That I'm Chris's favorite."

Nathan scoffs. "Favorite? More like he's into you."

My head jerks back. "What? No. *No* way." Instantly, I wish our publishing success was the only thing making me uncomfortable. Not this outlandish suggestion.

"You're joking." Nathan puts on a sort of pitying incredulity. "He checks you out every time we meet with him."

I flush, shuffling through memories of lunches near his office and drinks with our publisher. "He does?" I ask. I never noticed. Nathan did, though. I'm not sure what to make of that.

Nathan's eyes widen a little. "Does the observation *please* you?" He shifts away from me on the couch, everything about his posture defensive. He's acting . . . jealous.

"If it did please me, there'd be nothing wrong with that, would there?" It's a loaded question. There can't be anything wrong with my enjoying Chris's interest, not where Nathan's concerned. Because Nathan is married.

He pauses, like he's following the paces my mind just went through. "An agent sleeping with his client?" he asks, recovering. "I mean, it's *vaguely* unprofessional." His emphasis says *vaguely* is an understatement.

"Right. *That's* what bothers you." I stand, having reached the end of my patience with his scorn and skepticism. This conversation has gone haywire, unraveling in ugly directions. It didn't have to—we've received good publishing news plenty of times in the past—but for perverse, frantic reasons, I'm glad it did. I'm distantly guilty about ruining Nathan's enthusiasm, and so much more gratified I have this fight to distract me from the bigger questions of the call with Chris.

I've started to leave the room when I hear Nathan's voice behind me. "Why else would it bother me, Katrina?"

I round. My nerves have wound up into something darker, less forgiving. "It's my choice if I want to sleep with Chris," I shoot back, leaning into my frustration. It's not a direct response to his question, which is purposeful. I'm pissed he asked a question he wouldn't answer himself.

He leans forward. "So you *do* want to."

"Maybe! I don't know." I shake my head, exasperated. Honestly, sleeping with Chris has never crossed my mind. He's objectively handsome, though. Considering it now, it's not the *least* interesting idea in the world. But that's not the point. We're not talking about what we're really talking about. I'm done with it. "Let's get back to work," I say. "This *life-changing* book won't write itself."

Nathan stands. When he walks past me toward the dining table, his eyes flicker angrily with everything he hasn't said. His emotions will find their way into his pages later—I know they will.

42

Katrina

• PRESENT DAY •

NATHAN AND CHRIS have left the room, walking off in different directions.

I close my eyes. I inhale deeply. And I follow Chris.

I take the stairs two at a time, my heart rate picking up. When I swing open the door of my room, Chris has the gall to look surprised. "What the hell was that?" I ask.

Chris sits on the bed, reclining on his elbows. Carefree. "What was what?"

I'm in no mood for this dance. No mood to give him the benefit of the doubt the way I usually do when I think he's slighted me. When he's made dismissive references over dinner to how long it's been since *Only Once* was released, or when he makes some decision for the house without even telling me. "That kiss," I say, sharply. "I got the strangest sense it wasn't for me."

"Can't a guy kiss his fiancée after weeks apart?" He smiles his winningest smile.

"Sure," I reply. "If that's what it was. If it had nothing to do with Nathan."

Chris laughs. "Katrina, calm down. You know jealousy makes Nathan a better writer. I may not be his agent anymore, but I still know how to inspire him."

I open my mouth. Nothing comes out. The room suddenly feels slanted while years of conversations reorient themselves in my mind. Nathan and I used to joke about the attention Chris paid me in particular. When Chris and I got serious, I converted the jokes into signs. I found it comforting to think this was exactly where my life had been leading all along. Chris had carried a torch for me. It was obvious to everyone. The idea that we had something of a past, a history of innocuous flirtations, half connections and insinuations, gave me the sense of a future.

Except now, I'm remembering how often Chris's flirtations happened in the presence of Nathan. Worse, I remember the undeniable results. How wonderfully Nathan would articulate jealousy and longing and impossible, unnameable emotions.

I hear my voice come out hollow, choked. "Is that why you flirted with me before we were together? Only to goad Nathan's writing?"

Chris straightens. Smiling lazily, he stands and walks up to me. "Obviously, I was attracted to you." He places a hand on my hip.

I step past him, wanting his hands nowhere near me. It's morbidly funny how much I've wanted to see Chris, yet within fifteen minutes of him getting here, I can't stand to be in the same room with him, or the confident quirk in his lips, or the manufactured masculine scent of his shower products, or the rumbling murmur of his voice.

He faces me, frowning. "You'd be wise to be aware of Nathan's feelings for you," he says.

I search for jealousy or calculation in his eyes and find none. I can't help the sick shiver of pleasure I feel at Chris's warning—at what it implies. But the feeling is lost beneath disgust with Chris. With how he manipulated Nathan, how he used me to do it. Worse, how he's discussing another man's feelings for his fiancée like it's casual conversation or commonplace advice, like *Don't forget to lock the door* or *Remember to get detergent.* I don't even know exactly what he's advising, and the possibilities feel like gut punches. Should I use Nathan's feelings the way Chris did? Should I torture us both in order to write a better book?

I don't want to know. I don't want to finish this conversation. I don't want to confront how everything with Chris is falling dominoes of *I don't want.*

I head for the door. With my hand on the handle, I turn back. "You should've come to Florida because I asked you to," I say, each word boiling. "Not because of this interview." Before he can reply, I leave the room, slamming the door behind me.

43

Nathan

THE NEXT DAY, the day of the interview, I stand stiffly with Katrina on the porch. We haven't spoken since yesterday.

It's not her I'm avoiding. It's Chris. I've diligently kept myself out of the same room with my former agent, opting instead to spend the rest of the day writing in one of the other cafés in the neighborhood. Not the one where I went with Katrina. When the place closed for the night, I begged Harriet to let me come over. It was nearly midnight when I returned to the house, where I noticed Chris and Katrina's bedroom door closed, the lights off.

Now, we're shading our eyes in the morning sunlight, exchanging polite smiles with the reporter who's come to pry into every corner of our personal and professional lives. While Chris greets him and the photographer, I study our profiler. Noah Lippman is short, slight, collegiate-looking. He doesn't hide his baldness, and he's paired thin brown glasses with a well-chosen striped button-down. He reminds me of New York.

Chris invites them inside, where Katrina gives them a quick tour of the house while the photographer snaps photos. I stand in the living room, hands in my pockets. I'm familiar enough with press coverage from the *Only Once* promotional circuit. The plan for the day is straightforward—Noah will observe Katrina and me working together, capture some of our process, then move on to the interview. Chris will . . . I don't know, hover.

When we return to the living room, where Katrina and I will revise each other's scenes, she and I settle into the opposing armchairs.

The photographer speaks up instantly. "Sorry. Can you sit together? On the couch, maybe?" Chris, leaning on the doorframe, nods like we needed his permission.

Wordlessly, Katrina and I simultaneously stand. We move to the couch, where we resume reading, or pretending to read. My eyes skip uselessly over the words, the clicking of the camera shutter interrupting my thoughts. I notice Katrina's hands have started to sweat. She keeps pressing them to her skirt.

"How long of a piece are you planning?" Chris asks Noah loudly. "And you said it would be the front page of Arts and Culture, right?"

I roll my neck instead of rolling my eyes the way I want to. They can't possibly expect us to work like this. While Noah patiently confirms the details with Chris, I lean closer to Katrina. Like mine, her pen remains fixed in the same spot on her page.

Reaching over, I scribble a quick smiley face on her page.

She laughs a little, breathing out softly. The corners of her lips curl. She's unfairly cute, I catch myself thinking. The camera snaps four times in quick succession.

Katrina pauses, then she writes something in the corner of her page. Figuring she's editing, I try to return to reading until I feel her elbow nudge lightly into mine.

I glance over to read what she's written. *Where were you yesterday?*

I reach into her lap, putting my pen to her paper. *Hiding at Harriet's. Have a good night?* I write.

The light flees from her expression. I feel guilty I asked, although I suspect the real fault isn't mine. The dynamic between her and Chris today has been . . . off. Confirming my suspicions, she holds her pen over my pages, then circles the word *interminable.*

To our observers, it probably looks like we're engaged in intricate literary craftsmanship. Instead, for the rest of the hour, we pass notes like kids in class. It's not about anything, just entertaining each other. Saying without saying, *I'm here. I'm with you.*

It's the most we've talked since we returned from the club. I could point out how we're communicating in our writing again, the way she thought wasn't worth anything. But I don't. I just let this happen.

Finally, the photographer packs up his gear and goes to get coffee. Noah sits down across from us and places his recorder on the coffee table. The slim device is silver plastic, only the size of a pack of gum, yet strangely imposing. I feel Katrina stiffen next to me. Worrying the corner of her shirt, she darts looks in Chris's direction. He's moved out of sight in the kitchen, undoubtedly still able to overhear every word.

I don't know what happened with him and Katrina last night. Now certainly isn't the moment to ask, though. All I can do is fight to forget he's nearby.

Noah starts in with the softball questions—how we met, what our new book is about. Katrina and I play our roles perfectly, putting on the same friendliness we practiced on each other in our early days here. It's small comfort to know we're now united in performing for someone else. Thirty minutes into the conversation, our responses continue to come easily, in contrast to yesterday's practice run.

"How is working together again after four years apart?" Noah asks. I have to give the guy credit—he has a calm, patient way of deepening his questions. It's not hard to understand why he's the journalist writing features like this one. He adjusts his glasses and goes on genially. "Has anything changed?"

"I can't speak for Nathan, but I sometimes feel like no time has passed," Katrina says.

Her voice is gentle, and her words warm me. "I feel the same way," I quickly confirm. I meet Kat's eyes, and for not the first time, I recognize a quiet tug on the delicate thread connecting us. Out of the corner of my eye, I notice Noah jotting notes on his pad.

"Now, Nathan," Noah starts again, "you were famously quoted as saying Katrina's genius wasn't worth the torture of working with her." His voice hasn't changed. There's no hunger or salaciousness in his eyes. He's just doing his job.

My eyes flit guiltily to Katrina, who looks unfazed if a little withdrawn, her lips lightly pursed. We've never openly addressed my *New Yorker* interview. I doubt we have to, really—I show her every day how far from a hardship working with her is. Some truths are so obvious they don't need to be said out loud.

I lean forward on my elbows. We strategized for this subject. If we pretend the past never happened, the rest of the interview will ring false. "Look, it's no secret Katrina and I haven't always gotten along," I admit frankly.

"No secret, no," Noah replies patiently. "You both have, however, remained notoriously tight-lipped on the cause of your falling-out, despite . . . rumors."

I glance at Katrina and find her head turned yet again toward the kitchen. Her jaw is rigid. I know her expressions well enough to discern her thoughts have fled elsewhere. I just don't know where.

It feels like the floor is wobbling under me. Something is coming, but I don't know what. Despite my unease, I can only carry out what we planned for the interview. "You're asking if we had an affair," I say. The words feel like chewing on gravel.

Noah laughs. "Well, now that you bring it up."

In what I hope looks like innocent stretching, I nudge Katrina's knee with mine. I don't need her to rush to my defense. I just know I can't be the only one quoted on this subject. The gesture works, with Katrina straightening in her seat and refocusing on the reporter.

"We didn't have an affair," she says. Something is different. Her intensity is of a sort I've rarely heard. "Nathan was married to a very real person. To erase her for scandal and book sales disgusts us both."

Noah's eyebrows rise. I feel mine do the same. "Fair enough," he says. I watch him decide now is probably the moment he's waited for. "Let's set the record straight. You two never . . ." He waves his hand instead of finishing the sentence.

I fill in the empty space. "We were never together romantically."

"Then I have to ask," Noah says, "if feelings didn't get in the way, what was the reason for your split?" The journalist's gaze has sharpened. It's not predatory, just focused. He's nearing what he knows will be the real subject of his story.

Katrina's hands smooth her skirt, her knuckles white. Watching her, I struggle to keep my expression unconcerned. With forced nonchalance, I deliver the line we prepared. "We needed to grow as artists independently for a while."

"Of course. Tensions run hot, especially when success enters the equation," Noah says smoothly. "But why refuse to appear publicly together?" He smiles kindly. Immediately, I know he's prepared just the way we have. He's going to keep pressing until he receives an interesting answer.

"Living with someone for months, working creatively with a deadline—I'm not going to say there wasn't conflict," I reply.

Katrina holds up a hand. Her eyes are hard and fixed on the wall behind which Chris is waiting.

I don't know what she means until she speaks, her voice a stripped wire. "Nathan, I'm done. No more lies."

I look over, confused. For the first time, I realize I'm genuinely nervous.

Katrina's mouth is set. She stares Noah Lippman dead in the eye. "You're the first person who's ever asked me directly," she goes on. "I've heard the rumors, I've had conversations around the subject. But never has anyone asked me outright."

I feel like I've glimpsed a wave the moment before it crushes me.

"I'm asking you outright," Noah says.

Katrina inhales and exhales. "Four years ago, I *was* in love with Nathan Van Huysen. We did not have an affair, but you can imagine how it would have been irresponsible to continue our partnership."

The current pulls me under.

Noah watches her, openmouthed. Then he commences writing furiously. If Chris is still listening, he doesn't make a sound.

I sit there saying nothing. The roaring in my ears is deafening. Katrina doesn't look at me, like the confession wasn't for me at all. It's heart-stopping, hearing those words she's never spoken. I never thought they were even possible, not with what she did to me. Confusion and joy threaten to tear me in two. She loved me.

Loved, past tense.

The follow-up question doesn't come from my lips. It comes from Noah's.

"You loved him four years ago," he says. His eyes dart in the direction of the kitchen, to the fiancé listening in. "How do you feel now?"

Standing sharply, Katrina lets her hands hang relaxed at her sides. "How do I feel now?" She laughs a little. "I guess you'll have to read the new book. It's the closest Nathan and I come to honesty."

She walks out of the room, heading straight for the stairs.

I sit, silent. While the waters her confession plunged me into have started to calm, I'm still deep beneath the surface. I float, suspended. For the first time, the first moment I can remember of my entire life, not a single sentence strings through my thoughts.

44

Katrina

I WALK UPSTAIRS to my room, feeling like I'm dreaming. It's not a nice dream. I hear my heartbeat thundering in my ears. When I close my bedroom door, my breathing unsteady, I press my palms to my face. Heat sings from my skin.

I can hardly believe what just happened. Years of silence and lies, and I finally, *finally* told the truth. I was downstairs in this house I almost hate, listening to the reporter's questions, knowing Chris was hearing every word of the lines we'd specifically prepared . . . and I couldn't do it. I couldn't stand the thought of one more half truth passing Nathan's lips, not when he's spilled his soul onto his pages in ways he never would out loud. I couldn't stand my own lies, either. The ones I tell myself about my feelings for Nathan, so familiar I sometimes forget they're lies.

Above all, I was done lying to myself about my relationship. Lying awake next to my fiancé last night, I realized with searing clarity I hate what we've become.

I don't move when I hear the door open.

"That was *brilliant*," Chris says, moving into the room with evident delight in his quick steps. "You knocked it out of the park. Really. Liz is going to be ecstatic." His green eyes glitter when they fix on me, waiting for me to share the victory.

This dream isn't over. Its warped energy compels my next words. I look up, right into Chris's chiseled face. "You honestly think I told a reporter I was in love with Nathan to make Liz happy?" I laugh, harsh and humorless. "I'm done. I'm done with this. It's over, Chris."

I watch him, cataloguing his every reaction. He's stunned. Not hurt, yet. Indignation and defensiveness steal into his features.

"You're firing me?" he says.

I say nothing. I don't know how I could have possibly been unclear. In my silence, Chris steps forward with a smile like dark honey.

"Kat, babe," he croons, "don't be ridiculous. Even if you did fire me, I'd still be the agent on this deal. You know it's my contract."

I step back, like we're partners in a spiteful dance. "That's really all you care about, isn't it?"

"Should I be ashamed for caring about my career?" His demeanor has darkened. "I know you don't relate, Katrina, but honestly. The rest of us want to succeed. You just want to hide."

It is, surprisingly, what I needed. His cruelty is liberating. It opens up something in me, some spring from which joy surges forth. I knew what I wanted to do. Now I have the strength to do it.

"I'm not firing you, asshole," I say.

Wordlessly, I reach down to my left hand, where I wrench off the diamond engagement ring I've had for two very long years. I hold the piece of jewelry out to him, no uncertainty in my intention.

"We're done," I say softly.

Chris falters. I see some cord in him snap, and rage hurtles into his eyes. "Now that's a fucking joke. What? For Nathan?" He doesn't take the ring.

It's perfectly ironic. He's *jealous*? After weeks of saying I could do whatever I wanted with Nathan? Of course this is what gets to him. Chris wanted his future wife to be a writer. Having an affair didn't factor into it. But now, when that goal is taken from him—now, he's upset. "Not *for* anyone," I snap, placing the ring on the dresser. "Except for us. We don't work."

Chris squares his shoulders. "I stood by you when you were nothing. When you couldn't even get out of bed. When you cried to me, saying you'd never write again. When you weren't yourself, I stayed. Now, you're back to writing, and *you're* done with *me*? Fucking hilarious, Katrina."

"I *was* myself," I reply hotly. "You just didn't like who I'd become."

He slams his fist on the dresser, which rattles against the wall. The ring jumps. I can't help startling. I step backward, half fearful. While I know Chris would never hurt me, this conversation is going nowhere productive.

Nathan appears in the doorway, obviously having heard the commotion. I sense something raging under the flat stone of his expression. For a fragile second, his eyes meet mine.

"Chris, I think you'd better leave," he says. "Cool off."

Chris whirls. "This is *my* house. You may have fucked my fiancée, but you do not tell me what to do." He strikes the final syllables furiously.

Nathan doesn't flinch. "I saw Noah out," he replies calmly, "but I could invite him back in. I'm certain he'd find something of interest here."

Hate simmering in his eyes, Chris stares at Nathan. Like he's flipped some switch in frustration, he grabs his leather duffel in a rush. "We'll discuss this later," he says, his words for me and his eyes everywhere else, "after you've had a chance to think about what you're doing." Without offering me the chance to reply—and without picking up the ring—he strides out, his shoulder hitting Nathan's as he passes him.

His footsteps pound the stairs on his way down. Nathan heads into the hallway, following from a careful distance. I stay rooted in place. The room is silent. I hardly recognize the way my heartbeat picks up. Lightness fills my chest, spreading into my shoulders, lifting my head while I stare out the empty doorway.

I hear the front door slam, and all I feel is unbearable relief.

45

Nathan

I WATCH OUT the front window until Chris gets into his Uber X, the SUV's rear door flying closed behind him. My emotions are moving fast. I can't hold on to them, can't even name them. First Katrina's confession, then the words I overheard from their room, now her ex-fiancé leaving the house in a furious huff—it's nothing I ever dared imagine.

I walk upstairs. When I reach the doorway, I find Katrina having hardly moved.

Her face is flushed, her eyes weary. When I see her, one emotion finally overpowers the others in me. It's heartache. Not for myself—for her. I remember staring down the end of my marriage, standing exactly where she is, looking into the future and the past simultaneously from the place where they split. Whatever my hidden hopes and wishes, what Katrina's going through is not happy.

I don't know what to say. I don't know how to be here for her without seeming like I'm celebrating or gloating. Right now, I just want to be her friend.

After that . . . I'm afraid to admit what I might want to be.

Her eyes focus on me. She musters an exhausted smile, one I don't have the heart to return. "Well, I'm glad I never sent out invitations," she says.

Her humor, pained though it is, relieves me. I let out a laugh. "You didn't?" I joke. "I figured mine got lost in the mail."

She starts to laugh. Then everything catches up to her. I watch the realizations pummeling her, one on top of the next. Her entire vision of her life, vanished. The knowledge that this person she used to see nearly every day would become one she'd only speak to under the harshest of necessary circumstances. Her posture sags, not much—just enough that I know some spark sustaining her has gone out.

She drops down onto the edge of the bed, and her eyes glaze over. I stand, helpless. I want to tell her she'll be okay, that she'll feel like her life has fallen apart, but she can choose every piece with which she reassembles it. I want to tell her she deserves love she never had with Chris.

But I can't tell her those things. Because everything I say in this moment will be colored by her confession downstairs.

She needs space, not pressure to face what she said. To reckon with the new reality her words might have wrought between us.

"What do you want to do now?" I ask. It's a direct question, the kind she told Noah Lippman she didn't get enough of. While there's plenty we need to discuss, those conversations will come with time.

Which we now have, I realize. I don't need to leave her life when we leave Florida. Or . . . maybe she'll want to leave Florida tomorrow. Without Chris pressuring her, maybe she won't even want to finish the book. The possibility terrifies me. It's like I've just remembered I'm perched somewhere high over the ground, like I've just caught my first perilous glimpse down.

Katrina lifts her gaze, her expression now focused. "I want to write," she says firmly.

Her response floods me with a painful rush of relief. "Katrina, we can take the day off. We can take however much time you want off."

"No." She stands up. "I want to write now. Today. I . . ." She goes unfocused for a second, like the fragile scaffolding of her composure is shaking. "It's the only part of my life I understand." When she meets my eyes, I know what else she's really saying. We still need to sort out where we stand, but I understand what she needs. Sometimes processing emotions is easier on the page.

I feel undeniable pride hearing this resolve from the woman who'd retired from writing. She's finding herself, pushing past the ways in which we got in the way. I nod, letting myself smile.

"Then let's write," I say.

46

Katrina

• FOUR YEARS EARLIER •

WE'RE JUST DAYS from finishing *Only Once.* This has my emotions erratic, uncontrollable, like the needle on whatever internal sensor measures my feelings is wavering wildly. There's joy and relief, the inevitable counterpoints of finishing a novel, sharpened but simultaneously undercut by the expectations heaped on this book. Then there's looming depression I can see clouding the horizon. Without *Only Once* to work toward, to focus on each day, I'll be untethered, drifting out to sea. I'll return home, leaving this house, leaving this piece of my life. Leaving Nathan.

He sits at the end of the table, typing furiously, running his hands through his hair. It's the middle of the day, the summer warmth coating every surface of every room. Despite the heat, I feel a chill. I'll still see Nathan in New York, I know. It'll just be different.

Nathan breaks off typing, looking up at me. "Stuck on something?" he asks. "Is it because of my changes to the next scene—"

I cut him off. "No, it fits perfectly. I'm just done."

He pauses. "Already? Are you trying to make me feel threatened, Freeling?" He cocks his head, smiling slightly.

I grin. "Trying to impress you, more like."

"As if you don't impress me every day."

He returns to his computer like he doesn't know his words have warmed my skin. I privately soak in them. The moment doesn't last long. Sighing, Nathan closes his computer.

"I'm going for a run. Then I'll finish this scene," he declares.

"Okay," I say.

"Soon, um . . ." Something serious, even slightly uncomfortable, enters his voice. "We should talk about how much time we want to take before starting the next book. At this rate, we'll finish *Only Once* within the week."

The chill returns. Colder, deeper. Panic runs tremors through my hands, rattling my fingers, which I hope I've hidden well enough under the table for Nathan not to notice. I nod soundlessly, feeling pathetic. I just can't fight how little I'm looking forward to the life waiting for me outside Florida. I don't want to go home.

Nathan starts to stand.

I stop him, placing my hand on his thigh.

When he stills immediately, I recognize what I've done. I've never touched him this way, ever. Why I did now is something I understand only in the heated haze of instinct.

I'm not sure if it means anything. I'm not sure it *doesn't* mean anything.

"I don't want to take a break," I say. "I want to start the next book as soon as possible."

I meet his eyes. He swallows. The moment stretches, and I expect it to bend under the weight of so many unsaid things. But it doesn't. I remove my hand, knowing I've left it too long.

"I'd like that," Nathan replies. "What do you want us to write next?"

I hear the question within the question. Not which of our half-finished outlines I've chosen, which jotted-down plot I'm sparking to. What he wants to know has nothing to do with books.

Neither does what I say in response. It comes out breathless. "Anything. Everything."

In my head, I go on. I unravel hopes, hidden fantasies, precious imaginings. *I want a whole life with you. Not guilty sentences shoved under closed doors. Not characters speaking our secret confessions.*

Nathan and I are speaking in code. It would be completely outlandish to think anyone else would understand what we're saying in this discussion of what sounds like our writing career. But I'm not having this conversation with anyone else. I'm having it with Nathan.

And Nathan and I have been speaking in code for years.

The messages may have started innocently, the ways we would say *I'm grateful for you* or *I'm proud of you* in every "good line" we'd scratch onto each other's pages, or every check mark I learned to recognize meant Nathan liked something I'd written. Then they started to change. Started to deepen. They became the kind of messages *only* fit for code. Edits intertwining like embraces. Dreams on and off the page. *Sorry to steal your dress. But you look nice.*

I hold Nathan's gaze in the space separating us. Watching his eyes light up, I see the moment it happens. The fantasy in my head merges with the one forming in his. Suddenly we're filling in each other's hopes, detailing each other's dreams with devotion like I never would have thought myself capable of feeling. It's impossible for me to read his mind, to know his heart. But I do. Because we've had years of practice. Imagining together is what Nathan and I do.

It's how I know he hears everything I'm not saying. He confirms it when he speaks next.

"I'll need a couple weeks to . . . resolve things at home," he says. "Then, I'm yours."

More code, though not the sort only cowriters could decipher. When I felt the first flickers of something in my heart for Nathan, I wondered if I wanted him to leave his wife for me. I decided I didn't. It sickened me. I knew I needed to hide my feelings until they faded.

Except they never did. This veiled dialogue, this dance of intimations and looks, is the only way I could possibly imagine communicating this. The truth. The one I couldn't imagine speaking out loud.

I'm in love with you, Nathan Van Huysen.

It's been true for longer than I've wanted to recognize. Weeks, maybe. Maybe more, subconsciously. In the space of writing *Only Once*, something has shifted. I'd hidden it even from myself, especially from Nathan, until this one wild moment, when I could hide it no longer.

Now, Nathan *resolving things at home* still gives me no pleasure, but I know it's what's fair for everyone. Not that he's ever told me out loud his feelings have changed. If they have, though, we can't continue this way. Can't continue pretending we have two lives—with different homes, different relationships, different futures—when really, we've begun living one.

Nathan stands. This time, I let him. My skin still feels hot from where my hand rested on his thigh.

I don't know when it will stop.

47

Katrina

• PRESENT DAY •

NATHAN DIDN'T GO for his run. It's past midnight, and we're still writing. My vision stings from the searing white of my computer screen and the halogen glow of the overhead lights. Pink has started to spread on the skin of my pained knuckles.

Nathan, sitting on the couch, has made no move to head for bed. I have the sense he would stay here writing with me through the night if I wanted, which part of me does. I'm dreading returning to the bed I woke up with Chris in just this morning, slipping under sheets with his scent still on them. I know I'll have to, of course. I just don't want to. Here with Nathan, words spilling out from my fingers and into the story we're building together, is the only place I feel like I belong.

I'm writing scenes from Evelyn and Michael's divorce. I do so with the joyful recklessness I've felt coursing through me since I called off my engagement. For years, I was trying so hard to want only the things I thought were safe enough to have. But it wasn't wanting, I've realized. It was hiding. Hiding from myself, from what my heart craved so desperately it terrified me.

I'm not terrified now.

Seeing my computer's battery is displaying four percent, the flat metal underside hot on the skin of my knees, I close the screen instead of getting my charger. Straightening up in my armchair, I say, "Nathan."

He looks up. For someone who's obviously exhausted, he really is unfairly good-looking. I let myself enjoy the sight for a moment—why shouldn't I? Nighttime stubble shades the hard line of his jaw. His blue eyes gleam with lingering inspiration.

He notices my closed computer. "Done for the night?" he asks.

"You haven't said anything about what I admitted in the interview. I apologize if it was . . . a shock. I kind of figured you knew," I say. "Nevertheless, it wasn't the right way to tell you."

He slides his computer onto the cushion next to him and focuses on me. "I haven't said anything not because I didn't want to. But . . ." His eyes dart from mine for a second and return. "Shit, Kat, you've had a huge day. I didn't want to make it about me."

"I wouldn't mind if it were about you," I reply.

In the silence while Nathan studies me, I'm left with the whisper of the ocean. "Okay," he says.

He takes a breath. I know he's composing his thoughts, writing them out in his head, imagining them solid on crisp white pages.

"I'm not very good at speaking my feelings," he finally says. "I've known since I was young how much better I am on the page. In life I'm . . . less. I'm not the man I want to be."

"You're wrong," I say.

It cuts him off, halting the pages flipping in his mind.

"You're everything in person you are on the page," I continue, gathering conviction. Memories charge my words. Cafés and late nights and laughter. Sand and storms. "I've seen you. You're charming and graceful and . . . incredible." He flushes, pleased, color rising up his neck. "I just wish we spoke to each other somewhere other than . . . here." I pick up my computer, placing it on the coffee table.

He rubs the stubble I was just noticing. "It's just easy to say things you don't mean, and it's impossible to write anything but the truth."

"We write fiction, Nathan," I say gently. "It's not real."

"It *is*. How can you say what we write isn't real?" The intensity in his voice feels like an answer for the years of resentment he harbored for me. I can see now how we were standing on opposite sides of the truth, each of us alone. "Kat, really." He sighs, softening. "Is now the best time for this?"

"I'm done living my life waiting for the best time." It's a new decision, one I'm proud of.

Nathan doesn't flinch from what I'm saying. He looks me right in the eye. "Fine," he says. "Here's the whole truth. I thought I was over you. When you tossed me out of your life, I told myself you destroyed us. I believed it every day until I came back here. Writing about how pieces of love survive even the cleanest break, how you can never escape someone you gave your whole self to . . . Katrina, I don't know. I don't know if I wrote myself into this book or if the book uncovered something within me."

He drops his head into his hands.

Sliding out of the armchair, I don't fight the pull I feel toward him. My legs don't shake as I approach him. He doesn't look at me. Or maybe he won't. I need him to see me, though. I need us both to face this.

I sink to my knees in front of him.

I tentatively touch his arm. Finding me close, he startles. He doesn't pull away from me, doesn't move, doesn't dare breathe. "Maybe it's time we find out what exactly is real here," I say, my voice hushed.

His eyes dip to my lips, betraying him before he speaks. "Katrina. Kat . . ."

From sitting back on my heels, I rise onto my knees, my face close to his, my hands resting on the cool fabric of his pants. He spreads his thighs just wide enough for me to press myself between his legs. "I need to know," I murmur. Remembering our night in Miami, I don't close the distance.

I don't have to. I feel his resolve snap. His hands cupping my face, he crushes his lips to mine, every single word we've ever written prologue to this touch.

I wind a hand into his hair, knowing it's a favorite detail of his, one he's sent me in scenes like this one. I feel him exhale into me in pleasure, his lips sliding over mine. In return, he settles into long, deep kisses, his tongue brushing mine in only the suggestion of more. I smile, recognizing my own descriptions plagiarized on my mouth. We know exactly how the other likes to be touched. We've read each kiss, studied every caress. The result is the feeling of a first kiss with someone you've kissed a hundred times.

The whisper of the ocean sounds like a roar when I pull back. It's not because I don't want to keep going. I just know we shouldn't, not tonight, with Chris's departure still fresh, with his ring still on my dresser upstairs.

"Real?" Nathan's voice is a rasp.

"Yes," I breathe.

Nathan nods. His hair sticks up where my hand gripped him only seconds ago. "Where does this leave us?"

I stand, smoothing down my skirt. "I . . . have no idea."

We regard each other for a few moments, contemplating what just happened, neither of us speaking. It's quiet, not forebodingly, yet not quite comfortably. It's just the quiet of *before*. Finally, Nathan's lips twitch up. "We've been working without an outline so far. Why stop now?"

I start to smile. "No reason I can figure. Good night, Nathan."

I step toward the stairs. "See you in the morning," I hear him say behind me.

I feel my smile spread as I climb the steps. His words promise a world of possibilities. I let myself imagine each one, sketching out our future like a plot without an ending.

48

Nathan

• FOUR YEARS EARLIER •

I WATCH THE water under the clear night sky. The beach is empty, unsurprisingly. It's only me, sitting on the sand. The glassy ocean reflects the moon, ribbons of moonlight shimmering with the small ripples on the surface. There's something unnerving in the calm of being here, just myself, with this endless expanse. For the moment, it's mine, and yet I know it's very much not.

We finished the book today. Months of writing, outlining, discussion, and debate—ended with the final period on the final sentence. The white space following it no longer felt demanding. Only right. The ceiling fan spinning lazily, sunlight slanting in through the shutters, we were done. The book is everything I hoped it would be, the perfect mirror of what we'd envisioned in our heads.

It's extraordinarily rare, I know. Usually the creation comes out somehow skewed from what was planned, requiring some strange getting used to for the creator. Not *Only Once*. I feel like it's come from outside of ourselves, the way Michelangelo spoke of releasing his figures from the marble instead of sculpting them himself. I don't need publicists or editors to know it's going to be huge, either. I know it will.

When we finished our debut, Katrina and I celebrated by ordering too much food and trying to bake brownies. We fucked them up. I tend to underbake, while Katrina leaves every edge hard and crispy. Tonight, though, we didn't celebrate, I think because we knew bigger celebrations are coming. We quietly submitted the book, Katrina writing the email to Liz while I changed into my jogging clothes upstairs. Once I'd read it over quickly, we hit send without ceremony. I wanted to hug Katrina. I didn't. I told her I was heading out for my run.

Instead, I walked to the nearest beach. The evening cool enveloped me as I crossed streets, making my way through the quiet neighborhood. Everything felt strangely normal, dinners being finished in the windows of warmly lit dining rooms. The faint, grating hum of cicadas. When I reached the beach, I dropped down onto the sand.

I'm sitting close to the shoreline, facing out. The sand is cold under my legs, or my skin is on fire. I can't tell which it is. Inside the house Katrina and I have called home for the past couple of months, I feel like I'm constantly on fire. Like my mind is shredded from the effort of fighting my own thoughts. Like I'm waging war every second of every day on my deepest instincts, trying to turn myself into someone else entirely.

I'm losing the fight. I realized it last week when Katrina touched my leg. When she told me she wanted everything. *Everything.* I felt the innermost part of me wave its smallest white flag.

I knew what she meant. She knew I knew what she meant. It's Katrina. We've known what each other means for years, made a career of it. If I had to guess, I'd say she understood there was no room for miscommunication or uncertainty in the unsaid things we exchanged in our short conversation. Things I had tried to ignore in myself.

Finishing the book today, I knew I couldn't. I could taste my dreams coming true, and it made me realize how much *more* I wanted.

I stare out, following the black horizon. It reaches forever. My eyes wander over the scatter of stars, my mind wandering with them, elsewhere entirely. *New York.* Where we'll return, where we'll live our lives in parallel lines—latitudes running through exchanged emails written from separate homes, working lunches in our respective neighborhoods, conference calls on speakerphone—until finally, we'll reach our own horizons. Side by side but never crossing.

I want everything with her, too. The weight of this knowledge is physically painful. Not just the next book, the next contract, the next review. Not just more time in this house. I want to live my life entwined with hers, chasing her, leading her. I want to willingly allow my thoughts to stray to the soft skin on the back of her neck, or the way the ends of her hair stick to her sweat in the humidity. I can't keep writing with her, can't keep constructing this career with her. Not like this.

Because I'm in love with her.

I exhale, my head dropping to my chest. Just letting myself think those words splits open the dam within me, the feelings released rushing mercilessly over the floodplains of my soul. They're uncontainable. I couldn't ever possibly push them away again. Which means I need to face some harsh realities.

Melissa. My heart cracks for her, knowing what I have to do. I love her, if not in the soul-deep way I love Katrina. I don't want to hurt her. She's likely home right now, decompressing from her workday, heating up noodles from the place on our corner while Netflix plays. Distracting herself from her one-person dinner. The ordinary effort of it makes my eyes water. I thought I meant the promises I made on our wedding day. I'm realizing now that I didn't.

The thought casts me far out to sea. Its enormity is impossible to contend with, like looking out on ocean in every direction. There's nothing to do but let it swallow me. Tread water until I sink under.

And in the depths, I feel a new current pulling me down. Katrina—I don't know whether she feels the way I do. The uncertainty is impossibly powerful, consuming. We've never actually voiced feelings for each other. While I've guessed I could read her thoughts, and guessed she could read mine, I can't. Not really. We've exchanged the most personal writings one could, but I can't know for certain the emotions in them exist outside of ink on paper.

But whether she does or doesn't won't change the fate of my marriage. I know that now. I can't stay with Melissa, because I'm in love with someone else. If Katrina doesn't feel the same way, I'll lose my writing partnership *and* I'll lose my marriage, because it would be the worst sort of unfair to reduce the woman I wedded to a backup. A contingency.

If Katrina does feel the way I do . . .

The idea is unfathomable.

If Katrina does share my feelings, I'll make sure nothing happens between us until the final divorce papers are signed. Nothing, *never.* It's the one thing I can do for Melissa. I won't cheat on her.

Standing, I walk into the water. I can't confess my feelings to Katrina just yet. The enormity of them is just . . . too much. Feeling them, recognizing them in their own right, is like staring into the sun. Uncomfortable, even unmanageable. I need some sort of remove to keep them from wrecking me.

I've lived a lifetime of finding that remove in fiction. Putting these emotions onto the page is how I'll keep them from overwhelming me.

Besides, while I'm still married, the only way I can process these feelings is by writing them. I can put them into my craft, and Katrina will understand. She knows what I'm saying in every way I say it.

The water washes up, bathing my feet in the cold of complete clarity.

It shocks my system, the night narrowing down to what I need to do next.

I lift my head, finally feeling as serene as the ocean. Facing the sand, I walk up the beach. I'll return to the house, to my room, to my desk, where I'll pour my heart out, naked and vulnerable. The book is finished, but my most important work is not yet over.

I'm not done writing for the night.

49

Nathan

• PRESENT DAY •

I LEAVE THE house early the next morning, my sleep-fogged thoughts full of the *New York Times* interview, Chris's departure, my evening with Katrina. There's no way I'm hazarding crossing paths with her now-ex-fiancé, who's returning to talk things through with her today.

If I dwell on what their conversation might contain—on whether a night's sleep has changed Katrina's feelings, or whether the full arsenal of Chris's fraternity-president charms will weaken her resolve—I'll go wild.

Only the memory of her lips hot on mine steadies me. Or perhaps *steadies* is the wrong word. It was my happiest of dreams come to life. The kiss felt unreal and impossibly real, past whatever I could have conceived. The unbelievable softness of her lips, from which I'd heard laughter and phenomenal genius, now welcoming mine, letting me drink in her breath and the scent of her. The smooth skin of her cheeks. The way she moved, hesitant yet sure.

Now instead of imagining those details, I'm imagining losing them. I'm scared, and I hate it.

I flee from the feelings, driving with my convertible's top down into the neighborhood, which, remarkably, doesn't seem to know I kissed my best friend last night. Bicycles pass me on the other side of the street, their bells ringing. Seagulls cry. Music plays behind screen doors. The palm trees sway with what looks like relaxation. I fixate on the sights and sounds, and on Katrina's hand in my hair last night, until I reach where I'm going. I park the car and spring out of my seat.

When Harriet opens her front door, she sees me, and immediately, she smiles.

"You fucking did it, didn't you?" she says, sounding smug.

Without waiting for my reply, she nudges open the screen. I follow her inside. "What do you mean?"

"You're, like, *glowing.*" Harriet pulls a disgusted expression.

"No, I'm not," I scoff. I don't feel like I'm glowing. I feel like I'm incandescent, exploding with light.

Harriet is unmoved. "Don't bullshit me, Van Huysen. Did you two bang or not?"

I would laugh if I weren't entirely wrapped up in myself. Instead, I only feel my eyebrows rise. I dodge her gaze, walking farther into her entryway, where I inspect the vase on the table with interest. "We didn't—bang," I say. "We just . . ."

"Oh god," she moans. "You kissed. Somehow that's worse."

"How is it worse?" I ask, straightening up from the vase.

She gives me a flat look. "I can just imagine how romantic it was." She shudders. "It was probably tender and shit. You probably made a weird amount of eye contact. I'm guessing you haven't stopped thinking about it since."

I say nothing. I follow her into the kitchen, where I find champagne and a flute sitting on the counter. Smothering a smile, I face her. "Isn't champagne a little much for the occasion?"

Even for Harriet, the eye roll she executes is grand. "The champagne isn't because you kissed Katrina, asshole. It's because I sold a book." With sudden stiffness, she threads her hair over her ear. "Just got the news."

I'm stunned silent for a second. In the pause, she reaches for another flute and pours champagne for both of us. "I—" I falter, finally composing myself. "Congratulations, Harriet. That's fantastic."

She raises her glass in a quick *cheers* gesture, then sips. "Yeah, I'm pretty stoked, honestly."

"Why didn't you say you were writing something new?" The question surfaces from me once I've checked over my memories of every recent conversation with Harriet. We've talked about her teaching, her previous book . . . Nothing new. Before *Only Once* and everything, I remember how feverishly intense she would look when she was laboring on some new idea. They consumed her so much we couldn't help but discuss plot points, world details, or character choices whenever we would get together. The past few weeks have been the opposite.

She only shrugs in response to my question. "I wasn't sure how real our friendship was."

I open my mouth then close it.

There was nothing incriminating in Harriet's reply, nor is there in her expression. She waits calmly for my response. It's the nice counterpart to her cutting frankness and wit—she doesn't hide grudges or deal in ominous insinuations.

I set my glass down, feeling shitty for not knowing she'd been writing, shitty for giving her reason to not tell me, shitty for not even understanding that I had. "I'm . . . sorry, Harriet," I say, meaning it. I've relied on her one-sidedly—I mean, I'm standing in her kitchen *uninvited* because I drove over on instinct when I needed distraction. "It's my fault. Sincerely."

Narrowing, her gaze returns to me. "What's going on here?" She purses her lips, sipping once more from her glass. "We don't actually *talk about* our problems."

She's right. Now is different. "It's something I'm trying out," I say honestly.

She regards me, something surgical in her inquisitiveness, like she's peeling past my words to find their heart. "This is related to Katrina somehow," she says. Before I can reply, she waves her hand, flippant again. "On second thought, I don't want to know."

"I shouldn't have dropped our friendship because I couldn't face things with Katrina," I say, pressing past her redirection. While I'm not used to this kind of opening, I have momentum now. I'm not giving it up. "You have to know it wasn't about you."

"Yeah, that's the problem," Harriet returns, the first hint of frustration entering her voice. "It *wasn't* about me. Everything in your and Katrina's lives is about each other. Whether you're friends with me, whether you're not friends with me—it all comes down to what's happening between you two."

I rub my neck. Guiltily, I understand exactly what she's saying. I remember how often over the past few years I've congratulated myself on not missing my friendship with Katrina, on how much happier working on my own makes me, only to realize I was still . . . fixating on Katrina. Harriet's called me out on my myopia, and it feels like a kick in the gut. "I know I've been a shitty friend," I say feebly, "but I want to point out I've hung out with you this whole trip, even while Katrina and I hated each other."

"*Oh my god,*" Harriet snaps. "You literally never hated each other."

This stops me. *It felt like hatred*, I want to say. Except I don't. Because . . . I know, deep down, it never really did.

"You're writing a book about divorce," Harriet continues, "and somehow it's the most romantic book I've ever read." The gentle sincerity in her voice gets me to pull my eyes from the window overlooking her pool, where I've had them fixed like a penitent kid in the principal's office, and study her expression. She looks a little sad. "You and Katrina are incapable of hating each other," she says.

Heat steals up my neck, into my cheeks. Harriet's small smile confirms she's noticed. Was I really so easy to read? I've practiced nestling characters' innermost insecurities and instincts under layers of coping mechanisms, obfuscations, unreliable narration. Was every one of my own emotions just scrawled over me for everyone to see? I thought I was submerging them in fiction. It turns out I wasn't hiding anything.

Not the point, I remind myself. "Regardless, Harriet," I say. "You're my friend. I'm going to do everything I can not to fuck it up, but if I do, I want you to call me on it. Right now"—needing her to know I mean every word, I steady my voice—"we're going to celebrate your book deal. We're not going to talk about Katrina. We're going to drink champagne, and we're going to commemorate how fucking great it is my friend sold her next literary sensation."

Harriet laughs. I'm inexpressibly glad. Downing her drink, she points the rim of her empty flute in my direction. "I like that plan," she pronounces. "But first"—she narrows her eyes, sly—"I have to know. How was it?"

I'm opening my mouth to protest when she holds up a hand.

"*Do not* give me that I-don't-kiss-and-tell crap," she commands. "You're a writer. One way or another, you write every one of your experiences down for the whole world to read."

Defeated, I can't help grinning. It's extraordinary, really, how well Harriet has put into words what I'd hoped Katrina understood last night, what I was too full of feeling to express outright. She'd wondered whether what we had was real or fiction, but the question collapses into itself. Fiction comes from truth. It is a wonderful, imaginative, flourishing thing grown from a seed of real feelings, real desires, real fears. No artist ever creates from nothing. We work from what we've experienced, inspired by the unique piece of the world we see. It's why art cannot be replicated. And it's why what Katrina and I had was always real, even when it was only on the page.

"I'm not sure you want to know," I say.

Harriet smiles while she pours her next glass of champagne. "That good, then?"

Images and raw feeling flood me. When Katrina's hand was in my hair, I found myself in the eye of the storm and within the whirlwind at once. The ocean, the night, everything followed our rhythm, echoing how we breathed into each other. It was like fiction. It was magic and it was life.

"That good," I repeat.

"Gross," Harriet says fondly. "I'm happy for you. You certainly waited long enough."

The truth is, I would've waited longer. For Katrina, I would've waited forever. "Enough about me," I say instead. "Let's talk about your book. Tell me everything."

Harriet's smile softens. Her eyes start to sparkle. While she speaks, I hold dearly onto every word, hoping with every minute I'm showing her how I won't cut her out the way I wish I never had. It's nice—I feel present. With the pink flowers rustling out Harriet's kitchen window, the sunlight warming the room, I recognize I'm living my own life, the one I'm learning to pull off the page.

50

Katrina

• FOUR YEARS EARLIER •

WHEN NATHAN RETURNED from his run, his hair windswept, he rushed upstairs. I couldn't help smiling. It was perfectly Nathan. The night we turn in something huge, he's springing upstairs to start something. I recognized the fresh frenzy of inspiration in him. I've seen it in the seat next to mine on international flights, on mornings when he stands in front of his computer, coffee untouched on the counter, in his pajamas, too consumed by his ideas to move. It's incredible, if also unnerving.

I didn't hear from him for the rest of the night. When I return upstairs from grabbing a glass of water before bed, I notice his door ajar, his light still on. It's nearly eleven—I was reading, engrossing myself in one of the books I'd packed but not found the time to open.

Past the door, I see half of him. He's hunched over his desk, writing under the yellow light. I notice he's not on his computer. His hand flies over the page of the leather-bound journal he uses for brainstorming and freewriting whenever he's working through something big.

I knock lightly on the door, which swings open. "You seem inspired," I say.

He straightens up. When he spins to face me in his chair, I falter. His expression is unusually electric, even for Nathan. "Yeah . . ." he says. "Just finishing something. Are you going to sleep?" He seems to force his words past ideas or feelings moving impossibly fast.

I don't know how to read his demeanor, whether he's distracted or excited or nervous. Why he would be nervous, though, I can't figure.

"I'll stay up for a bit," I say uncertainly.

"Good. Great," he says emphatically, like my response was very important. "Wait one second." While I linger in the doorway, he returns to his journal, where he scrawls one more sentence then caps his pen. I'm confused when he rips the page out, tearing it carefully so the edge is neat.

Stunned silent, I watch him stand. He looks the page over briefly before his eyes find mine. The molecules in the room seem to still while he walks the single sheet over to me. For the next few seconds, we face each other, saying nothing. I have the wild impression he might kiss me.

He doesn't, of course. In one rushed movement, he shoves the page into my hand. "I'll be up for a little while," he says. "If you want to . . . discuss this."

I nod, searching his expression. Something is different. I feel I'm on the edge of a precipice I can't see, just waiting to step into open air. Whatever waits past the drop I know instinctively is nothing Nathan will say out loud. He's returning to his desk, closing his journal.

The single page feels hot in my hand.

51

Katrina

• PRESENT DAY •

I've been sitting in the swing on the front porch for the past hour, watching the road. Chris has come and gone. He took his ring with him.

When he got here, we walked into the front room, where we sat in some sort of mutual understanding that our conversation wouldn't be fit for the friendlier, more private rooms of the house. My bedroom was his bedroom no longer.

I was prepared for the conversation to be unpleasant. It was, but not in the ways I'd expected. Chris had donned professionalism like a shield. Sitting up straight, his large frame nearly filled the front window. While my shorts and shirt were nothing out of the ordinary, I noticed how precisely he'd dressed, a lightly patterned button-down under his linen blazer. The only cracks in the façade were the dark rings encircling his eyes when he removed his gold sunglasses.

He wasn't emotional. He didn't try to change my mind. Voices were never raised. It hurt a little, how he wouldn't even fight for me. But he hadn't fought for me in years. If he had, we'd be married, or maybe just happier. I definitely wouldn't be in Florida, writing a book with Nathan. It's pointless to imagine the possibilities.

When Chris and I had said everything we needed to say, the room went quiet. He stood up from the couch. I walked him to the door, where I gave him the ring with dry hands. Not following him onto the porch, I let the screen door shut behind him.

For someone who's explored divorce and infidelity plenty in fiction, I was surprised to feel like I learned something from the end of my engagement. But I did.

I learned sometimes relationships don't die. They just don't grow. Kept from sunlight, from nourishment, they never flourish. Nothing is different today from how Chris's and my relationship has been for years. He was an easy presence in my life, someone who gave me the appearance of contentment. A walking résumé for a husband. He was successful, handsome, and smart. He was involved in my career—which wasn't hard since he was my agent. Above all, I knew he would never leave me.

I didn't know then what I do now. Never leaving someone isn't the same as loving them.

I lean into the swing, letting my head rest on the cushions, soaking in the sun. More conversations are coming, past curves in the road I can already make out from here. About our house in Los Angeles, what involvement he'll have in my literary career, the untangling of four years of life with another person. The prospect doesn't worry me, doesn't wind knots into my stomach or leave my muscles sore from stress. Chris was a future when I felt like I had none. Now I'm realizing I have as many futures as I want. I'm free to focus on one I've chosen, not one I've clung to like a life raft.

Hearing Nathan's car pulling into the driveway, I open my eyes. I smile when he cuts the engine, the Porsche's growl going silent. A lifetime ago, I sat right here, waited for and watched Nathan drive up exactly this way. It strikes me how many versions of us this neighborhood has seen. Younger writers tackling something new together, friends unsure how their relationship was changing, spiteful former colleagues forced into each other's company—and finally, whatever fragile, hopeful thing our relationship is now.

Nathan gets out of the car. On his way up to the porch, he skips the middle step. His eyes find me. When I beam, he physically relaxes, like he honestly thought I could be feeling any other way right now.

"Tell me you're not smiling because Chris won you back and you've set a date for your wedding," he says.

I hold up my ringless hand. "With that imagination, you should be a writer," I reply.

He laughs. It's loud, joyous, real. The sort of laugh I find myself caught up in—enough I nearly don't notice when he gently catches the hand I held up. Our humor subsides into soft smiles while he holds my fingers firmly in his.

"He's going back to LA," I say.

He nods. "What about you?"

Nathan's question holds several unsaid others. He wants to know if I'll be okay, if I'll have to endure nights down the hall from my ex-fiancé. There's more, though. He's feeling out what I want my future to look like.

My eyes leaving his, I glance to the house above us. "I'll have to move properly eventually," I say, "but for now, I might stay here for a while."

"Tell me when you want me to leave," Nathan says. There's no hidden spite in his voice, only understanding. "I would never want to impose."

I look right into the ocean blue of his eyes. "I think we have unfinished business first, don't you?"

He pulls me to my feet, which puts us very close together. His free hand finds my hip. If his eyes were the ocean before, now they're the midday sun sparking off the waves. I feel like I've never seen him this happy. Not when we've written something he's proud of, not when his publishing dreams started to come true.

I lean forward, pressing a kiss to his lips, marveling to myself. *I get to do this now.* It feels unreal, or half real, like I'm on the edge of a fairy tale. The dizzy expression on Nathan's face says he knows the feeling. Holding onto his hand, I lead him into the house.

We pause in the living room. When his eyes find mine, I only smile. I've felt lucky on plenty of occasions for what a wonderful writer Nathan is. For how he pushes me, fills in for me, inspires me. I don't know if I've ever let myself feel lucky for what a wonderful man he is. I let myself now. Facing me, he's like I've seen him on countless other mornings, looking comfortable in his white polo and gray shorts, watching me intently.

His voice is low, unsure. "Do you want to write?"

I laugh. It's comical how much we're not on the same page right now. While his eyebrows crinkle in confusion, he starts to smile. I nod to answer his question, saying nothing. There's something charged in the warmth of the room, static electricity stored in soft fabric. He releases my hand to pick up the pages he was editing this morning then sits on the couch.

Looking at him, I revel for a moment. For the first time in years, I know exactly what I want.

Stepping up to him, I put a hand on his pages. "No," I say, pushing the pages to the side. "Not like that."

I climb into his lap. My movements are slow, deliberate, showing him exactly what I mean. He takes me in, his expression greedy, his eyes lightly shocked in the best way. Like this is a fantasy he's kept even from himself. Heart pounding, I place my hands on his chest, feeling how firm he is. Warmth spreads through me. My limbs melt, my breath catching. When his hands slide up my thighs, skimming over skin and under my shorts, I feel the tremor in his touch, and suddenly every inch of me wants to shiver in this heat. Our eyes locked together, I lower my lips with obvious intention.

We collide, waves crashing, striking the shore—his hand rising swiftly, instinctively, up my back, pressing me to him while I kiss him. He leans into me, his mouth meeting mine. His other hand moves to hold my hair from falling forward. I grind my hips into his, where he's hard, unmistakably and urgently. Feeling light-headed, I pull back from the kiss to focus on his belt buckle.

He watches me. "I have a feeling we're about to become very unproductive."

My fingers fumbling the cool metal, I laugh. "Sorry our book was late, Liz. We were having vigorous, frequent sex."

He lifts my shirt over my head. I raise my arms with the same sort of instinct I feel driving his every movement. I want the garment off, nowhere near us, immediately. He uses the opportunity to press one quick kiss to my lips. "Don't even joke about it," he says.

"About what? Our book being late?"

"The other part." His hands dig into my hips.

"Do I seem like I'm joking?" I reach my hand down between us, watching his eyelids flutter closed while he lets out his breath, his grip on me tightening. "I'm not."

While I touch him, his mouth moves to my neck, causing me to arch my back into the contact. His fingers slide to my stomach, then sink lower, stroking me over the fabric of my shorts. I close my eyes. Knowing it's Nathan's fingers slowly undoing me, Nathan's lips meeting mine, feels like fiction—the kind you read with a hand between your legs, not the kind you get to taste on your tongue.

We pull back, panting and flushed. The mood shifts suddenly, like storm clouds opening up, the humidity splitting into rain. Gone is the humor, replaced by need. I stand up. While his stare drinks me in, I undo the button of my shorts, letting them drop to the floor.

Then I walk upstairs.

52

Katrina

• FOUR YEARS EARLIER •

I READ NATHAN'S pages standing in the middle of my room, lightheaded. I'm not sure if I'm imagining what's written, whether fever or fantasy have shifted the characters of something mundane into what's on the lightly creased paper clutched in my hand. When I finish my first read, I pause, then return to the opening lines, going slower, reaching to understand.

I don't recognize the characters' names. There's a man, Nick. A woman, Kelly. They're poets in New York City. It's no idea Nathan's ever pitched to me, probably one of hundreds I know he has hidden in his iPhone, or maybe something brand-new that's taken hold of him just now. His style runs within the syllables like electricity.

He's started right in the middle of a scene. Nick waits outside Kelly's door in the pouring rain. Slick with water, he's given her a letter, which he demands she read right in front of him.

Kelly,

While I write this, I feel the words in me desperate to come out. Pressing up to the gates of my pen, demanding to be written. But K, just because they're coming fast or fluid doesn't mean the feelings they express have reached me recently or easily. You're reading the direct line to my deepest truths. The fact they're finding their way onto the page quickly doesn't mean they haven't been burning in me for so long I don't remember when they started.

Honestly, I think every single word I've written since the day I met you has in some way been leading up to this. To you. To say you changed my life is the kind of understatement I could never permit myself to put in writing—you changed my entire world. You reached inside me with your words and your stories and wrote yourself onto my own soul. Before you, I was whole. I was one being, one heart. Now, I'm half of everything and greater for it.

I'm in love with you. I know we can't be together. Not yet. But if you tell me you feel even remotely the same way, then we will. Maybe you've never considered it, but I find it hard to believe that my feelings, screaming in my head night and day, leaking into my writing with a vulnerability that would embarrass me if your eyes weren't the ones reading them, sound only like a whisper to you.

If this is a surprise, forgive me. Read this. Consider everything, and write to me. I will understand whatever it is you tell me.

Writing alongside you is my greatest joy. Is it greedy to want more? You've changed every hope and dream I've ever chased—revised them to something smaller and yet more infinite. I want to write our lives together, K. To make each of my days a page written in your hand. To craft the chapters of my future with you in every word. Because I've realized a life lived with you is the best story I could ever tell.

Yours,

N

When I finish my second read, I find I'm crying.

Yours, N. Of course, he means "Nick."

Of course, he doesn't.

Overwhelmed, I sit down on my bed. I feel not quite in control of myself, the tremble in my lip, the force of the emotions clutching my windpipe. I feel like my heart is expanding so fast it hurts. The writing is stunning. It's the profoundest proclamation of love I've ever read. Which only moves me more. Because I know in every syllable, every choice, this could only ever have come from Nathan.

From Nathan, to me. These aren't just characters. He's talking to me through the page. They're his feelings—his feelings for me.

It's tremendous, terrifying joy. Everything I've been trying so hard not to hope for. Now I'm holding in my hands an entire future, a life, a dream. They feel as fragile and as real as the paper they're written on. I pause, the reality washing over me.

Then I rush to my desk. I pull one sheet of paper hurriedly from the printer. Pressing the tip of my pen to the page, I take a moment to figure out what I'm going to write. How to continue the story, to give *Kelly* her reply. I know what I feel. But the idea of giving those feelings voice is like contemplating the first brushstroke of the Sistine Chapel.

Of course I love him. I have novels' worth of what I want to say. Paragraphs and paragraphs, pages and pages I could compose from the stray thoughts I've caught in the corners of my mind when I'd let my guard down. Nathan wrote that his words were *pressing up to the gates* of his pen. My feelings are lined up behind the gates of my heart, except they're not pressing. They're pounding.

But when I focus on the page, nothing comes out.

I can't write. I find myself imagining precisely what will happen when I do.

I'll have everything I want.

The reality cools my mind. I push myself to render the details, just like if I were writing a scene. Nathan will return home, where he'll end his marriage. Then, after some weeks, some impossibly short time . . . he'll return to me. And he'll never leave. He's courteous enough that he'll give Melissa their apartment. He'll use my bathroom, watch TV from my couch, sleep under my white duvet. With me. I'll have him, then and forever.

In a year, *Only Once* is going to come out and be a huge success. I can feel it. Every single page is electric. The echo of finishing it today hasn't stopped reverberating in my ears. It'll change our careers. Change our lives.

For my entire professional life, I've stared up the side of this mountain I'm climbing with Nathan, finding clouds obscuring the summit. Now, the clouds have parted. The way is clear. I imagine reaching the peak not long from now, imagine how it'll feel gazing down from the dizzying height. I'll be struggling in the thin oxygen.

I feel paralysis seeping in even now. I *can't.* I can't have everything at once, everything I've ever wanted.

Especially not when Nathan's put his promises into words like these. Whatever he thinks he feels is too wrapped up in a story he's telling himself, the story of us. It's plain in the pages in front of me. He couldn't even put his feelings for me down without fictionalizing them. *That's* how real they are.

But real life is everything else. Everything continuing on once the story ends. I'm not certain which one Nathan wants, the story or the everything else.

The pen falls from my hand. What I've been feeling this summer was, I realize, just the ominous pull of the current. Now I'm swept off my feet. Sucked out into very deep water. The future is overwhelming, suddenly *here*, daunting and mine to lose. And I'm thrashing furiously under the surface, not sure which way is shore. And I'm *scared*.

Because the true, true horror, the one seemingly no one realizes but me, is that once you have your dreams, all you have left is the chance to lose them. It's inevitable. Losing writing will hurt. Losing Nathan—

It's like some switch flips in me, leaving me unfairly furious. He put his words down on paper, where they're fucking perfect, immaculately unmistakable—where they're fiction.

Where they're easy to destroy.

I walk downstairs, my heart pounding, my head memorizing every single word written on the page in my hand. The living room is dark. One forgotten coffee mug sits on the side table. There's something foreboding in how normal everything looks, like it's ready to be disrupted. I walk to the fireplace we've never once used.

Hands shaking, I reach for the lighter.

This way, Nathan can return to his wife, to the life that's real. This way, I'll fall from a lower height, one I can survive.

It takes me two tries for the lighter to spark in the dark frame of the fireplace.

When it does, the flame burns steady.

53

Nathan

• PRESENT DAY •

KATRINA WALKS FIVE or six steps in front of me. In the hallway, I follow her outline, my heart like a drum.

She leads us into my bedroom, not hers. The choice is inspired, of course. It's utterly sexy, the confidence, the self-possession of taking me to *my* bed to sleep with me. When I walk in, she's sitting up on the bed, wearing nothing except her underwear. Her eyes fix on me with gentle invitation, her legs folded loosely under her—the legs I've watched her reposition countless times while we work, except now they're bare, only one soft triangle of fabric separating me from what I want.

I linger in the doorway, trying to memorize every detail. The waterfall of her hair spilling over her shoulder, brushing the tops of her breasts. The hinting curve of her rib cage under her bra.

But my body wins out. I'm pulled forward, hands finding those curves, my lips crushing to hers. She kisses me fiercely, clinging to me, her hands taut in the fabric of my shirt.

Which I tear off. I catch her leaning forward in one smooth motion, reaching—her bra falls, her wonderfully soft chest meeting mine when I pull her to me. When I reach up, caressing, the small, gasping moan I hear escape her undoes me.

"Fuck," I say into her neck. She lifts her chin, the motion perfectly synchronous with mine, like we've practiced this dance. It might be because we have in dreams—I know I have. But I don't think it's why we know each other's movements before they happen. Why her fingers find mine to interlace over her breast. Why she knows to spread her knees when I reach to cup her lower down.

I think it's the gift of being *us*. We've expected, examined, chased each other's instincts on the page so often we've internalized them. We write like we're one. Now, we're moving like we're one.

"Yeah," she pants, nodding. "Fuck."

I laugh while I figure out why this is funny, pausing only to join her in quick, deep kisses. "I'm glad we agree on the word choice," I say.

She grins, then pretends to contemplate, leaving me to continue kissing her neck. "Hmm," she says. "Now I'm not sure. Could we try a few synonyms?"

"I'll have you trying plenty of synonyms when I get these off," I say, tugging her underwear up teasingly from her hip. She laughs, spontaneous and real, and it's the greatest sound I've ever heard. It makes me crush her to me, feeling her small body shake with the echoes of humor and delight—which of course change to a pleased whimper when skin meets skin down the whole length of our chests.

She pulls away from me. From the spark in her eyes I know instantly she's not done with the joke. "No elaborate metaphors, okay?" she demands. "When you talk dirty to me, I want it *normal*. No trying to win the Pulitzer Prize. Just sexy. Got it?"

"Good note," I reply with faux-fancy respectfulness, imitating the tone everyone would use in creative writing courses. "Just sexy. I'll workshop it in."

"Yeah." Kat nods. "Workshop it in, Van Huysen."

We've separated for this repartee, her fingers still interwoven with one of my hands while my other holds the inside of her thigh. Her eyes smolder into mine.

I feel the moment when we realize we really, really want to return to kissing. We rush forward with new fevered intensity, everything sweeter for the pause. She reclines flat on the comforter, her hair splaying out while I shower her with kisses, over her collarbone, her stomach, the upper hem of her underwear.

I feel dizzy. Dizzy from the impossibility of the dream I've walked into, from how this passion is past every romantic scene we've written together. This is what's left out of the idiom. Sometimes life is *stranger* than fiction, but sometimes it's incomparable in other ways. Sometimes it's a heaven that the false fire of imagination could never capture.

The strip of smooth skin between Katrina's hip bones and the tops of her legs isn't just real. It's the sexiest thing I've ever felt, forcing me to run my hands over it once, twice, up her thighs, before hooking my thumb in her underwear to drag them off. She responds, exhaling unconsciously, tipping her head up.

Then she's pushing herself back toward the pillows, hurriedly. I remember the conversation we had four years ago, writing *Only Once*, on precisely this subject. *The first time . . .* she'd said. *After all the waiting, I wouldn't want to wait longer.*

I move fast, shucking off my shorts and underwear, practically vaulting to position myself over her. "Um—" she interjects quickly.

"I know. No metaphors," I exhale.

"No." She puts one hand on my upper chest. I look up. I feel like she holds my entire world in the dark pools of her gorgeous eyes. "Do you have a condom?"

I digest the question, worried for a moment—I do *not* want to put this on pause, although for her I obviously would. "Yeah," I say, remembering.

Katrina nods. Her expression doesn't change. "Get it," she instructs me. Part of me notes how perfectly Kat the request is. It's like her writing. Direct, efficient. I love her for it.

I'm suddenly enormously grateful for this thought. I love her for it.

I love her.

"Hold on," I say. I scrounge in my shorts for my wallet, unfolding the scuffed leather to pull out the single wrapped condom inside. Flush with relief, I return to her, half kneeling on the bed while I open the wrapper. I'm surprised when she reaches forward.

"I want to," she says. She grasps the latex in her fingers.

Wordlessly, I nod. She does.

I reach one hand to gently sweep her hair from her cheek. The other runs the length of her—the mesmerizing reality of her, from the slope of her breast to the stretch of her exposed side to the curves farther down. I feel charged, unsteady. I'm not in control, and every single second my eyes wander over the soft subtleties of her naked body, I'm pushed further past myself. Her hand lingers on me, and then she reclines once more while I position myself over her.

She looks up, her lips parted softly, her eyes saying *now*.

Now.

I've never felt so much of her, felt so close to her. Everywhere we meet, my skin is feverish. She enfolds me, leaning into this moment, joining us.

I feel like my very soul is on fire.

• FOUR YEARS EARLIER •

I HEAR KATRINA'S door open and close. Everything in me coils, winding up for whatever will happen next. In every second, my hopes leap from impossible highs to crashing lows. Every creak of the house or whisper of the wind feels somehow significant, either warning or promise. I wish I knew which.

I wait for her to slide something under my door. Or to knock. Or to say my name. Whatever form my fate will be delivered in. In the near silence, my room feels like a prison, my fears and desires fighting to escape the four walls. With every passing second in which nothing comes, it gets harder. Finally, when four minutes have gone by, I stand up. I wonder if she's left the house. Feeling restless, like I have to know, I walk to my door.

When I reach the stairs, I smell it.

The earthy warmth of kindling, the faint whisper of smoke. The smell of fire.

When I hear something crack—the sound splitting the quiet of the house—I hit the stairs, my feet thundering down the steps. I recognize the light vermillion glow dancing garishly on the wall.

I feel like I'm watching myself, like I've flipped forward in the pages of my own life. I've read this part. I know what happens next. I've spoiled the ending.

Katrina is kneeling in front of the fireplace, her hands empty, her eyes fixed on the golden parchment curling and catching flame in front of her. The heat consumes what I've written, welcoming it into the fire. She faces me, her expression empty. I meet her stare, and an entire conversation is spoken in utter silence. She doesn't want me. She hated what I wrote to her, enough to destroy the words instead of just disregarding them.

No, that's not right.

I feel a separate fire catch in me. Because I understand what's truly happening here. If Katrina felt nothing for me, she would just say so. We would want to have conversations, figure out how to navigate our writing career going forward. She might even want to be friends. There's only one reason to *burn* what I've written. She's betraying herself. To destroy what I wrote could only mean she doesn't want to face what it makes her feel. Because she *does* feel something. But she would rather hide, would rather pretend the words we've exchanged this summer were only a game.

It leaves me physically ill. This is the woman I love, who I think might love me. Who's chosen to hurt me instead of confronting our feelings honestly.

Without speaking, I walk upstairs. With even, efficient movements, my heart hammering, I open the drawers of my dresser, shoving my belongings into my bag. I know I'm leaving possessions behind, but I don't care. Returning downstairs, I feel every second hitting me with force. There's nothing impulsive or instinctive in my decision. I'm conscious of the finality of my every step, the permanence of this choice.

When I pass through the living room, I don't look Katrina's way. She doesn't say anything, doesn't try to stop me. I walk out of the house, leaving whatever was between us to crumble into ash.

• PRESENT DAY •

I'M COMING TO life in ways I never have, ever. I move with Katrina, or we move with each other, or—I don't know, not now, when I feel like my consciousness has shattered into pieces, each one charged with sensation.

It's impossible to focus on every part of her. I'm forced to experience them in a kaleidoscope of moments, her leg rising while she rolls her hips forward, my hand grasping her thigh, then her head tipping up, leaving me opportunity to press my lips deep into her neck, her scent overwhelming.

I pull back. Our hands move to the pillows. Our fingers interlace.

While I look into her eyes, I know she is spread out underneath me. Her stomach, stretching uninterrupted to where we meet. Her legs, entwined with mine. The knowledge without the visual—I continue staring into her dark irises—is intoxicating in its own way. I press my forehead to hers, watching her eyes close while her fingers dig into my hands.

I don't know what the fuck we were saying, *synonyms* and *workshopping in* her *just sexy* note. I'm speechless. Katrina is speechless. We're just rhythm, instinct, heat. It's ironic, a couple of romance writers rocked so far out of ourselves we have no words. Nevertheless, it's what's happening.

She moves on top of me, my hands reaching urgently for her in the moment we lose contact. When she sinks down on me, I know I can't draw this out as long as I want. This view overwhelms me.

She sucks in a breath, and once more I'm locked in our perfect synchrony, reading her every intention, matching her every move. I press deeper. She reaches her hand to my chest, bending to capture my mouth. I've surrendered myself to Katrina countless times. Each page I give her, submitting my words to her red ink. Every discussion of our career. She's directed the course of my life, and I'm better for it. Right now, pinned beneath her, I feel it with complete certainty. I would put myself in Katrina's hands forever.

When she shudders, the motion rips through her. I watch, holding her in every way I can. I'm desperate to remain right here, like this, until finally I'm overcome. I lose myself in her.

What comes next I could only call perfect contentment. The sun streams in the windows, my sheets strewn everywhere. I collapse gently into Katrina. Remembering we're here, in Florida, right now, is head-spinning in its wonder. This is real. This is us. This happened. I hug her to me, her head resting near my heart.

She holds me, our chests heaving together. I know with complete certainty this has only stoked the fire between us. The flames lick ever higher. When I glance at her, Katrina catches me looking.

She smiles, and my heart ignites.

54

Katrina

I'M IN NO hurry to leave Nathan's bed. So I don't, even though it's the middle of the day. Even though we have work to do.

"Any notes?" Nathan asks next to me.

It takes me a moment to process his question. Like when you're a kid and you see your teacher on what's obviously a date at the table next to yours, the contexts misaligned so dramatically that your mind is wiped blank. "Notes?" I repeat.

He rolls onto his side, his eyes lit with humor. "On my performance."

"Seriously?"

"Katrina, you know how much I love feedback. Yours in particular."

I laugh. His grin is boyish in a way I've never seen before. Nothing like the intentional charm of his author photo. His dimple frames the corner of his lips, and there's an eager openness in his expression that I can only interpret as genuine happiness. I know he expects me to play this game with him a little longer, stretch out our wordplay the way we both love.

I can't, though. Not while his smile is making me embarrassingly soft. "No notes. You were . . . It was perfect."

He catches my hand, kissing my knuckles. "It was," he says.

There's no way I'm leaving this bed, I decide. I'll work from here. Possibly forever. I pull on my underwear, wondering if he's watching—he definitely is—then throw my shirt on over my head. Settling into the pillows, I curl up, grabbing the pages I need to edit from the nightstand. Nathan follows my lead, spreading out across the foot of the bed, shirtless and barelegged except for his briefs. The sun warms the room.

I feel good. It's so simple, yet so profound I don't focus on it for fear it will flee under scrutiny.

An hour passes, two, while I work on the pages, sneaking glances at Nathan typing on his computer. I let my cheeks heat remembering his hands everywhere, feeling every inch of me. His mouth kissing my breasts, gentleness and care fighting with hunger in his every movement. I felt good with him, too. Myself. Swept up in the best possible way.

"Getting lots of work done?" Nathan asks, not looking up from his computer. His lips curl conceitedly.

I drop my gaze, smiling despite myself. Busted. It's impossible for me to focus right now. What's more, I'm stuck. The change this scene needs won't reveal itself, my mind too jumpy and too wrapped up in itself for me to find the fix. I set down the pages, not really frustrated the scene has stumped me.

"I have writer's block," I say. "I need a shower." I spring out of bed and head for Nathan's bathroom. I'm expecting him to repeat his usual refrain—*writer's block doesn't exist.*

Instead, he doesn't speak until I've reached the doorway. "In my bathroom?"

I round on him, smirking. "You mind?" I don't wait for his reply. Walking into the bathroom, I leave the door open.

I turn on the shower and step in. Under the hiss of the hot water, I let my muscles unwind, hoping my mind does the same. The shower is my favorite place for inspiration. The invigorating warmth combined with the rhythm of water on tile, the repetitive rinsing and lathering, the quiet meditativeness tricks the mind into creativity. Suddenly, the scene you're not even thinking about unfolds in some corner of your consciousness.

Facing the nozzle, I close my eyes, enjoying the spray running down me. When I hear the door softly close, I smile. Moments later, I feel Nathan behind me. I spin to face him, raising one eyebrow.

"What? I have writer's block, too," he says.

I laugh. "Sure you do." Nathan rolls his eyes, but his hands run down my back. I sink into the feeling, letting my own hands run up his chest. Though I'm still fearful of dwelling on my own thoughts, of one I'm certain—I've never felt this way before. "Tell me something," I say softly.

"*Hmm?*" he hums close to my ear.

"What was it like to write on your own again?"

He pulls back to look into my eyes. It's several seconds before he speaks. "It felt . . . incomplete. I don't know how many times I had to fight the instinct to send you a chapter, how often I thought, *Katrina will do this scene better—I'll leave it to her.* Only to remember." His eyes dim.

His words wind into me so deeply, I nearly forget his hands cradling me under the rivulets of water. "You don't need me, though," I point out. "You wrote something wonderful on your own."

The light returns to his eyes, electric. "Oh, I need you." He steps closer, pressing himself up to me, showing me exactly how much. I can't help being impressed. Pleased, too, knowing what it promises. "What about you?" His question is soft. "Did you really write nothing these last years?"

I settle into his embrace, resting my head on the plane of his chest. I couldn't compel myself to put ideas on paper, where they could be read, where they would've started to want things from me like completion or recognition. "I wrote," I say, "just only in my head."

His fingers find my temple, brushing gently. "To be in there," he murmurs.

"You already are," I say in a heartbeat. "Not a day went by that I didn't think about you. Nathan, I—"

There's plenty we have to discuss, the past hiding underneath what we have now. We've built a bridge over the high cliffs where we've stood, separated for four years. While it stretches the gap, it's shaky, new, and the drop is long. Our past is still there, waiting for the slightest wrong step.

Nathan crushes his lips to mine. I know what he wants. I always know what he wants, can predict what he'll like, can hear his voice in my head. When I write, and not only when I write. I hear it now. *The past can wait.* I fall into the kiss, letting him know I agree.

We stay under the water, enjoying, exploring while the minutes slip past us.

It's when Nathan's lips lower to my neck, his fingers trailing down my stomach, that the idea sparks in my mind. I step back sharply. Nathan watches me with concern. "Did I do something wrong?" he asks, his voice unguarded.

I shake my head. Working through the idea, checking every facet, making sure it fits, I finally decide—it's perfect. I smile. *Oh, this is good.* "I figured out the problem with chapter thirty," I say, speaking quickly. "It's the setting. We put it in the wrong place."

Nathan laughs. "Katrina, seriously? I do not want to discuss chapter thirty right now." He looks playfully indignant. "Is that what you were thinking about? I'm insulted."

"I wasn't! I swear," I insist. "In fact, I was so *not* thinking about it that I figured it out."

"So you're saying . . ." Something smug settles over his expression. "I distracted and relaxed you enough you got over your writer's block?"

"Yes," I confirm.

"Intriguing." He fixes his eyes on me, delight and mischief cascading into them. "Well, here's to more writer's block in the future. I'll be happy to help *whenever*." When I shove his shoulder lightly, he pulls me closer. "Tell me you're not even thinking of leaving this shower to rewrite chapter thirty."

I reach down. "I can wait."

55

Nathan

We go out for dinner. Katrina and me, going out for dinner. Except it's not just hitting pause on the day's work to refuel. It's a date. It's kind of a first date, in fact.

We've done plenty of things that looked like, or even felt like, dates in the past. I've spent a small fortune on the hipster-café coffee I've consumed in this woman's presence. Once in Italy, needing two hours of not talking to each other, we went to the movies, not realizing there wouldn't be subtitles. We stayed and enjoyed the cinematography. On the walk home, we pitched each other ridiculous ideas to fill the gaps in the plot we hadn't understood.

Those weren't dates, though. Dates hold intention. They're not just occasions—they're declarations. *I'm interested.* Romance hides in every quiet pause, every noticed glance.

Or, sometimes, it doesn't hide. It's out in the open right now, in the way I hold Katrina's hand over the table, the way I catch her lingering glances, the way I spontaneously lean forward to kiss her after dessert. We'd been to Knot and Key before (the small seafood restaurant in our neighborhood), because we've gone to every restaurant within walking distance. Last time, we bickered in the dim candlelight over plot points in *Only Once*, and I had the clam chowder. Tonight, suffice to say, I did not have the clam chowder.

I memorize each detail of the night. Katrina in her black dress, the oil paintings of the ocean, the netting on the walls for our decorations. In every caress I give her hand, every second I stare into her eyes, I feel like I'm asking if she really wants this. In every smile she sends me, she says she does. I want to believe her.

But the past is here, with us now. Scars don't stay closed in such matters. They're waiting to be reopened, ready to bleed over everything nearby when they do. Part of me wants to ignore it. To pretend it never happened, to retreat into the safety of this perfect present. The other part doesn't want to have doubts with Katrina. I don't want to be with her and fearing the day those old wounds tear into us.

I need to know. It's nothing I'll ever figure out on my own, no peace I'll ever find without pushing us both, without putting the questions in front of Katrina. I need to risk her reaction. To risk her setting everything we have on fire once more.

On the walk home, the breeze cooling us in contrast to the heavy-scented warmth of the restaurant, I lead her a different route. The sun hasn't yet set. I feel curiosity in her demeanor until we reach my destination. She tenses, waiting a few steps from me.

We're in front of the independent bookstore. The one where we ran into each other weeks ago. Expecting her reaction, I speak gently. "Let's go in."

"I'm sure they're closing," she replies hesitantly.

"So we'll be quick." I don't pause before what I say next, my real purpose. Doing everything I can to project nonchalance, I pull her hand gently toward the store. "Come on," I say, my voice light. "We've never signed *Only Once* together."

This is honestly sort of impressive, when I give it thought. We managed not to sign one single copy of our international bestseller together. But then, the post-release promotional rollout of *Only Once* was pockmarked with stubborn refusals and mutual hostility. Whenever there were signings or book festivals, one of us would agree to attend, and the other would summarily decline. I'm anticipating the way Katrina falters in the doorway, her hand pulling free from mine. The last time we were here, she wouldn't even go inside for fear of being recognized with me. Now I'm asking for even more.

I don't let her hesitation slow me down. I'm not waiting. While I wish we were walking home, too, I told myself on the way to dinner I wouldn't waver. Katrina is either in or out. One day, today or tomorrow or the next, we'll have to either face what we've done or hide from ourselves forever. Only one path has a future.

I walk into the store without her.

Holding my breath, I wait. I study the store to distract myself until I hear the door open behind me.

When I feel Katrina by my side, relief cascades over me. I hold out my hand, which she takes with damp fingers.

"I just like being a *reader* in bookstores," she says, sounding nervous. "Not an *author*."

"How exactly do you plan on publishing another book, then?" I face her, half smiling. I'm going for levity, even though it's sort of a serious question. From Kat's expression, I know she does not feel the humor. She chews her lip, her eyes like clouds over the ocean. I realize it's because she hasn't thought that far into the future. I'm somewhat sorry I made her. Somewhat not.

We reach the fiction section, where—there it is, still face-out. We stand in front of the shelf, saying nothing. It's the closest we've ever been to our past. It sits there innocently, a physical reification of what we did to each other. Four hundred and thirty-six pages of fraught memories, this small window of white type on dark blue framing different versions of ourselves.

I feel the book wedging between us, bringing back the fever in which we wrote it. The day it rained at the beach, the night we finished, the fire. It's suffocating. I feel Katrina lean away from me. The book's presence is palpable, imposing. I'm desperate to cut through it, forge my way back to her.

"I hated the cover when I saw it," I say.

She startles. It's exactly the effect I'd hoped for. When her eyes find mine, there's not just curiosity in them. There's the faintest flicker of something else. She knows what I'm doing, because she knows me. "Really? Why?" she asks.

"It just wasn't what I'd envisioned," I reply. I'd hoped for black-and-white photography. Thin type. I'd imagined this book and its promise tirelessly enough that I'd created in my head every detail of the cover.

Katrina lifts her gaze from me, reluctantly bringing it to its new destination. The book. She steps closer to the shelf, to the copies face-out. We're surrounded by pastel walls and plush carpet, yet her movement has the caution of someone reaching the end of a diving board. I exhale just a little, not loudly enough for her to hear my relief.

"It's the perfect cover," she says quietly.

I draw back, genuinely curious. I never knew she loved the cover. But then, there's plenty I don't know, painful swaths of memories we'll never make together. I don't know how Katrina responds to reader questions. I don't know if she ever read our reviews or what she thought of them. There's so much I don't know.

But I might have the chance to find out. This seemingly casual conversation is proof. We're doing this. We can invite the past back into our lives in these little pieces. It doesn't have to destroy us.

"I know that now." My voice softens. "But at the time . . . nothing looked the way it was supposed to."

Katrina says nothing. She stands there, unmoving—like she's okay.

"Let's bring these up front and sign a few," I say.

Her reply is immediate. "No."

While quick, it's not quite convincing. It's instinct, not intention. I don't know how I know. I guess it's my considerable new experience with Katrina when she's really pissed off or resistant. This window isn't closed. "Katrina, we wrote this. We created it together. Why do you hate it?" I ask.

"I don't. I don't . . . hate it." She fidgets, touching her hair, shifting the shoulder strap of her bag. "I just . . . Here." She reaches into her purse and pulls out a pen. "Let's sign it and leave it without saying anything. Someone will find it. It'll be a surprise. A secret." Something wild has caught the edge of her voice. It's half excitement, half desperation.

She holds out the pen.

I pause. It's not the scene I wrote in my head when I led us in here. But it's something. I nod, taking the pen from her. Grabbing the copy from off the shelf, I open the front cover, where I place the signature I've scrawled on thousands of pages exactly like this one.

This time, I leave room for Katrina. I return the pen to her. She waits, the felt tip lingering in midair. Then something in her solidifies. Swiftly, she adds her own mark to the page, the tips of her *K* crossing into my name.

We hear footsteps approaching, and Katrina snaps the book closed. She shoves it onto the shelf. I can't help smiling. The whole thing is ridiculous, imagining someone catching us defacing our own book. If someone did question us, we would literally just point to our pictures on the back cover. They would probably move the signed copy to the front. Hell, it would probably be the same kindly bookseller I met weeks ago.

But I don't say any of that. I walk quickly out of the store, following a giggling Katrina, even letting myself glance over my shoulder for fabricated interlopers. When we get outside, I double over laughing. Partly from how ridiculous we're being, partly out of relief. We faced a big piece of our past, looked it dead on. It feels like one step into the future.

56

Katrina

We walk home, the sun starting to set, the sky marbling with pale yellow. Shadows stretch long on the sidewalk. When we reach our porch, I wait while Nathan unlocks the door. I know what he was doing in the bookstore. Know why he was doing it, too.

I can tell he's comforted by how our visit to the bookstore went. Which doesn't frustrate me, exactly. I'm just worried he's not being realistic. If he thinks signing a single copy of our book will repair the enormous rift in our past . . . Well, I'm not looking forward to him figuring out it won't. Our history is ugly. It's huge. It's daunting.

It's why I don't follow when he walks into the house. I linger on the porch, the humidity enveloping me like a blanket, but not a comfortable one—the point when it's covered you for long enough you start to feel feverish.

Noticing I haven't joined him inside, Nathan pauses, facing me.

"I don't hate *Only Once*," I say. "It's a wonderful book. I'm proud of it."

"Okay . . ." Nathan hasn't lowered his keys. They shift in his fingers. Waiting for me to continue, he looks comfortable but cautious.

"But whenever I think of it, I'm reminded of how much everyone expects of me. I just wish I didn't feel constantly in competition with myself." I swallow, wishing saying the words made me feel better. It doesn't. It just makes them feel more real.

Nathan takes my hand, looking relieved. I've seen so many sides of him. The guilty husband, the intense creative, the cocksure literary celebrity. The openheartedness in his expression right now is so profound, so loving, it hurts. "You're not. Besides"—he smiles—"I have to tell you, what we're writing now is just as good. Maybe even better."

I dodge his gaze. "It doesn't matter," I reply, the first hint of harshness in my voice. "One day it won't be. One day I'll disappoint . . . everyone."

I'm including myself in *everyone*. The public pressure of releases like ours is enormous, undoubtedly. But disappointing our editor or reviewers or readers is not the only fear I fend off when it chews my nerves raw. Writing is the only thing I'm special at. If I lose it, in a way, I've lost myself.

I watch Nathan realize this is a real conversation, not a passing worry. He faces me fully, returning his keys to his pocket. "Katrina, I'm not going to lie to you and say you'll never disappoint anyone. You will. But you can't live your life afraid of it."

His words sound gentle, but even the gentlest press of a bad bruise feels like a blow. Without wondering if I'm being fair or understanding, I let defensiveness flare up in me. "Don't act like I'm the only one who's afraid," I fire back.

He drops my hand. "What's that supposed to mean?" he demands.

His demeanor says he knows.

"It means you hide in your writing. You told me you loved me in fucking fiction, Nathan. While you were married."

There it is. The first invocation of the shadow that has covered our relationship—or lack thereof—for years. I thought I would regret this moment, thought I dreaded the shadow rearing into reality. I don't. Despite how destabilized, how profoundly shaken, I feel, I'm glad I'm crossing into these waters.

"I didn't hide," he replies. "I knew you would understand, and you did. I bared *everything* in what I wrote. And you burned it, because it terrified you. You can't turn this back on me. You're the one who panicked because you wanted what I was offering you. If you lost it, it would hurt. So you chose to destroy it and pretend it didn't exist."

"I had to!" I nearly shout. I don't care if my voice carries past the porch, don't care if our neighbors hear the culmination of Nathan's and my half-decade-long drama. Like someone's ripped the door to my heart off its hinges, I want everything out in the open. Spoken, not written. "Your letter was . . . beautiful. Perfectly crafted. The best writing you'd ever done."

He huffs a bitter laugh. "I didn't realize that was a crime."

My breath wavers. He really doesn't get it, not even now. "I don't want some perfectly crafted love story. I can't live up to it! There's no final page in life, no point where we kiss and everything is happily-ever-after. We can't be contained in neat phrases or nicely designed covers. We're not characters. We're people. I couldn't be with someone who only wanted the story version. I wanted—I *want*—something *real*, and I'm not convinced you can handle real."

Rage flickers in Nathan's eyes. It's been some time since I've seen him look this way. He's noticed the subtle shift in the conversation. We're no longer only in the past. We've dipped our toes into the present, into the problems I know will follow us wherever we go from here.

"I did give you something real," he returns. "I loved you. I still fucking love you. How can you tell me what I can't handle? I know better than anyone that love is flawed. That it can break."

I step farther from him, crossing my arms over my chest. He doesn't move, feet planted on the house's doormat.

"Here's what you really don't want to hear," he goes on. "What we have *is* a fairy tale. It is a dream come true. *And* it's imperfect. I wish you could understand it can be both. Fiction is fiction *and* it's real. They're not opposites. They live within each other." His voice is raw, his expression naked. While anger is the fire in him, I recognize pain is the kindling. "The worst part is, I think you love me, too. I think you know we're soul mates. But we'll never be together as long as you're afraid of your own happiness."

The roaring in my ears overwhelms me. I was wrong when I imagined Nathan's anger was a fire. It was a knife, one he's stuck into the smallest, quietest part of my heart. He's opened up the center of me, where I hide sad secrets even from myself. It hurts deeply, enough I can't possibly keep up the conversation.

So I don't. I turn around and walk right off the porch, into the evening.

57

Katrina

• FOUR YEARS EARLIER •

I'M WAITING FOR my date in one of the most obviously, intentionally hip restaurants I've ever been to in Brooklyn. The place has nothing on the walls, midcentury-modern furnishings in whites, grays, and light woods, moody electronic R&B pumping from speakers into the close-quarters dining room.

I focus on the details, hoping they'll distract me. I should have canceled. My stomach is in knots, my head chaotic. I know I won't enjoy myself—not when I'll be spending every minute trying to vanquish the thought of Nathan's *New Yorker* interview, which published earlier today. When it hit the internet, I told myself not to read it. Every minute since has been a test of strength, and I feel myself weakening.

I check my phone. He's late.

Frustrated, I shove it back into my bag. They haven't brought menus yet, which is unfortunate. I could have read the prices of every esoteric option before inevitably deciding on the one least likely to further upset my stomach. Instead, I dutifully refocus on the décor, my eyes jumping restlessly from corner to corner. I won't have to wait long, I reason. It'll be fine. What's five, or ten, or even fifteen more minutes when I've spent the entire day resisting?

But letting my guard down was the wrong move.

Before I know what I'm doing, my hands fumble for my phone again. I click through to the interview.

I devour every word, reading the *New Yorker*'s gaudily old-school font like it's my death sentence. Nathan could have written this himself, I observe ruefully—the eloquent literacy with which the story sets up its premise, the former cowriter now striking out on his own. They've even got one of the *New Yorker*'s trademark caricatured renderings of their subjects. I wish I could say it looks ridiculous, but it only looks like him. His spry swoop of hair, his sharp chin, some crackle in his eyes even the casual drawing couldn't help capturing.

Minutes pass. I keep reading.

The restaurant disappears while I immerse myself in the interview, hearing Nathan's voice through the screen. When I reach the end, I robotically close the tab and shut off my screen. I return my phone to my purse, feeling cold in my fingertips. I don't reread the story.

Writing Only Once *was one of the worst times in my life. Katrina Freeling is a genius, but I'm not sure the genius is worth the torture of working with her.*

The words should hurt. I know it's what he meant—to hurt me. Yet when I wait for the pain, it doesn't come. Maybe it's because I know I deserve what he said. Maybe the worst wounds don't hurt until the shock wears off. Maybe I'm just numb.

"Sorry I'm late."

I look up. Chris stands over me, one hand on the back of my chair, smiling. I force my expression into pleasantness and tilt up my head when he leans down to kiss my cheek. In the moments while he sits down opposite me, I work up a smile of my own. "It's no problem," I say.

"How are you? You look beautiful." He studies me with intent eyes. *Chris likes me,* some voice in my head says with surprised clarity. *Nathan had been right.* I push the memory away, irritated to have thought of Nathan.

"I'm great," I lie. "I'd say you clean up well yourself, except you always look sharp." This part is not a lie. Chris does look good. He's a man of broad shoulders and clean lines, which tonight fit perfectly into his obviously tailored gray blazer and white dress shirt. It's a simple look, and it succeeds in its understatement.

I'd invited Chris to dinner on a whim, one I didn't know until now whether I'd regret. We were texting last weekend, me with the TV on, some innocuous HGTV show to stave off my boredom. My loneliness, too. He made a publishing industry joke, and . . . I don't know. When a little light flickered into my mood, it was enough. Nathan will think I did it to hurt him. I don't think I did.

He grins, pleased by my compliment. "Can I just say how thrilled I am we're finally doing this?" he asks.

I hope my eyes shine back at him. Seeing him has steadied me some. I've stopped focusing on the interview. With the candle glowing in the middle of the table, I feel something new, something I could get used to. It's not the empty calm of every day in the months since I returned from Florida without Nathan. It's different. This feels firm under my feet instead of like floating in endless fog.

"Me, too," I reply. I think I mean it. This is going to be better, I tell myself.

It has to be.

58

Nathan

• PRESENT DAY •

WITH OUR FIGHT echoing in my ears, I don't follow Katrina off the porch. I don't even watch her stalk off into the sunset, doing what she does. Pushing us apart for flimsy, worthless reasons and hiding from the damage. Instead, I head directly up the stairs, hitting each step heavily. Whether I'm running from or chasing my feelings, I don't know.

I ignore the discomfort of being in this house without her. It's our space but not *mine*. Even though I've been living here for two months—waking up in the bed down the hall, brushing my teeth over the sink—right now, I feel like I'm intruding. The windows feel watchful, like they're looking in instead of me looking out.

While the sunset is starting to shock the sky orange, I reach my room. It's instinct to drop into my chair and open my laptop. I'm ready to write everything raging in me, to put this heartache into words. To process and move through these feelings using this psychological blood-letting onto the empty white page. I open the document with ritual focus. Preparing myself, I fix my eyes on the unwritten first line.

I can't put my fingers on the keys.

I just can't do it. Resistance I'm unfamiliar with holds me in place, keeps me from writing. This hurt is mine and Katrina's. It belongs only to us. No one else. For once, I want to live the pain instead of dressing it in fictional clothing. It might heal cleaner. It might make me better.

Resigned, I close my computer and sit alone with the wound in my heart.

59

Katrina

Under the red sunset, I step out of my car. The beach opens in front of me. It's the same one where Nathan and I got rained on four years ago, where I realized how much I wanted him to kiss me.

Pulling off my shoes, I walk onto the soft sand. It pools over my toes welcomingly, like it remembers me. The wind plays weakly with my hair. I drop down, sitting with my knees bent, hating how pleasant the evening is. There's no sign of storms. The few clouds in the sky have caught the violent colors of the sunset, gashes of pink on an orange backdrop. It's perfect.

I'm not the only one here. There's a woman doing yoga in the corner of my view, a couple walking hand in hand close to the water, families packing up umbrellas and beach bags. In moments like this, it's so hard to reckon with everyone else's life just continuing on, independent of mine, of how I feel I've pushed myself once more right to this familiar crossroads.

I find I'm crying, tears streaming down my face. I could just leave, I realize. Not to return to my home in Los Angeles with Chris, but I don't have to be here. I don't have to finish this book. The only reason I'm in Florida, writing with Nathan, was to save my relationship, which is gone now. If I want out, there's finally nothing forcing me to stay.

Wiping my eyes, I feel without flinching the weight of what I'm considering. It's not every day you reevaluate everything. The breeze blows over the sand, shifting the sea of footprints into new shapes. For years, I chased dreams of literary success, then realized how fragile they were once I'd caught them. I put my dreams elsewhere, into a relationship that would become a marriage that would become a life. Now, I'm not chasing anything. I sit, letting the emptiness envelop me.

Nathan's words fill it. *You're afraid of your own happiness.* He said it like an insult. He doesn't understand how *not* ridiculous my fear is. Happiness *is* terrifying. I'd hurt much less in the long run if I pushed Nathan out of my life, deleted our book, found something safer to chase. I imagine my modest, frictionless existence. With the earnings from *Only Once,* I could move to the city of my choosing. I could go to grad school, spend my time reading, surround myself with people who aren't writers.

I press my forehead to my knees. I'm really considering this. It's the second time I've walked right up to the promise of what our career could be, what *we* could be. It feels like it's going to be the second time I don't take the final step.

But it has to be this way. For me, it does. I just need to sort out how I'll keep from coming back to these frightening heights again and again.

I'll just change, I promise myself. I'll learn how to more carefully keep what I want most out of the corners of my vision.

It needs to start now. Quietly, I pack up my unfurling feelings for Nathan.

I focus on the sounds of the wind and people splashing in the water.

The minutes pass. Despite the calm I feel, I'm not convinced it will last. Like I'm not out of the woods, only closing my eyes to them.

Then, in my head I hear—first words, then sentences.

I don't know that happiness is the goal, really. Not always. It's a woman's voice. The reply is in a man's. *If we're not doing this to be happier, then why, Evelyn?*

To find out who we are again, Evelyn says.

I laugh to myself. It's dialogue. I'm writing dialogue.

The realization is so funny to me that my laughter shakes my whole body. My tears turn sweet.

The calm dissipates. What replaces it is surer, stronger. It's something innermost finding its way forward, uninvited. Even with nothing left, I'm writing. Writing remains. Maybe it's my own answer. Maybe it's simply me. I'm doing it not because it promises an unfraught future, because it's free of pain or peril—I'm doing it because it demands to be done.

For the first time, I contemplate the possibility of reconciling myself with those consequences. Instead of imagining paths of retreat, I try to put my writer's mind to work imagining paths forward.

I understand, genuinely, that I can't avoid crashing after feeling joy. It's just the way I'm made, I know. Depression and anxiety will be there. I can't simply choose to live without them—like I can't simply choose to live without writing.

What I can do is . . .

I push myself to force this possible future into focus. What I can do is protect myself while I pursue what I love. I have to face the fact the fear *is* coming. I've felt it in recent weeks like I did before *Only Once*—tremors before tidal waves. What I need to do is use what I have to stay upright. I have knowledge of myself. I have courage. I have my therapist, with whom, I decide, I'll schedule weekly calls surrounding the release.

I'll need them, because I'm finishing this book. Because it's coming out, and it's going to be good.

I stand, swiping the sand from my legs. I don't let my eyes linger on the horizon, now decked in the final embers of daylight. If I write, if I finish this book, it's because I want to. Which I do. I have my direction. There's nothing left to hide behind.

I walk back to my car, back to Nathan. Back to my life.

60

Nathan

I RUN.

I follow every street in our small neighborhood, hoping I get lost somehow. I pound the pavement in ways I never have before, the effort cutting my windpipe raw. The curbs of each corner fly past me, indistinct, while I push myself ever harder.

When Katrina left without a word, I did the only other thing I could instead of writing. I grabbed my running shoes and headed out, directionless. I couldn't sit in the house with her gone, wondering if she was even coming back.

Finally, on the verge of collapse, I have to return home. When I do, her car is in the driveway. Despite myself, relief rushes into my pounding heart, fear following close behind. I speed up my steps. If Katrina's here, it means something. I just don't know what. I'm simultaneously unable to process and hyperconscious of the details of the night, the solitary hum of some insect, the crescent moon overhead. On the porch steps, I tell myself how this will go. I won't let history repeat. I'm different now, and I think—I hope—Katrina is, too.

I walk in the front door, listening. The house is silent. There's no sign of her on the first floor. The lights are off. The room is still. I climb the stairs, every creak of the wood conspicuous in the quiet. Reaching the upper level, I find her door half open.

I pause outside. I didn't hold back with her on the porch, and although I want to hide the emotions in me that feel too big to contain—want to write them down, pull them out of myself onto the page, where they're easier to comprehend, where I can hold them at a distance—I won't. Which means I can't hide from her now. From whatever she has to say to me.

I knock gently on her door. It swings open, revealing her sitting at her desk, typing quickly on her computer. She's barefoot, sand speckling her ankles. She went to the beach.

I don't think she notices when I step into her room. She's focused, fixated on whatever she's writing. I wonder for a second if it's some warped parallel of what I wrote to her four years ago. Some damning scene rejecting me and what we might have. I'm done having this conversation in fiction, though. When I speak, my voice is fragile. "Can we talk?"

She stops typing and spins to face me, her eyes shining brighter than I've seen in days. In years, maybe.

"Of course," she says. I hear the same change in her voice. She sounds full of confidence, renewed in some ineffable way. "I want to talk. I want—" She cuts herself off and stands up. "I've realized exactly how much I want."

Wild emotion seizes me. Whatever she was writing, it wasn't a rejection. I can read it on her face. I know what I'm feeling. I know what it demands. Following the impulse, I reach for her hand.

She squeezes my fingers firmly. Then she pulls her hand free with an apologetic smile.

"But first, I want to finish our book," she says.

The skin of my hand is cool where her fingers left mine. I study her expression, surprised by the subject change. She's indecipherable. "I don't understand," I say gently, recognizing how unusual this is with the person whose mind I've learned to read.

"I want to show you I can finish it. I want to show myself. I need to face this, Nathan," she replies. She doesn't sound scared, just determined.

I nod. It's wonderfully easy, following Katrina wherever she leads. "I'll write anything with you," I say.

She smiles, the expression seeming to radiate through her. "Thank you." Saying nothing more, she starts to turn to her computer.

"And us?" I ask.

She stills. Her features cloud. Nevertheless, I see her struggling to look past the clouds instead of staying lost within them. "I have to know there is an us outside of writing. With Chris I was the bestselling-author trophy fiancée. I need to know you want to be with *me*, not just a co-writer who will help your career."

I take my time before replying, understanding what she means. There's never been me and Katrina without our writing career. Writing is our entire life together. But while I may have fallen in love with Katrina through our writing, it wasn't because of the copies I thought she'd sell. It was because I saw her in her words. *That's* why I love her. And I want to prove it to her.

"Katrina, we can walk away from the book," I say, and it feels easy. "You're worth more to me than a *book deal*. Than a lifetime of them."

"No." The immediacy and quiet resolve of her response surprises me. "I want to finish the book," Katrina continues. "It's important to me."

While unpacking this vibrant change in her is tempting, I can feel our conversation has momentum I don't want to lose. Instead I refigure my idea. "So . . . so we separate them. The writing, and us. We finish the book first. We put us on pause until we do."

This is *not* easy for me to say. The thought of holding myself back from Katrina for even one minute more—to say nothing of the remainder of our word count—is painful. It's the right decision, though.

"If you want this, then we start us as *us*, not as cowriters," I conclude.

I'm comforted when relief mingles with the caution in Katrina's eyes. "That means no putting into our writing everything we're not saying to each other," she warns me with a half smile. "No angry edits. No late-night love letters written in someone else's voice."

I hold my hand over my heart, returning her smile. "I promise," I reply. "When I want to say something to you, I'll *say* it to you. When the book is done."

"I look forward to it." She seems forlorn for a moment. I feel the same way. It's a short goodbye even though neither of us is leaving. Then something new catches her eyes, making them sparkle. "How quickly do you think we can write this ending?"

A small laugh escapes me. "I'm not sure." The coming weeks stretch before me in my head. I foresee eight-hour writing sessions, working breakfasts, bleary-eyed evening edits. If I thought I worked compulsively before, it'll be nothing compared to what's to come.

If I thought I was grateful for my partner before, it will be nothing compared to what's to come.

"I'm glad there's two of us, though," I say.

Katrina meets my eyes. "Me, too."

61

Katrina

WE DEVOTE OURSELVES with newfound vigor to finishing the book. Weeks go by. We write by day, edit by night, punctuating our routine with dinners with Harriet and walks to get much-needed caffeine.

We don't kiss. We don't even touch. It's hard sometimes—when I stand in Nathan's doorway to trade pages, my memory will return to his bed, or when his shirt rides up while he's stretching, I have to sit on my hands. I'm not ungrateful for the clarity of purpose it's given our work, though. We write for ourselves, not for each other. Of course, there's no keeping your soul out of your prose entirely. Nor would I want to read writing with no personal imperative. But there's a difference between letting your feelings and realizations inform your words and writing the secret messages of your heart with one reader in mind.

It's healthier. For the first time in years, it lets me feel in control. It lets me love what I'm doing. I sprint through ideas, enjoying every weary night and inspired morning. I'm not afraid of this book going out into the world, either. I'm excited.

I keep waiting for this persistent joy to end. It never does. Finally, after weeks of invigorating and exhausting work, we reach the closing scenes. We're working in the dining room, me and Nathan and Harriet, our collection of portable fans fending off the late-night heat. I'm my usual combination of physically spent and emotionally charged, my wrists hurting, eyes bleary, my computer keys filthy. I'm laughing with Harriet while we implore Nathan not to use the phrase *existential prophylactic* in our book.

It's not going well. Nathan's digging his heels in.

"Seriously, Nate," Harriet says, not sounding serious. "Be better than 'existential prophylactic.'"

Nathan cringes. "*Nate?* I haven't been called *Nate* since summer camp before sixth grade."

Harriet wags a finger at him. "You'll be Nate to me for the rest of my life if you stand by this choice."

Looking pained, Nathan pauses lengthily before holding up his hands. "Fine. I surrender."

"Wow," I say, laughing. "I never thought of threatening to call him Nate. You're a genius," I tell her.

Harriet stands, collecting our empty wineglasses and walking them to the sink. "I know," she says over her shoulder.

"Don't get any ideas." Nathan's looking at me now, and something passes in the warm air separating us. It's playful, friendly, and more. Intimate, even. I wink, enjoying the easy familiarity.

Harriet returns, grabbing her computer and her three overfull notebooks, which she shoves unceremoniously into her bag. "I'm off," she says. "Hey, have you decided what you're writing next?" She asks the question casually despite the layers of uncertainty surrounding the subject.

I'm proud of how I don't instantly clam up or nervously spiral. When I glance at Nathan, he's watching me patiently, without pressure. From the compulsively productive Nathan, I recognize his patience for the gesture it is. "Not sure yet," I say honestly. I walk Harriet to the door, pausing in the entryway out of Nathan's view. "I want to write something, though," I go on, softer, in the incomplete privacy of the hallway.

Not reaching for the door, Harriet studies me. "I'm proud of you," she says. "I'm proud of both of you. You're so . . . Well, it's like you're actually friends again. I have to ask"—she eyes me seriously—"was the sex horrible? It's the only explanation."

I purse my lips to hide my grin. Conscious of Nathan in the dining room, I reply quietly, "It was very *not* horrible. Kind of life-changing, if I'm honest."

Harriet's eyebrows rise. "Care to elaborate?"

I hear Nathan's chair scrape on the floor in the dining room. "Later," I promise her, unable to stop the fizzy warmth the memory of the two of us gives me. "Let's get a drink, and I'll tell you everything. I'm . . . I'm not leaving Florida anytime soon," I say.

Harriet's expression softens. I'm touched by how genuinely glad she looks. "Deal. A drink, just us," she says, then her eyes go familiarly wry. "I can tell I'm going to need to get drunk to hear these details." She swings the door open and walks into the night, waving over her shoulder.

I return to the kitchen, grateful I've repaired more than one friendship over the past months. When I reach the counter, I find Nathan's printed something for me. He's quietly loading the dishwasher with his back to me. I pick up the pages. Above the first chapter header he's written, *WHERE WE'LL END?* The paper printer-hot in my hands, I read the words over a couple of times, thinking, then look up.

"Is this a question?" I ask him.

He drops the final pieces of silverware into the dishwasher. "It's a title," he says while he closes the door. Facing me, he looks like he's working hard to keep his expression light. "Though I suppose when we finish, we'll need to figure out our own answer to the question."

He's right. But for now, we're not finished. For tonight, I decide I'm focusing on the pages in front of me instead of the questions a little further ahead. "It's perfect. Night, *Nate,*" I say teasingly, waiting for my reward, which comes when his cheeks redden. He rebounds quickly, pointing one lazy finger in my direction.

"'Very *not* horrible,' was it?" He repeats what I told Harriet with unhidden pride. "'Life-changing,' even? Please, support that statement. Details, figures, comparisons are all welcome."

I roll my eyes, but I'm laughing. Nathan grins, not pressing the point.

I leave him in the kitchen and head up the stairs. Entering my bedroom, I feel light and eager in familiar and unfamiliar ways. The title stares up from the chapter in my hands, and I realize—it's a question I already know the answer to.

62

Nathan

• SIX YEARS EARLIER •

I HATE READING my work aloud. Wedged between perfect strangers on the lumpy sofa in the house where we're staying, the smell of damp wood pervading the chill in the room, I'm dreading the next hour. It's the first day of the New York Resident Writers' Program, and I'm miserable.

Driving through the small town nearby on my way up, I was looking forward to this. I expected the workshop would consist of valuable mentorship, the opportunity to work in the quiet outside the city—two weeks of solitude. Instead, it's only been hours of rushed introductions, hearing dozens of my fellow writers pitch me their novels, and finally, icebreakers. I've heard where everyone's from, heard strings of higher education acronyms so numerous they sound like code. We've shared our desert-island poems. We've grouped up in fours and found out what we have in common—we're all writers. It was torture until I heard we'd be reading our work out loud. Now I'd prefer coming up with goofy pneumonic devices to remember everyone's name.

The one person I met this morning who seemed interesting, and who didn't promptly pitch me the next Great American Novel, isn't here. Harriet Soong is probably doing something useful instead of wasting her afternoon listening to moody excerpts poorly read.

Frankly, I'm not interested in making friends here. I have friends. Better, I have a fiancée—the luster of this thought hasn't faded in the three months since I proposed to Melissa. The reason I'm here is that simply nothing I'm writing is coming out the way I want it. I'm missing something. I've chosen this workshop because Carter Gilroy, *New York Times* bestseller turned *New York Times* critic, is teaching. It's Carter's feedback I want, not critiques from twenty MFA students. I'll suffer trading pages—I know I'll have to—but I draw the line at reading for everyone.

No one would notice if I left now, would they? I could head up to my room, get some writing done while my stuffy roommate overdramatizes his prose for the group. Extricating myself from the couch, I walk swiftly for the door, trying to project the impression I have a good reason for doing so.

A woman standing in the entryway stops me. "Are you leaving, or just going to the bathroom?" she asks.

I vaguely recognize her, though she wasn't in my icebreaker group this morning. She doesn't have the academic airs of many of the people here, myself included, with my stiff oxford shirt and leather loafers. The woman's plaid flannel is untucked from her jeans. She watches me with dark, intensely inquisitive eyes, curls of brown hair falling free from her loose bun. "Sorry," I say, realizing I missed her question. "What?"

"Your seat. Are you giving it up?" She nods slightly into the room.

I glance behind me, noticing every couch in the small space is occupied. "Oh, right. No, you can have it," I say. There are a couple other people standing in the back. The layout of the house this program runs out of is claustrophobic. It was once a private home, and alongside the antique furniture and old-money decoration, it has the cramped proportions of historic dwellings.

The woman doesn't move for the seat. "So you're bailing, then?"

"Um," I say, surprised by the directness of her question. I immediately resent the nothingness of my reply. I'm better in writing, which this girl, the entire workshop, will soon learn. Just not now, at a public reading.

She cocks her head, something simultaneously vivid and delicate in her expression. "Look, I don't want to take your seat if you're just going to pee or whatever. I can stand. Don't sacrifice your couch for some girl you don't even know," she says, the edges of her mouth curling up.

I laugh, which coaxes the girl's smile wider. "I'm bailing," I confirm.

She brightens. "Excellent. I really didn't want to stand. These readings can go on forever."

"Hence my bailing." I start to slip past her out of the room.

Her voice stops me. "You're not curious?"

I pause, curious, just not in the way she means. "Now you're trying to get me to stay? Pick a theme—" I leave off the sentence, realizing I don't know her name.

She sticks out her hand. It's delicate, her nails unpainted. "Katrina Freeling," she introduces herself.

"Nathan Van Huysen," I supply, taking her hand. Her fingers grasp mine with brisk firmness. Not every handshake is indicative of the person, but this one, I think, is. It's just like the portrait of this girl I've sketched in the past thirty seconds. Everything with her is intentional, thought-out, direct.

"I'm not trying to convince you. The couch is legally mine now," she informs me. I have not stopped smiling for several moments now, I note. She goes on. "I just wonder why you'd come to a writers' workshop to hide in your room."

"I'm not hiding. I'll be writing," I clarify. "Which, if I'm not mistaken, *is* what you're supposed to do at a writers' workshop."

"Writing what?"

I blink, once more struck by her directness. There's no prejudgment in Katrina Freeling's expression, no competitiveness like I've seen in many of my peers today. She's just interested. "You haven't heard enough pitches today?" I press her lightly.

"I guess not," she replies, her eyes sparkling. "What's your book?" she asks. It's familiar shorthand, the favorite question of publishing people. The business card of this world.

"Nothing yet," I confess. "Just thoughts, feelings. I'm hoping to find a story here."

"*Ah.*" Her voice is playfully pitying, yet I know she means no offense.

"*Ah* what?" I narrow my eyes, still smiling.

"You don't have something good enough to read out loud."

"Yes, I do!" I laugh. I feel it's important she knows this.

She puts one finger to her chin, faux-contemplative. "If only there was a forum in which you could prove such a statement . . ." Mischief catches her grin. I recognize her joke for what it is. She's daring me to stay. In response, I cross my arms over my chest, pause, then look past her into the room.

"Someone's taking your seat," I inform her. "You better go explain your— What was it? Legal entitlement to the sofa."

She looks over her shoulder, where one of the guys from the back of the room is settling onto the couch. Her eyes returning to me, she shrugs. "Oh well. Guess I'll stand." One of her full eyebrows raises lightly. "You better get out quickly, though, before they start."

I see one of the fellows step up to the front of the room. Katrina's right. I don't have long. "What are you going to read?" I find myself asking.

She smirks. "Nathan, if you're curious, you'll just have to stay."

I scoff in the same unserious way she looked pitying of me earlier. "You overestimate my curiosity."

"Do I?" she replies immediately. "Let's find out."

With remarkable timing, the fellow who's standing up calls for silence. I purse my lips, feeling pulled in opposite directions. If I return to my room, I could get so much done. It's the perfect amount of time to get down the scene idea I had on the drive up. I should slip out—if I stay, I'm trapped here for probably hours. But . . . the girl watching me not inconspicuously keeps me here, stuck in place. I promise myself I'll wait until she's read, then I'll leave. I'll duck out to go to the bathroom, and I won't return.

Except when they start taking volunteers, Katrina doesn't raise her hand. For the next torturous hour, she continues not raising her hand while I endure uncomfortably personal essays and alternating purple and pretentious prose. Finally, like she's decided I've served some sentence, Katrina walks to the front, throwing me a wink on her way.

She starts reading, and she's effortless, fearless. I'm a little surprised to discover her short story is a love story right in the literary-commercial sweet spot. It's not unlike the kind I write. Not unlike it at all.

I'm enraptured. I soak in her every word, hearing how similar it is to the styles I love but with Katrina's own personal flair elevating it. While she reads, I have the surprising urge to hand her everything I've ever written and beg her for feedback. Suddenly, peer criticism can't come soon enough. She has exactly what I've been looking for. If she could teach me or even—

I find my thoughts pulled off track by her words, derailed by the force of what she's reading. I let myself enjoy the new path she's cutting in my head, the characters she's rendering, fully formed and captivating, the voice she wields with refined precision. I shouldn't be surprised her writing is so like herself, or what I've seen of her so far. *So far.* It's my silent, unconscious promise to myself.

She finishes, her final sentence echoing in my ears. The room claps, but Katrina's not focused on them. Her eyes find mine, her smile challenging.

But I don't need daring. Not now. I raise my hand immediately. If I read, I can ask her her thoughts. If I'm really lucky, I'll captivate her enough that she'll read more of my work. On my way to the front of the room, our shoulders brush as I pass her. I'll read my writing for the whole room, because she's in it. Because really, I'm only reading for one person.

Katrina Freeling.

63

Nathan

• PRESENT DAY •

THERE'S CURIOUSLY LITTLE ceremony in finishing a novel. In most cases, they end like they began. There's no fanfare, no applause, only swelling emotion hidden beneath more ink on more pages just like the rest. Maybe your coffee gets cold, maybe you don't check your phone or your email for a while. Otherwise, the world continues to turn, while your personal, private story ends.

Katrina and I write the final chapter of *Where We'll End* sitting next to each other on the dining table bench. It's half past noon. The day is gorgeous, sunlight searing in our windows from the pale sky. My coffee is, in fact, cold. I know I won't remember these details. I never do. When I'm writing, I imagine the end of each story so vividly, there's no surprise when, finally, it comes. It's how endings should work. In some ways, you should know them from the very first page. They're the culmination and subversion of everything proceeding, the satisfaction of expectations and the joy of the unexpected.

We're writing the ending together, the way we started this book, side by side, with one voice. I read over her shoulder while she works on the scene. I'm close enough I could kiss the curve of her neck, which I resist, like I have every day for the past three weeks.

Evelyn and Michael sign their divorce papers. They tell each other they love each other one last time. Then Katrina pauses, fingers hovering over the keys. Understanding she's hit a creative wall, I wait while she gently hands over the computer for me to continue. I do, picking up the scene like I'm singing a harmony to what she's writing. The characters kiss with real emotion—with all the feeling they have left.

Katrina reclaims the computer, seizing it compulsively. I have to smile. I will never not love seeing her inspired this way, like every inch of her is energy. She finishes out the final paragraphs, describing how Evelyn and Michael's love has changed form, burned then dimmed, how it will never go out completely. How they'll carry its embers with them even as they leave each other for good.

I watch her put down sentence after sentence, anticipation growing in me. The last weeks of writing have been wonderful in their way, full of collaboration, inspiration, and joy. Seeing Katrina every morning, her eyes gleaming with excitement for the work, making tea for her while she prints our pages, doing the dishes together with our inspiration playlist on. Lingering in the hallway each night once we've said good night, watching her smile softly while she shuts her bedroom door.

It's been perfect in every way except for one.

Even now, we're deliberately not touching—no elbows grazing or shoulders colliding accidentally. The intentional inches separating us feel charged, like there's static electricity jumping the chasm, connecting us where physical proximity doesn't. Whenever I've watched her bedroom door shut, it's been the same. I find myself wishing I could kiss her good night. Sleep beside her. Feel her skin on mine. When this is done—only paragraphs left now—I'll learn whether I've done those things for the last time.

She hits what I know is the final line, and a small gasp escapes her. Shooting her a quick grin, I move the computer over for my own contributions. While Katrina follows my work, nodding, I shift sentences, change emphases, break up paragraphs, and combine others. The whole process is silent, spoken only in the perfect understanding we have of each other.

"Is it—" Katrina starts.

"Done," I finish.

Everything stops. Everything keeps going. While the ocean rustles outside, while someone's wind chimes ring distantly, I sit, contemplating the closure of this story we've created. This time, I know, comes with the possibility of starting several other stories with Katrina.

Her grin fills her whole face. I know instantly, innately, where it's coming from. She fought her way back to herself. I find I'm mirroring her expression, my cheeks aching.

"Let's send it in," she says excitedly. "We can explain it's a very rough draft, and we know it'll need more work."

No way would I ever object. "Let's do it," I reply immediately. Once the draft is in, we can get to what really matters. It takes me two minutes to compose the email to Liz, my nervous excitement leaving a trail of typos I know Katrina notices. I attach the draft, the file named only *Where We'll End.*

Before I hit send, Katrina puts her hand on my arm.

"I love you," she says.

"I love you, too," I reply. I meet her eyes. There's nothing original in the declaration, nothing perfectly crafted, no elegant metaphors, no profound prose. It's a sentence every writer has used, one every person has spoken. It's ordinary, common. And it's perfect. The sentence captures what I couldn't in hundreds of my finest pages. I wouldn't change a word.

I hit send. Katrina leans in, finally closing the fragile gap. She kisses me, a gentle press of lips. I'm washed clean of everything except the sensation. It's not an answer, just a feeling.

"There," she says softly. Her eyes shift to the computer. I catch something fleeting cross her expression. Not even I know her well enough to discern what it is. "It's done. Our contract is complete," she continues.

I realize we're thinking the same thing. I've often felt with Katrina like I could read the pages of our story, following the plot from outside of myself. Right now is one of those moments. I'm struck by how similar the scene we're living is to the one we just wrote. This could be where *we* end, if we want. We could walk away from each other like Evelyn and Michael, closing the cover on these chapters of our lives.

I desperately don't want it to end here. The idea is a cold spike driven into the center of my heart. It renders me nearly breathless, leaving me grasping hungrily for whatever future will have her in it. This could be the end of everything.

"Fuck that," I say, inelegant and sure. "I didn't do this for the contract. I want you."

I swear I see tears in Katrina's eyes. She gives me the same half smile she did when I first ran into her six years ago. "Good." Her voice wavers like her heart is full. "Because I'm not done writing our love story yet."

When I kiss her, crushing her to me, losing myself in her scent and her skin and wanting every inch of her, it's with the passion I've withheld for weeks—for years. It's the kind of kiss that closes a book. But this time, it doesn't.

This time, it's only the beginning.

Epilogue

Katrina

• THREE MONTHS LATER •

IT'S FIVE MINUTES past when I should have shut my computer. I'm rushing to write down new ideas, hardly hearing the rolling rhythm of my fingers flying over the keys. When we turned in *Where We'll End*, I wondered in the dark corners of my mind whether new stories would find me. It's something I discuss with my therapist, with whom I scheduled those weekly visits. So far, though, they have. I've woken up most days with them in my head. Right now, I know if I don't get my ideas down before I leave, I'll be distracted in the meeting I'm about to be late for.

Pausing momentarily, I pull up the sleeve of my black turtleneck, which I've paired with the long skirt I bought for today's meeting. It's the kind of outfit I wouldn't have worn in Los Angeles, where fall is really just summer dressed in different colors. The kind of outfit I missed when I moved.

I race the clock in the corner of my screen, wanting to capture one more thought. My words come crisp, clear, luminous onto the page. It's one of those creative moods I know I need to chase when they come. In the midst of my rush, I hear the bedroom door open behind me. Familiar footsteps pad down the hall, toward the office where I'm working.

"*I'll never write again*, she once said," I hear from the doorway.

I face the direction of Nathan's voice. He's framed in the entryway, and he looks disarmingly handsome. He's shaved for the meeting, something he doesn't often do because he thinks his usual stubble looks writerly. His tan from Florida has faded. He doesn't look worse for it. In fact, they could put him in catalogues for the gray cowl-neck sweater he's wearing.

I meet his gaze. "If I gave it up for real, would you still love me?"

He crosses the room, giving me my answer in a long kiss. "You already did for four years, and I didn't stop loving you."

"You did not love me those four years." I laugh, leaning into him while he moves lower to kiss my neck.

"I did," he insists. "Come on, Kat, would I make this up? It's terribly cliché. Carrying a torch while I pretended I was over you? If I were rewriting the story of our romance, I'd be more original."

I grin, giving into his doting logic. Whether it's true isn't important. It's a good story, and one we've both chosen. Fiction doesn't only come from life. Sometimes, it's the other way around.

It's been three months since we left Florida, since I packed up my life in Los Angeles and Nathan his in Chicago. We live in Brooklyn, where we should have been together from the start. Sharing a career and a life isn't easy. We fight, we let creative differences spill into hurt feelings, we work hard to repair what we mess up. It's no fairy tale, no succinct happily-ever-after. But it's worth it.

Nathan checks his phone. "Shit," he says, straightening up. "We should've left by now."

Closing my computer, I sigh, guilty. We're headed to lunch with our publisher and Jen, who now represents us both. Officially, we're celebrating. The *New York Times* profile came out this week, announcing *Where We'll End* and featuring our interview. Neither Nathan nor I have read it. The email sits unopened in my inbox. We don't need to read whatever rumors Noah Lippman has decided to stoke or dispel. We know the truth now, the one that's only for us.

I slide on my boots, then follow Nathan to the door. He stops to pet James Joyce, who's presently nuzzling Nathan's shin. I swear, the only one more infatuated with this man than me is my cat.

On the sidewalk, I breathe in deeply, enjoying the New York fall rushing into my lungs. I missed this, like so much of my life. We'll return to Florida soon, though, to write the proposal for the next book we hope to sell. We'll stay in the house—once our prison, now our refuge, memories living in layers within the walls. We'll see Harriet. I can't wait.

While the wind shakes the red trees outside our place, Nathan puts his arm around me. He pulls me close. "Should we get a cab?"

"Can we walk by the bookstore first?" I ask. We picked this apartment because it's a two-minute walk from one of our favorite independent bookstores.

Nevertheless, Nathan looks incredulous. "Katrina! We're going to be so late."

"On the way back, then," I concede.

Nathan eyes me, saying nothing. I don't pout, though I'd really hoped we could slip into the store. Even so, I know Nathan senses my disappointment. Of course he does. He stares into people's souls for a living. "In and out," he says, relenting. "As fast as possible."

I kiss his cheek, excitement lifting me onto my toes. "I'll tell Jen we're running ten minutes late. Just, so many books came out this week I want to read. There's—"

"The new Taylor Quan and the Cassandra Ray Smith," Nathan finishes. His grin lingers on me a moment too long. "What if someone recognizes us in there?"

I tighten my grip on him. "Then we'll sign some books and confirm we're together," I say easily.

Nathan raises an eyebrow. "Confirm we're together?"

"Do you want to stay a secret?"

Nathan laughs lightly, more to himself. "Were we ever a secret?"

"Only to ourselves," I say.

"So when I propose to you," he says, "should I do it in a bookstore?"

I nearly stop on the sidewalk. My mouth drops open a little. Nothing comes out. I close it, then start over. "Hilarious," I say, studying him. He's serious, despite having wrapped the question in a joke. I know because, while he's playing casual, he's watching me too intently.

"What about in the finished copies of our book?" he asks, once more serious and not.

I'm only just holding onto my composure, joys I couldn't possibly catalogue crashing over me. "Our book about divorce?" I remind him.

"Good point." He pauses, his eyes drifting contemplatively. Unsatisfied, he turns to me. "Care to brainstorm this with me?"

I shove him, delighted. "I will not cowrite your proposal with you."

"Damn," he says ruefully. "Well, I'll figure something out. Soon." His gaze darts to me on the final word, watching for my reaction.

"I look forward to it," I say softly.

"Yeah?" His question is immediate, his voice searching, even vulnerable. I have to smile, my heart cracking happily. Everyone talks up the proposal. Not enough is made of whatever this is. The preproposal. It's wonderful in its ordinariness. Proposals are for candlelit dinners and champagne. Preproposals are for sidewalk conversations and running late. They're one of the small moments you don't find in stories—only in real life.

He's still waiting for my answer. "Ask me first," I tell him.

"Fair enough." He has the stupidest, most wonderful grin. His shoulders straighten while he walks, his head a little higher. I feel like my entire self flows into our joined hands.

We've written the rough draft of our love together, the draft with loose ends, unfinished edges, mistakes every other page. But every writer knows there's magic in revision, where your work changes from a manuscript into a book. Where intentions, emotions, missed connections coalesce into something complete. It's where what you mean to say becomes what you have said. The characters deepen, the details shine, the prose sparkles. Suddenly, from nothing, you find your story.

We're in the revision now, Nathan and me. The second draft. Each next one will only improve, becoming more nuanced, more honest, more profound. More us.

We reach the bookstore. Nathan walks up beside me, where he's been so often before. Before we ever kissed, before we traded pages, before the new book. Before fire, thunderstorms, calmer waters. I love even our roughest draft. I love every fraught page we've rewritten to get to here. Because in the end, the best part of a love story isn't having it. It's getting to keep writing.

While Nathan holds the door open, I walk into the bookstore, inspired not by what I'll find on the shelves or put onto the page but by every new day.

Acknowledgments

It's intimidating venturing into a new genre, especially with a story so personal and close to our hearts. We could not have done it without the support, love, inspiration, and hard work of everyone we would like to thank here. *The Roughest Draft* could not have existed without you.

We conceived this idea on our honeymoon while discussing how our agent was probably relieved we'd finally put rings on our writing partnership. When we returned home with the spark of this idea, the manuscript only came together because said agent, Katie Shea Boutillier, encouraged us to keep pursuing the concept. We're endlessly grateful to you for believing in this new genre for us and in this story, which could not have happened without your pushing us on every character and motivation. None of our stories ever do.

What's more, thank you for representing with grace this novel in which certain literary agents come off, uh, not awesome. Had Nathan or

Katrina loved their agent the way we do you, passages of the book would read much like this one.

The most joyful part of this journey has been, without a doubt, finding our new Berkley family. This starts with Kristine Swartz, who we knew from our first phone call perfectly understood the novel we hoped we could craft here. Your insight and sense of the book's positioning and identity is incredibly inspiring, and your friendship has made a publishing house feel like a home.

We've been honored and moved to be embraced by our entire Berkley team. To Vi-An Nguyen, thank you for a cover so stunningly perfect it inspired a whole new scene in the book. To Christine Legon, Mary Baker, Megha Jain, and Erica Horisk, thank you for bringing this book from the *literal* roughest draft to this gorgeous novel. To Jessica Brock, Danielle Keir, and Fareeda Bullert, thank you for reaching readers with your extraordinary work.

One thing that never changes is the importance of wonderful friends. Aminah Mae Safi and Bridget Morrissey, you two aren't friends—you're family. Thank you for pandemic weekly video calls and making us not want to slingshot ourselves into the sun. Seriously, you light up our every day. The best decision we ever made was going out to the desert with a group of people who'd literally never hung out together before. Maura Milan, doing writing sprints with you and catching up on our progress every day is the only way this book got outlined in time. Between working out story beats with you and trading video games, your friendship helps us "keep on keeping on." To the rest of the LA Electrics, thank you for group chats and movie nights, publishing advice and shared joy.

Rebekah Faubion, thank you for being a fabulous human and for your early read and insight on this manuscript. Everyone needs an agent sister like you. Gretchen Schreiber, thank you for always being there for venting sessions even when we're living in different states. Diya Mishra, your enthusiasm for this story was a real lift when we needed one.

Gabrielle Gold, our oldest friend, thank you for so much, book- and non-book-related. We're honored and overjoyed to be part of the romance family—Rachel Lynn Solomon, Jen DeLuca, Lyssa Kay Adams, and Emily Henry, thank you for welcoming us in!

To our family, thank you for fostering the love of writing and stories that inspires and sustains us in everything we write.

Finally, our readers new and old—everything we write is a love letter to you.

Keep reading for an excerpt from

Do I Know You?

Available now!

Eliza

SAY SOMETHING.

I watch my husband out of the corner of my eye, imploring, wishing he would end the silence filling our car. In the window past him, the ocean glitters, unchanging. The California coastline should inspire wonder, with its rippling cliffs and its crystalline expanse, even when you've spent hours watching the water through the windshield. Instead, the thing I notice most is how it just keeps going.

Say something.

Graham doesn't. He drives, his long fingers clamped on the pebbled leather of the steering wheel, his posture stiff. The quiet, interrupted only by the occasional *whoosh* of cars passing us, prickles over me like the start of a sunburn.

Is this how this week will be?

I told myself it wouldn't. I've told myself that pretty much every day since Graham's parents handed us an envelope over dinner containing a weeklong, all-expenses-paid romantic getaway at the Treeline Resort to celebrate our fifth wedding anniversary. I convinced myself the week would be wonderful instead of awkward or claustrophobic. What couple wouldn't want to celebrate five years of marriage at a five-star hotel famous for its romantic ambience?

The quiet filling our car says it knows. Determined, I fight off my discouragement. I wish Graham would speak up, would offer something up into the silence—even comment on the weather—but he doesn't.

It's not only him not speaking, I remind myself. Screw sitting here waiting. Maybe I need to be less narrator, more main character.

I clear my throat. "We're doing good on—"

"Just three hours to go—" Graham quickly cuts in.

"Time," I finish, then wince, hearing the unintentional overlap of our voices. It's less like cutely finishing each other's sentences, more like two supermarket shoppers coincidentally reaching for the same shelf. Less unison, more collision.

I don't blame him for cutting in, for intuiting exactly what I was going to say. Every exchange my husband and I have managed in the past twenty-four hours has consisted of nothing except this one meaningless subject. When we should leave, how long the drive is, whether we should take Highway 1 or the 5 freeway. Unable to help myself, I glance over, wondering whether Graham shares my desperation to change our conversational flat tire.

He does. He shifts in his seat like someone's stowed rocks in the soft leather cushion under him.

I remember the way I described Graham Cutler to my friends and my parents fresh off our first dates. *He's tall,* I'd said. *He's got blond hair, a cleft chin, intelligence in his eyes. The kind he could use to eviscerate rhetorical weaknesses, but he doesn't, not with me.* We'd met and chatted with each other on a dating app, and when we got together in person, these observations were the first I connected to the personality I'd gotten to know on my phone.

The problem is, they're what I hear now. Observations. I've been married to Graham for five years, and when I look over from the passenger seat, my mind does nothing except reproduce the list of identifying marks I jotted down in my head when me met. *He's tall. He has blond hair.*

It hasn't been this way forever—in our newlywed years, Graham turned, the way spouses should, into swirling slideshows of happy memories, never-ending excitement to catch up over dinner or share something funny one of us found online.

Gradually, though, it's gotten harder to feel like I *know* the man seated next to me, despite knowing I love him. It happened not through fights or rifts, but through late work nights, quick conversations instead of real ones. Our starkly different careers don't help—the high-profile San Diego law firm where Graham is planning to make partner, the many audiobooks and voice-acting jobs I've recorded in the past five years. Complacency converted into unspoken questions and discussions never had. Five years into our marriage, I'm left with only my catalogue, once eager, now rote. Learned. Repeated.

He's tall. He has blond hair. He is my husband.

Part of me wonders whether Graham's mother gave us this gift knowing we're having difficulty finding the spark. Helen has never been a particularly generous gift-giver despite being a member of the Marina del Rey yacht club. When I got home and Googled the hotel, seeing the price per night confirmed her meddlesome motives.

Of course, Helen's response would be to force us into this situation, which is frustrating in principle no matter how much I might be looking forward to cucumber water in the lobby. The Cutler family way is to walk through fire, while mine is to walk in the other direction. It's why I haven't spoken to my sister in months. I don't *enjoy* retreating—I've just concluded it's the safest thing for me. For everyone.

No, I chasten myself. *Eliza, you will enjoy yourself, damnit. You will not surrender to three more hours of traffic-related small talk.*

My internal pep talk surges confidence into me, like I felt when I spontaneously shoved my new lingerie into my suitcase under my running shoes and my e-reader. It's red, lacy, and designed for exactly one purpose, which is *not* day-to-day functionality. My best friend, Nikki, gave it to me to celebrate this anniversary. While packing this morning in the bedroom of the house we rent in San Diego's summer cottage neighborhood of La Jolla, I chose to ignore how out of place the lingerie was in the present context of Graham's and my marriage, how far we've started to feel from spontaneity or surprise. *I'm going for it,* I decided, stashing the collection of lace and straps in my suitcase.

"Hey," I say, latching onto a conversational handhold. "I wonder if this hotel has milkshakes."

Every sliver of my focus is on Graham's reaction to this subject change. When he smiles, despite the sun shining through the windows since we left our hometown's morning fog behind, I feel warmth for the first time in the hours we've been on the road.

Until he replies. "Milkshakes?" he repeats, cool confusion in his voice. "Why would we want milkshakes?"

My heart plunges. Right off the cliff outside. Right into the endless ocean. I wonder if Graham knows what he's done. His straightforward stare says nothing of my dashed hopes.

"I don't want milkshakes," Graham goes on. "I want *banana* milkshakes."

I hear myself laugh. The sound is quick, echoing joyously in our car. Now Graham grins fully, half Cheshire cat, half high-school boy pleased to have earned his crush's laughter. *I'm the crush,* I remember delightedly. I'm not just the person he goes to bed with—I'm the person he still plays games with.

On the first night of our honeymoon, we lost track of time exploring the streets of Honolulu, only returning to our hotel famished with five minutes until room service ended. The understandably perturbed kitchen staff explained they'd cleaned up for the night except for the ice cream supplies, and guests had polished off everything but, inexplicably, the banana ice cream. If we wanted, they offered, they could make us banana milkshakes.

We did. We spent the first night of our honeymoon watching midnight descend over the water, drinking banana milkshakes.

"What will we do if they don't have them?" I reply, pitching my voice breathily, putting on the register I used for the wonderful new historical romance novel I just finished recording. Today, I'm a damsel in milkshakeless distress.

When Graham replies, I recognize the gravitas of his client-phone-call voice. "I think we have clear claims for tortious vacation interference or negligence of frozen treats," he informs me. "Wrongful death if my wife perishes from banana milkshake deprivation is harder, but there's precedent. Depends on the inclinations of judges in this circuit."

"Better hit the books then, Mr. Cutler."

"Will do, Mrs. Cutler."

"Is this pro bono work?"

"Out of the goodness of my heart, Mrs. Cutler," he promises.

I smile, relaxing into the passenger seat, the stress releasing from my shoulders. I shouldn't feel so relieved. It's just—so many of my conversations with Graham lately, while pleasant, have felt insubstantial. Missing something. Like the filler dialogue I sometimes record for video game parts instead of the main story. Banana-milkshake banter felt real. It felt like *us*.

Emboldened, I pivot in my seat, crossing one white sneaker under me. The canopy of trees unexpectedly soaring over this stretch of road filters the sunlight in patterns while we drive, speckling the dashboard in ever-changing leopard spots. "For real," I prompt my husband. "What do you want to do when we get there?"

I watch the moment it happens. Graham's expression doesn't change—the relaxed hint of his smile, the fixture of his eyes on the road—except, something *does* change. Some secret spark shuts off in him. Photographs of sunlight look like day, but they offer no warmth. Nothing grows in the sort of false light now glinting in Graham's eyes.

"I don't know," he replies with forced casualness. His hesitancy is its own flashback, reminding me of his studious reserve when we first met, when courtroom experience hadn't yet put confidence into him.

I press on, patiently struggling. *We were just having fun, weren't we?* "Well, *I'm* just looking forward to having the gorgeous room to ourselves. The ocean view, the trees, the hot tub . . ."

Graham just nods.

"This is going to be good for us," I say, then immediately regret my choice of words. I can't ignore the implication in them. Saying this trip will be *good* for us is prescriptive. It's vitamins served on a silver platter. I sound desperate, chasing the nameless shadows creeping into the corners of our marriage lately.

"It will," Graham says. It's the end of the conversation.

When the road swerves, my thoughts do the same. I retreat into sudden insecurity, ignoring the spectacular path our car is now winding into the sagebrush mountains. Are our memories the only things we have left? If so, why even go on this trip? Why drive these six hours into the green hills of Northern California if we're only going to cloak ourselves in reminiscence when we get there?

No. I refuse to give up. We haven't even gotten to the hotel. I know retreating would be easier, occupying myself with the sample I need to record—

Right then, I get the perfect idea.

The sample my producer sent me is not video-game dialogue. It's not nonfiction essays. It's not commercial voiceover. It's . . . sexy. Very sexy.

Maybe it could reset the tone for this trip. Loosen Graham up.

It could be, dare I say, fun.

Glancing up, I find my husband still focused on the road. "Hey," I say innocently. "Would you mind if I record something?"

Photo by Sue Grubman

Emily Wibberley and Austin Siegemund-Broka met and fell in love in high school. Austin went on to graduate from Harvard, while Emily graduated from Princeton. Together, they are the authors of several novels about romance for teens and adults. Now married, they live in Los Angeles, where they continue to take daily inspiration from their own love story.

CONNECT ONLINE

EmilyAndAustinWrite.com